The woman was halfway up the tree, damn it!

With every inch her toes lowered, Laura's black linen skirt crept higher above the knee.

Sweet heaven. Who would have thought that little Ms. Women's Lib—Ms. Judge-My-Talent-For-Yourself—had the legs of a Las Vegas showgirl? Alec slid an appreciative gaze from thigh to instep, then shook himself.

"Unless you *want* my son to witness your death, Ms. Hayes, kindly stay still." Grasping the ladder in both hands, he notched his foot on the bottom rung.

Laura glared down like a treed cougar ready to leap on his neck. Confused, Alec instinctively sought the nearest male for an explanation.

His son peered at him over dangling sneakers. "I don't think she needs your help, Dad," Jason said. "She can climb pretty good...for a girl."

"*Too Many Bro...* ...k—fast-paced, funn...
...Susan Mallery, ...de

"Jan Fr... ...ion with characters who st... ...g at the reader's heart."
—Alexandra Thorne, author of *Lawless* and *Boundless*

ABOUT THE AUTHOR

After years of writing advertising copy, Jan Freed decided if she could make washing machines sound glamorous, creating irresistible heroines should be a breeze. She admires "strong, gutsy women who safeguard traditional values against all odds." And certainly, Jan's first published heroine reflects that "John-Wayne-in-panty-hose" attitude.

Jan, who co-owns an advertising agency with her husband, Gerald, lives in Texas with their children, Stephanie and David. She'd love to hear from readers and invites you to write her at: P.O. Box 5009-272, Sugarland, Texas, 77487.

Jan Freed

Too Many Bosses

Harlequin Books

TORONTO • NEW YORK • LONDON
AMSTERDAM • PARIS • SYDNEY • HAMBURG
STOCKHOLM • ATHENS • TOKYO • MILAN
MADRID • WARSAW • BUDAPEST • AUCKLAND

ISBN 0-373-70645-6

TOO MANY BOSSES

Copyright © 1995 by Jan Freed.

To Gerald,
the partner every woman dreams of finding,
and I've been blessed to keep

CHAPTER ONE

TWO SENTENCES into the phone conversation, Alec McDonald yanked open his desk drawer and rummaged for his Tums. "I understand your concern, Mrs. Pennington. But Jason won't fall, I assure you. He's as agile as a monkey." *And twice as mischievous.* "Lure him down with something he likes. Tell him to come watch cartoons or something."

"In other words, reward him for misbehaving?"

Where the hell were those Tums? "Look, Mrs. Pennington, I have a very busy schedule this morning. Can't you—"

"Climbing a thirty-foot tree is *not* in my job description. You're the boy's father. I need assistance. Just where would you advise me to go?"

He swallowed his blasphemous suggestion. Replacing Jason's last two baby-sitters had been difficult enough. "Don't go anywhere. I'll be home as soon as I can, all right?"

"Well ... so long as I'm not held responsible." She sniffed. "I hope you have a tall ladder."

He didn't own a step stool. "Everything's under control. Please tell Jason I'm on my way. If he shows the good sense to climb down, call me on the car phone. The number's on the refrigerator. Goodbye, Mrs. Pennington."

"Hmph," she grunted, and hung up.

Charming woman. Her references had been impeccable, but Lord, she was sour. Of course, Jason could try the patience of a saint.

Digging into his pocket, Alec found the missing roll of antacids and thumbed a tablet into his mouth. Calm. He must stay calm. That was what Houston's largest advertising agency paid him for, after all. To remain cool and logical in the midst of chaos. Compared with the self-indulgent tantrum his creative director, Tom Marsh, had thrown not ten minutes ago, Jason's prank was a minor insubordination.

Yeah, right, McDonald.

Exhaling through his teeth, Alec closed his eyes against the pain, guilt and love whirling on spin cycle in his gut and fusing into one complex emotion he couldn't begin to sort out.

How he could manage more than one hundred employees with ease, yet allow himself to be manipulated by a six-year-old boy baffled and embarrassed him. In the two months since Jason's arrival, Alec had been unable to break the pattern. Today's escapade was a prime example.

Leaving the agency would help, he assured himself. A few more weeks and he would make his move. All he needed was—

"Excuse me, Mr. McDonald. Your ten-o'clock appointment is here," his secretary announced through the intercom.

Appointment?

God, what a morning.

Frowning, he jabbed a button. "I've got a minor emergency at home I've got to take care of, Sharon. Cancel my appointment and clear my schedule through lunch, would you?"

"But, uh, what about Ms. Hayes, sir?"

Odd. His secretary never questioned his instructions. "You'll just have to reschedule Ms. Hayes for another day." He scanned his calendar. "Friday at eleven o'clock looks good."

Hayes... Hayes... He searched his memory. Oh, yes. Some junior copywriter from the creative department. He'd canceled on her once already, he remembered with a twinge of guilt. Or was it twice?

No matter. Either way, this morning's schedule was in the toilet. And he still had to lure his son onto solid ground. Not *safe* ground, though. He'd been lax with the boy long enough.

Scooping up his briefcase and untouched coffee, Alec strode to the closed door and shifted both items to one hand. Before he could reach for the knob, it twisted violently and whooshed toward his groin. He sprang backward, grimacing as hot coffee sloshed over his hand and across his chest.

Sharon gasped. "I'm so sorry, Mr. McDonald!"

Incredulous, he stared down at the brown splatters branding his starched white shirt.

"She was trying to force her way in, you see, even though I *said* you weren't available. I tried to block the way, but..." His secretary twisted the pearls at her neck. "Oh, dear! I had no idea you were close to the door."

"That's all right, Sharon." Alec kept his voice even. "But if you'll get rid of this cup, I'd appreciate it. And see what you can do about wiping down my briefcase."

As she bustled forward, he lifted his gaze over her neat gray hair and froze. Lion gold eyes watched him with the unblinking intensity of a cat eyeing a pigeon. The sensation was not pleasant.

"If there is any apology due here, Sharon," he said, "I hardly think *you* should be the one giving it."

The stranger's slightly tilted eyes narrowed to glittering slits, emphasizing their feline quality. He wouldn't have been at all surprised to see a tail switching somewhere beneath her skirt.

Alec waited for a response, lifting a single eyebrow when it became apparent there would be none. His secretary threw him an I-told-you-so look before slipping out the door.

"Ms. Hayes, I presume?" he asked coldly.

She was taller than average and willow slim, with dark chestnut hair pulled back into some sort of braid.

"That's right. I'm Laura Hayes."

Her voice was a rich contralto and slightly raspy. Like a cat's.

She stepped forward. "I'm the lowly copywriter who's worked eight months on company newsletters and ads for the Yellow Pages just waiting for a chance to join the Regency Hotels account team." She took another step. "I'm the woman who found out nobody touches that account without your permission. And yes, I'm the appointment you've broken four times in a row without so much as an explanation, much less an apology."

She stopped an arm's length away, her invisible tail twitching steadily. "What I'd like to know is just who you think *you* are, to treat anyone so rudely?"

Alec blinked, not sure he'd heard right. She met his glare with one of equal outrage.

Drawing himself up to his full height, he gave her the cool assessing look that had rattled everyone from mailroom clerks to agency principals. "If I'm not mistaken, Ms. Hayes, I'm your boss. I don't explain my actions to anyone who doesn't pay my salary, and you won't get anywhere near the Regency-account team without re-membering that. Nor will you touch that account unless you learn to curb your impulsive behavior.''

Her gaze wavered and dropped to the floor.

Alec released his breath. She had a nice straight nose, he noted magnanimously, and the kind of mouth that de-served a second glance. Her full bottom lip quivered now with emotion. He watched her lashes slowly lift and pre-pared himself for her dismay, possibly even tears. Any-thing but irreverent glee.

''You've got to be kidding, right?'' she said on a choked laugh. ''You cancel four appointments with me at the last minute and then call *my* behavior impulsive? Don't you think that's—'' She stopped, crossed her arms and peered at him closely. ''Do you do that on pur-pose?''

Alec wondered about the woman's IQ. ''Do what?''

She flung a hand toward his forehead. ''That eyebrow thing. Do you raise it and look down your nose all the time, or is it just me?''

Alec felt like he'd stumbled into a carnival fun house. He mentally groped for balance.

''In answer to your first question, Ms. Hayes, I never kid. And I'd call your behavior not only impulsive, but incredibly foolish for someone in your position. Or have you forgotten so soon who I am?''

She rolled her eyes. ''Oh, puh-leeze. First, I get a su-pervisor who turns out to have tunnel vision, then a boss who turns out to be a...a...'' Her gaze zoomed in on his left eyebrow and lit with inspiration. ''A castaway from the starship *Enterprise*.

''Well, Spock, sorry to have disturbed your morning. But you know how emotional we humans get when we're treated like machines.'' With a swirl of black pleated skirt, she turned and swept through the door.

Of all the impertinent... Alec followed her, inhaling the faint scent of lavender in her wake. ''Wait just a minute, Ms. Hayes. What's so important that you'd risk your job for it?''

He reached out and caught her shoulder. From the look she directed at his fingers, they might have been bird droppings. Not until he lifted them did she slowly turn around.

''My job is at risk?''

To his amazement, Alec felt his face heat.

She sighed. ''Oh, well. Mr. Marsh will be furious with me for trying to talk with you, anyway.''

''Tom Marsh doesn't want you to see me?''

''Not in this lifetime. That's why getting an appointment with you has been so nerve-racking. I've had to wait until I was sure he'd be gone from the department before scheduling a meeting. And then when you canceled each time...'' She shrugged eloquently.

Alec weighed his options. Not twenty minutes ago—knowing full well Sam Parker was on the verge of moving the Regency Hotels account elsewhere—Tom had presented yet another set of stale layouts for the all-important Regency campaign. Puzzled as much as frustrated, Alec had ordered new layouts be turned in by three o'clock tomorrow afternoon.

This woman was, in her own words, just a lowly copywriter. But if the idea of her seeing Alec sent a bee up Tom's butt, it was worth investigating.

''Look, Ms. Hayes. I was on my way home to take care of a minor problem. But if you'd like to ride along with me, we can have that meeting on the road.''

She assessed him frankly, neither coy nor intimidated as most women were in his presence.

"You'll have twenty minutes of my undivided attention. That's how long it takes me to drive home."

Suddenly aware of their audience, he raised an eyebrow. "Through taking notes, Sharon?" When his secretary's dentures clacked shut, he nodded. "Good. I should be back by one. You can reach me on my car phone until then."

All business, he retrieved his newly buffed briefcase and turned toward the elevators, pretending not to see Laura's impudent salute to his back. In the interest of time, he would ignore her disrespect for now.

But he rather looked forward to showing Ms. Laura Hayes the value of self-discipline in the near future.

THE WITCH went back inside. Jason let out his breath and swung his legs in the air. When she'd stood under the tree and yelled up at him, he'd been scared by the mean look on her face. But he hadn't climbed down.

His dad was coming to get him.

He wriggled, then bounced his bottom against the branch and rode the seesaw motion. It was sort of like how he'd felt since coming to live here. Nothing around him stayed still anymore.

He'd been kind of scared on the airplane ride to America. But some pretty ladies had fussed over him the whole time, so it wasn't too bad. One of them had led him down the ramp to a tall dark-haired stranger. Jason knew it was his dad 'cause the man's eyes were like looking in a mirror.

For a minute, Jason had seen something that made him feel important. Needed. Even loved.

Then his dad thanked the lady, and the special look was gone. He'd watched for it, waited every day for it to come back, but his dad didn't look at him much after that first time. So Jason had learned what he was supposed to do. Mind the baby-sitter and play with his toys—his dad bought him whatever he asked for—and stay out of everyone's way.

That was what he was supposed to do.

Instead, he did bad things, mean things he never would have done to Nanny Howard. Like taking money from purses. And putting doodlebugs in bedroom slippers. And climbing trees to miss the school van. He'd felt kind of guilty doing stuff to the first two baby-sitters.

But not to the witch. The witch hated him. And he hated her.

Shivering, he tilted his face toward the sun. The little pieces of blue showing through the leaves weren't warm at all. Everybody said Texas was lots hotter than England, but he didn't think so. He'd never felt this cold there.

His stomach growled and he hugged it tight. He should've eaten the witch's yucky oatmeal right off before she'd called him a brat and taken away his bowl. Scrunching over, he studied the ground below and waited.

His dad was coming to get him. And maybe, just maybe, he'd give him that special look again.

LAURA WAITED for Alec between the parking garage and high-rise office building as instructed. A strong gust of March wind swept through the alley, carrying a nose-wrinkling mixture of jasmine blossoms and exhaust fumes.

She loved this time of year, before sweltering heat and humidity forced her to scuttle between air-conditioned environments as quickly as possible. Raising her face to the cloudless sky, she felt a surge of optimism.

Month upon agonizing month of frustration had led to today's outburst in Mr. McDonald's office. She couldn't wait any longer for someone to give her a chance. She had to *take* it.

Living in Houston did that to people, regardless of where they were born. The "can do" attitude that had survived the oil and gas bust of the eighties now spurred an economic revitalization that had earned Houston the title of Cinderella City. Like her adopted town, Laura intended to make the most of her second opportunity.

Alec surprised her by pulling up curbside in a late-model Chevy Silverado, instead of the expected status import car. She took one look at the gleaming black truck and promptly salivated. All-terrain tires, fog lights, bucket seats, four-wheel drive—it had all the bells and whistles lacking in her family's battered pickup.

Someday she would present her father with such a truck, Laura vowed. She would help pay off the debts and be guilt free to pursue her dream of establishing her own agency. But first she'd better convince this Alec McDonald of her value to Harris, Bates and Whitman Advertising.

Inside the cab, Alec leaned across the passenger seat and opened the door. She ignored his outstretched hand and boosted herself up, landing smoothly in the leather cushion.

He sent her a curious glance. "Looks like it's not the first time you've done that."

"My dad's driven a pickup for as long as I can remember. When I was little, he'd start rolling down the road whether I was in or out." Laura smiled at the thought of Grant Hayes's notorious impatience. "After being dragged through gravel ruts a few times, I learned how to hop in any way I could."

Boarding a pickup wasn't the only thing her dad had taught her. She could almost hear him now. *Just because you jump into situations feetfirst, Laura Jane, doesn't mean you have to leave your head behind altogether.*

Forcing her mind back to the present, she fastened her seat belt and glanced out the window. They were heading straight for the Galleria area. The city's second downtown boasted a concentration of fine shopping complexes, restaurants, luxury hotels and high-rise offices. If Alec lived anywhere close to this West Loop area, he earned a heftier salary than she'd thought.

Stealing a quick peek at him, she cursed her quick temper—even if it *had* been totally justified. Alec McDonald was everything she'd heard. Arrogant. Cold. A credit to his Ice Man nickname. Why, he hadn't so much as thanked Sharon for polishing the briefcase she'd extended like an offering to the gods. Despite that, his middle-aged secretary had twittered like a lovestruck teenager under the influence of those spiky-lashed sapphire blue eyes.

Laura shifted ever so slightly toward the steering wheel, bringing Alec into her peripheral vision.

So the man was attractive, she admitted.

Her gaze dropped and traveled the six feet plus from his polished leather shoes to his wavy black hair, lingering at scenic points in between.

Okay, very attractive.

She wasn't impressed. After all, she'd been raised by two of the most ruggedly handsome male specimens in Texas. And it wasn't her dad or brother's good looks Laura had found comforting those first years after her mother died. She remembered the spontaneous bear hugs and big awkward hands combing her hair, buttoning her small coat and wiping away her tears.

Alec turned his head and caught her staring. A raven black eyebrow lifted in the now-familiar gesture. "If I'd known this is how you'd spend your twenty minutes, Ms. Hayes, I could have given you a snapshot and been done with it. You've got fifteen minutes left." He adjusted his rearview mirror a fraction. "I suggest you use them wisely."

Laura felt the blood rush to her head in an equal mixture of anger and embarrassment. She *needed* this man, she reminded herself. Pride be damned. "I'd like to apologize for my earlier behavior. I don't barge into offices as a general rule."

His mouth twitched once before melding back into a granite line. "I get the impression you're not happy at Harris, Bates and Whitman, Ms. Hayes. Surely you realize I have no direct line of authority over your position?"

Hypocrite. "On the contrary. You made a point of letting me know exactly how much authority you do have in this agency. And if I'm not mistaken, Mr. McDonald," she said, mimicking his earlier tone perfectly, "you're my boss."

His jaw was very lean and square. Especially when his teeth were clenched.

"True enough. But why come to me for help? I'm not exactly known around here for my sympathetic shoulder."

Laura bit back a crack of laughter at that understatement. To date, three women under his supervision had resigned in tears. As long as his marketing brilliance continued to bring in accounts like Regency Hotels, no one dared take him to task.

"I had two choices," she admitted. "Scrap the last eight months of my life and start over at a new agency. Or trust your sense of fairness and put my fate in your hands."

A small movement drew her attention to the long tanned fingers resting lightly on the steering wheel. She stared as his thumb rubbed slow lazy circles against the padded leather.

"Brave woman, considering Kleenex is standard issue for my female staff." His eyes were the deepest hue of bluebonnets....

"Wh-what?"

A car horn blasted from behind, jerking her gaze from his.

"My reputation," he explained, as if speaking to a dull child. "You're not afraid of it?"

"I haven't cried since I was a little girl. I'll take my chances."

Years of masculine companionship had taught her to give as good as she got, Laura assured herself. Besides, her father's recent heart attack left her no choice. She would walk on burning coals if it would help ease his financial burden. And the fastest way to send money home was by earning a promotion with her current employer.

Laura drew a deep breath. "As a businessman, Mr. McDonald, would the idea of your company wasting a valuable resource upset you?"

"You've got my attention."

"I know this may sound conceited, but I'm too talented to waste on jobs that require the imagination of a slug. If I was allowed the opportunity, I could contribute a lot to this agency."

"Go on." His tone was noncommittal.

"When I was hired, Mr. Whitman told me there would be plenty of opportunity for advancement."

"Mr. Whitman?" He threw her a sharp glance. "Didn't Tom Marsh hire you?"

"No, he didn't. One of my professors at UT had gone to school with Mr. Whitman. He arranged for the interview. I never talked to Tom until my first day on the job."

"It's customary for low man on the totem pole to get the jobs no one else wants. Did you expect him to promote you right away?"

"Of course not!" She straightened and drummed her fingertips on the molded armrest. "I expected to earn my stripes like anyone else before working on more important accounts. And for eight months I've given the most trivial assignments my one-hundred-percent best effort." Her fingertips stilled as her words sped up. "But at what point will I be allowed to move up the totem pole? Last month Jim Reese was promoted ahead of me to the Capital Computer account after only three months with the agency."

Laura was beginning to read Alec's implacable face more easily. He obviously doubted her abilities. "If you'll take the time to compare Jim's performance with mine," she challenged, "you'll see why I filed a complaint with Human Resources."

Alec frowned. "I was never notified about a complaint."

"Mr. Marsh likes to work out staff problems 'quietly,' which to him meant ignoring my requests for more challenging assignments. Eventually I got so desperate I started submitting unsolicited ideas on the Regency account. Just to show him my capabilities."

A flicker of interest crossed Alec's face. "What did he say about your work?"

She turned toward her window. "He tossed it in the trash without even looking at it. He said that he would be the judge of when I was ready for more challenge." Laura curled her fingers at the memory. "That I'd better not go running to Mr. Whitman, either, or he'd make me long for the days of Yellow Page assignments."

"If you want to be successful at Harris, Bates and Whitman, Ms. Hayes, you'll have to develop a tougher hide," Alec said in a lecturing tone. "Perhaps another agency would suit you better."

She blinked, then ground her teeth. Hadn't he heard anything she'd said? "You don't seem to understand. I can't get a higher position somewhere else by showing a portfolio of Yellow Page ads. And by now everyone at the office, including Tom Marsh, knows about our little tête-à-tête. Do you honestly think he would let me leave without trying to get even? I won't be able to land a decent job at any top Houston agency after today."

It was only a slight exaggeration. Mr. Marsh had enormous influence in the Houston advertising community. He'd won a wall full of awards for the agency, although none in recent years. A discreet call here and there, and she would be blacklisted without any recourse.

Alec kept his gaze on the road. "Perhaps you should have thought of that before sneaking behind the man's back and kissing up to me for a promotion."

Laura's outrage rose like bile, obliterating everything but her need to wipe the patronizing expression off his face. "*Kissing up to you?* I went on the offensive, you pompous bigot, just like you would have done in the same situation. Only you can't get past the fact I'm a woman long enough to see this meeting was my only chance of building a future here!''

She was scarcely aware of the truck turning. When the vehicle passed through the ornate wrought-iron gate of a magnificent redbrick Georgian house, her anger dissolved into uneasiness.

Alec switched off the ignition and shifted to face Laura. It took all her courage not to turn away. He studied her intently, as if he didn't quite know what to make of her.

"You're wrong, you know." Amusement danced in his eyes. "Under the circumstances, I can understand why you bypassed Tom. And I'm not a pompous bigot, either."

One corner of his mouth kicked up slightly, deepening a masculine dimple in his left cheek.

"I'm a *smart* pompous bigot." He sobered quickly. "But I'm afraid I can't reward you for insubordination."

Her heart plunged. It was a long moment before she could speak. "Is this how you get your jollies? Getting people's hopes up so you can knock them down?"

Many a former schoolboy would recognize the look she gave Alec then. Laura Hayes always came up swinging.

"You'd be wise to reconsider your decision," she said, pleased to see Alec's relaxed slouch slowly straighten. "You can and should reward me. First, because I'm talented. Second, because I've honestly earned a chance for more responsibility. And last, because . . ."

"Don't stop now, Ms. Hayes. I'm fascinated."

She narrowed her eyes. "Because unless you assign me to the Regency Hotels creative team, I can virtually guarantee that you'll lose the account before the month is over."

He regarded her incredulously. "Are you threatening me?"

She raised an eyebrow. "*Smart* pompous bigot, aren't you?"

Alec lifted his right arm to her seat back. The deceptively innocent movement pulled fine worsted blue wool taut across his shoulders. Clearly it wasn't padding that made them seem a mile wide. His big body radiated anger, wrapping her in an oppressive embrace.

Dear Lord, what have I done? She swallowed hard. "D-don't you have a problem here at home to take care of?"

"My problem will sit safe until I get to it," he assured her, leaning even closer. "Don't change the subject, Ms. Hayes. I'm extremely interested to know how a junior copywriter could affect the fate of this agency's largest account."

His scornful gaze drifted down her department-store ensemble. She resisted the urge to cross her foot over a deep scuff mark no amount of bone-colored shoe polish had been able to hide.

Raising her chin, she treated him to her own scathingly slow inspection. "Some people in this world, Mr. McDonald, are not dependent on *connections* to pave their way to success."

Alec had been married to the daughter of founding partner John Bates. Agency gossip said that even after the divorce, John had favored Alec over other staff members, including Paul Whitman, also a founding partner.

Laura ignored the small twitch in Alec's cheek and folded her hands. "Whether you admit it to me or not, we both know Sam Parker is fed up with this agency's lackluster creative efforts." She slid him a wry glance. "It doesn't take a CIA agent to know he's inches away from defecting. You need someone working on his account who can turn the situation around. If Mr. Marsh hasn't done that by now, quite frankly, I doubt he ever will."

Alec's upper lip curled. "Let me get this straight. A woman with a whopping eight months on the job is going to do what a man with twenty years' experience hasn't been able to accomplish?"

She studied him coolly. "Exactly what bothers you more, Mr. McDonald? My gender or my lack of experience?"

Without moving a muscle, he loomed darker and larger. "Your complete lack of respect bothers me a lot, Ms. Hayes. A hell of a lot. Just what are you suggesting I do? Fire Tom and promote you to creative director?" He eyed her with distaste. "Or is it *my* job you want?"

Laura sniffed. "The only thing I want—the only thing I've ever wanted from this agency—is the chance to practice my craft. Give me something more challenging than a Yellow Page ad and judge my talent for yourself. If I fail, I'll resign without a peep."

"And if you succeed?" He arched a skeptical eyebrow.

Just watch me, Spock. "Then I'll have gone where no man has gone before. Even one with twenty years' experience."

Laura's smirk froze as his teeth bared in a humorless smile. She'd jumped in feetfirst again and as usual left her head behind.

"Very well, Ms. Hayes. If you really want that assignment, you've got it." He searched her eyes almost anxiously. "You *do* want it, don't you?"

Laura's scalp prickled. "Of course."

In the place where her instinct dwelled, a faint drumroll sounded.

Ready...

"Well, then, Ms. Hayes, here it is. I want a multi-media campaign concept for Regency Hotels that is designed to increase occupancy by twenty percent over the next year."

Aim...

"It must be totally different from anything we or any other agency has done for them before. I'm looking for innovative ideas...and practical applications. Any questions so far?"

Her mind was a black hole. Fortunately her tongue was used to navigating without a captain. "No. You've been very clear."

"Excellent!" Alec's gaze leapt to life with the first real gleam of pleasure she'd seen, then dropped to inspect a thumbnail. "Oh, and Ms. Hayes?"

It could have been an afterthought, a minor detail remembered, but Laura was beginning to know the man.

Fire, you son of a bitch!

"I want it on my desk by three o'clock tomorrow."

CHAPTER TWO

ALEC HITCHED the clanging aluminum ladder tighter under one arm. He would kill the kid. No—that was too merciful. He would take away Nintendo privileges for a week. Jason would consider that a fate worse than death.

As if dealing with the outrageous Ms. Hayes wasn't enough for one day, once again Alec had failed miserably as a father. Jason had stared down from his perch in the backyard's ancient pecan tree and flatly refused to move. Logic, threats, an offer to buy him the video game of his choice—nothing had budged his obstinate little rear.

Now Alec felt the impotent fury and self-disgust of a parent who has sunk to bribery and still lost. Thank God his neighbor had been home to lend an extension ladder. With luck Alec just might be able to get himself and Ms. Hayes back to the office by one. After all, he mused with a burgeoning grin, she had a challenging new assignment to tackle.

Unbidden, the vision of Laura accepting her impossible task with quiet dignity invaded his mind. There had been a strength of purpose in the set of her mouth and chin he'd almost admired. And those exotic eyes . . .

Alec frowned at his train of thought. The woman was a troublemaker. An undisciplined, self-serving hotshot looking for an easy route to glory. He'd given her exactly what she deserved.

Clattering toward his backyard fence, he eased the ladder's top rung through the open cedar gate. Somewhere around the sixth rung, the contraption jammed on a protruding hinge, squashing the hell out of both his thumb and any remaining good humor he possessed. He stumbled free of the gate and glared at the towering tree fifty feet ahead.

A stream of giggles drifted down from its dense canopy of leaves. Unbelieving, his gaze traveled first to one bone-colored pump, burrowed in the grass beneath spreading branches, before locating its mate a few feet away. As if flipped off in haste, the shoe lay upside down with its heel pointing skyward like an accusing finger. He groaned inwardly.

She was up in that tree with Jason. Just how she'd gotten there, Alec didn't know. But now he had not only one, but two errant children to retrieve.

Dragging the ladder behind him, he plowed a fifty-foot trail to the tree trunk and propped his cumbersome load against the bark. Slowly, dreading what he would see, Alec raised his gaze.

The woman was halfway up the tree, damn it. And from the look of things, on the verge of breaking her fool neck. His anxious gaze darted higher, recorded his son's safety, then swung back to the shapely derriere swaying toward him. As one slim foot stretched down, his interest quickened.

With every inch her toes lowered, Laura's black linen skirt crept higher above the knee. Several runs sprouted from a gaping hole in the heel of her panty hose. He followed them up a trim ankle and nicely curved calf until...

Sweet heaven!

Who would have thought that little Miz Women's Lib—
Miz Judge-My-Talent-For-Yourself—had the legs of a Las
Vegas showgirl? He slid an appreciative gaze from thigh
to instep, then shook himself. She was certainly acting the
part of a bubblehead.

"Unless you want my son to witness your death, Ms.
Hayes, kindly stay still," he bellowed.

Laura's entire body jerked, including her supporting
foot. She groped to reestablish hand- and footholds before glowering down under her billowing cotton sleeve.
"The only one who'll get me killed is you, Mr. Mc-
Donald. If you'll get out of my way and stop yelling, I'll
be fine."

Alec frowned. Delving into his pocket with one hand,
he located his last antacid tablet and popped it into his
mouth. Until today, he probably hadn't raised his voice in
three years.

"I appreciate your heroics, but you could get hurt."
Shrugging out of his suit jacket, he placed it carefully on
the grass. "Stay put and I'll come get you."

Grasping the ladder in both hands, he notched his foot
on the bottom rung and looked up. Laura glared down
like a treed cougar ready to leap on his neck. Confused,
he instinctively sought the nearest male for an explanation.

Jason peered down over dangling sneakers, his alert
blue eyes rimmed in thick dark lashes. "I don't think she
needs your help, Dad," Jason said. "She can climb pretty
good—for a girl."

Alec's gaze dropped lower to where Laura was perched,
narrowed on her smug expression, then lifted back up to
Jason. "*How* good, son?"

The boy shifted his weight, unmindful of the swaying
branch beneath him. Dappled sunlight dusted his wheat

blond cap of hair. "Well—" he hesitated, his ego obviously battling with admiration for Laura's skill "—almost good as me. Wasn't her fault the branches got too small way up here."

Sensing a flurry of movement, Alec lowered his gaze just in time to see Laura touch down on a gnarled branch stretching parallel to the ground. She pivoted and faced him squarely, planting feet and fists Peter Pan style. *So there,* her impudent grin said.

Something hard and tight inside Alec loosened a fraction.

He scowled. "I believe I asked you to wait in the truck until I came back, Ms. Hayes."

Her grin faded, replaced by an exasperated glare. "You left me in a hot truck with the electric windows rolled up—and no keys, I might add. If I were a dog, Mr. McDonald, you could be arrested for cruelty." She sat down in a huff, feet dangling, and made a show of adjusting her skirt.

Suppressing a smile, Alec crossed his arms and leaned one shoulder against the bark. "As long as you were risking your neck up there, why didn't you bring Jason down?"

"I moved down to a bigger branch, Dad," Jason volunteered. "She said I wouldn't like bein' a pancake." He peered at Laura and giggled infectiously, as only a six-year-old can.

Alec watched the exchange through narrowed eyes. The two were certainly chummy. His son had never looked at *him* like that.

"I warned you once about your impulsive behavior, Ms. Hayes." He let his gaze slide over her disheveled appearance, lingering on her torn panty hose. "Don't expect me to pay for clothing damages."

Her unrouged cheeks bloomed roses, intensifying the rich brown hues in her eyes and hair. Against a fluttering green backdrop, she looked as natural and vibrant as spring itself.

"*I* was more concerned about your son's safety than about my clothes. That twig Jason sat on could have snapped any minute. Your ladder wouldn't have helped a broken neck."

Alec calculated the distance from Jason to the ground and felt a sharp skewer of alarm. He shifted, ignoring the bite of rough bark beneath his shoulder. She'd responded to Jason's danger, and he'd treated her abominably in return.

"Where I grew up, we climbed fire escapes, not trees," he explained. Staring somewhere in the vicinity of her feet, he lowered his voice for her ears alone. "I've never climbed a tree in my life."

The admission embarrassed him. God only knew why he cared what this woman thought. But for some reason he did.

"I didn't mean to imply you didn't care." Laura matched his quietness. "It's obvious you love Jason very much. And he certainly loves you."

He raised an eyebrow. "For someone who loves me, he has a hell of a way of showing it."

She pointed a finger overhead and swung her legs. "You mean *this?*" Two enchanting dimples appeared briefly. "He couldn't show it more plainly if he sent you a singing telegram."

With nonchalant ease, she pushed off the branch and fell feetfirst in the lush grass. Brushing twigs and leaves off her skirt, she walked slowly toward him and met his eyes in unmistakable challenge.

"Why do you think he insisted on you being the one to get him down?" she asked.

Alec strove to maintain his casual stance against the tree, nearly failing when he looked down at her upturned mouth, the lips pink and slightly parted. For the life of him, he couldn't make a sound.

"You're a *smart* guy. Figure it out."

Turning, she plucked her shoes from the ground. "Oh, and Mr. McDonald?"

Despite her innocent tone, Alec tensed.

"Do it by three o'clock tomorrow, won't you?" With a definite smirk, she ambled toward the gate, pausing halfway to shout over her shoulder, "Bye, Jason. Your dad has to drive me back to the office now, so be a good boy and come on down, okay?"

The silence stretched. Alec released a long vindicated breath.

"Okay, Laura," Jason said.

To her credit, she resisted looking at Alec before continuing toward the truck. He stared at the gate long after she'd passed through it. For the first time since issuing Ms. Hayes her impossibly difficult assignment, he wondered what tomorrow would bring.

AT TWO-THIRTY the next afternoon, Sam Parker stared eagerly at the door leading into the executive offices of Harris, Bates and Whitman Advertising. McDonald wasn't expecting him. Of course, Sam had planned it that way. Unexpected visits revealed the truth behind the makeup. If you caught a woman without her "face" on and she was still beautiful, you knew it was the real thing. And he was beginning to suspect that under the concealing talent of Alec McDonald, the face of Harris, Bates and Whitman was as ugly as a baboon's ass.

Seconds later, the solid oak door opened to reveal Alec's tall frame, his hand outstretched. "Sam," he acknowledged with a wry smile. "What a pleasant surprise. If I'd known you were coming, we would have rolled out the red carpet."

Exactly, my boy. "Nonsense. I had an appointment in the area, so I thought I'd stop in and see how that little problem I discussed with Paul is coming along."

"Couldn't be better." Not by so much as a blink did the marketing vice president indicate it was highly unusual for Sam to drop by. "I'm afraid Paul is in Austin right now. But why don't we go to my office and I'll give you a status report?"

"Fine, fine."

Sam followed Alec down a hallway of charcoal gray carpet patterned with tiny pink squares. The walls were covered in mauve silk, seventy-five dollars a square foot if it was a dime. He knew, because he'd just vetoed something similar for his property in Denver. No wonder conference calls and meetings like this cost him a hundred bucks an hour.

Sam's teeth clamped tighter around his cigar. If the agency couldn't cough up a viable campaign today, after two previous failures, he'd have to turn in his ninety-day termination notice and hire a new agency.

Alec led the way into his office, motioned Sam to sit down and settled himself behind his desk. "Okay, Sam, why don't you tell me why you're really here?" He leveled one of his infamous cut-the-crap looks.

"I told you, Alec. I came to see what's being done regarding the campaign you're sticking my hotel's name on. 'See' being the operative word here."

"I'd rather wait until our scheduled meeting to show you the details." Alec leaned back and clasped his hands over an enviably flat stomach. "We're still polishing the rough edges at this point."

Sam's sharp bark of laughter spit the mutilated cigar free of his teeth to land on the edge of his lower lip. "I'm not exactly known for my polish, son. If anybody can see past the rough edges, I can." He plucked the cigar from his mouth and ground it decisively into the ashtray Alec had pushed forward. "Let's not play footsy, boy. If you can't show me anything now, I might think some outside free-lancer was supplying this agency's creative work—which, by the way, you assured me your staff could handle."

"I assured you that this agency would get the job done," Alec corrected. "How we do that is our problem, not yours. But since you insist on checking into our hotel early, don't complain to management if your room's not ready." He reached over to an intercom and jabbed a button. "Sharon? Please call Tom Marsh and tell him to take his work to the small conference room, instead of my office."

Alec glanced at his watch and rose. "Shall we?"

Sam followed his account supervisor down the hall, wondering at the man's phenomenal self-control. Any other suit would be sweating bullets now at the possibility of losing his business.

Three months ago, when word had leaked out that the twenty-six-million-dollar Regency Hotels account was up for review, his life had become a circus. Suddenly agencies from all over the country wanted to take him to lunch, give him a tour of their "shops," show him their "reels." He'd seen enough dog-and-pony shows to make P.T. Barnum contemplate selling insurance.

Fed up, Sam had finally made an offer to the recognized advertising mastermind behind Economax Lodge's thirty-percent increase in market shares. When Alec had declined on the grounds it would be a conflict of interest with his existing client, Sam had simply gone over his head to strike a deal with Paul Whitman.

Alec paused in front of a doorway and gestured for Sam to enter. A teak table surrounded by black leather club chairs dominated the room. Two easels supported large art boards, shielded now from curious eyes by a cover flap.

A silver-haired man rose from the end of the table. In addition to wearing one of those ridiculous jackets with leather elbow pads, the dandy sported a bow tie. Sam didn't trust men who wore bow ties. To top it off, the guy's eyes—ice blue, opaque and edged with a circle of dark gray—were downright creepy.

"I don't believe you've had the pleasure of meeting our creative director," Alec said. "Sam Parker, meet Tom Marsh."

Those strange eyes locked with Alec's a moment and narrowed, then flicked Sam's way. Cripes, the man gave him the willies.

"How do you do? Would you care for some tea?" Tom gestured toward a fancy coffee and tea service, frowning when Alec poured himself a cup of coffee and sat down.

"No, thanks," Sam said. The creative director's nasal accent placed him north of Oklahoma, a grave offense in Sam's book. He grasped the hand being offered and inwardly grimaced at the soft contact. As quickly as business etiquette allowed, he released Tom's hand and sat down.

Alec's manner turned brisk. "I'd like to say a few words, then let Tom explain his creative concepts and strategy to you."

Ignoring Tom's obvious surprise, Alec launched into a review of the agency's accomplishments to date. Sam had to admire the smoke screen. Unfortunately the most brilliant account management in the world couldn't make up for a weak creative message.

"All mechanisms to begin an aggressive advertising campaign are in place and functioning smoothly. I'm sure you'll be pleased with this new concept," Alec concluded. "Tom has been working hard on a *fresh* approach. I'll let him take over from here."

Sam shifted in his seat, glad he wasn't on the receiving end of Alec's glacial stare.

Tom cleared his throat. "Regency Hotels' basic strengths have always been excellent service, luxurious appointments and spacious suites. Past advertising has focused on your founding slogan—The Standard In Royal Treatment—as a way to capitalize on those strengths."

He flashed Alec a defiant look. "Mr. Whitman and I see no reason to tamper with tradition. The fault is obviously not with your message, but with a lack of visual support to lend the message credibility."

He pushed his chair vigorously away from the table, rolling on solid brass castors to the base of the left easel before standing up. With an affected flourish, he lifted the cover flap.

Four magazine-ad layouts glowed like jewels against the black art board. Everything about them was first-class. The design, images and copy sent the clear message that if a hotel bears the name Regency, it's worthy of royalty. The creative theme had served Regency Hotels admirably for thirty years.

Too bad his founding hotel was *thirty-two* years old.

Sam's shoulders sagged. He felt betrayed, as if he'd gone to a gourmet restaurant and been served a microwave dinner.

Alec stirred in his chair. "I thought I asked you to redo those layouts," he said in a soft chilling voice.

Tom paled and thrust out his jaw. "As I said, Mr. Whitman agreed with me that wasn't necessary." He pointedly ignored Alec and turned to Sam. "Of course, these are only illustrations. Once people see the unique beauty of Regency Hotels in the new photographs we'll take, they'll believe our claims of superiority. Technology and computer imagery have come so far since the hotels were last photographed you wouldn't believe what can be done to disguise flaws."

"Are you saying that we need to alter photographs to make Regency Hotels look good?"

Tom appeared startled, then wary. "No, of course not. Regency Hotels are known for their exceptional beauty."

"Then why do we need to spend thousands of dollars for new photographs to show people what they already know?"

"These photographs will show them better. Interesting angles. Dramatic lighting. People will want to *frame* these photographs." A bead of sweat glistened at Tom's left temple.

Sam slammed a fist down. "I want people to *sleep* in my hotels, not frame them! The rules have changed, God help me. I can build the most beautiful hotel in the world, sink everything I have into it. And in six months' time a Marriott or Carlson or some other megacompany will have built three more just like it. If the old advertising theme still worked, I wouldn't need a new agency." He knew he was yelling, but it had been pure hell the past year watching occupancy rates plummet, in spite of all his efforts.

Glancing at the second easel, he sighed with resignation. "I don't suppose you have anything revolutionary hiding under there, do you?"

Tom's face tightened. "It appears you've already closed your mind to this particular campaign. Although I think you should reconsider its merits."

There was a tense silence as each man adjusted to the implications of the meeting. The account relationship was finished. Hell, they all knew it.

Tom glanced at Sam. "You're not looking for something revolutionary, Mr. Parker. You're looking for a miracle. Well, let me be the first to wish you good luck," he sneered, his silver irises glowing malignantly. "Because you're definitely going to need it."

Sam withdrew a new Havana from his inside jacket pocket and calmly bit off one tip. His gaze followed Tom's huffy departure from the room before turning back to Alec with true regret. He struck a match and pulled deeply, silently, until a fat grub worm of ashes inched slowly toward his mouth.

Alec lifted his cup and shoved a saucer forward just in time to catch the crumbling mass. "Now what?"

"You've left me no choice, Alec. Unless you're a magician and can pull something out of the hat better than *that*—" he pointed at the exposed layouts "—this meeting, and my company's association with this agency, is finished."

A tiny spark of interest, a vitality Sam had never seen before in the other man's eyes, flickered to life. Without knowing why, he found himself suddenly hopeful.

Alec held up a pencil like a cautionary finger and stretched to the center of the table. Pulling a sleek black phone toward him, he dialed an extension.

"Sharon? Did my three-o'clock appointment show up?" Listening with that curious gleam in his eye, he tapped his eraser against the table. "Yes, yes. Please apologize for me. But don't let her leave, yet. In fact, send her here to the conference room as soon as possible." He nodded. "Good."

If Sam didn't know better, he'd swear the legendary Ice Man was nervous. "Just what are you trying to pull, McDonald?"

"Pull? Pull," he repeated, chuckling to himself. "You wanted a rabbit, didn't you, Sam?"

A sharp rap sounded on the door.

Alec sobered, lifted his pencil theatrically and waved it toward the door like a wand. "Abracadabra."

SHE WAS GOING to be sick. Right on the polished teak table. Dragging in a breath, Laura almost gagged as the thick faintly sweet fumes hit her lungs and empty stomach.

She'd spent eight hours at an all-night computer center preparing a seventy-page presentation, complete with color graphs, before rushing home with barely enough time to shower and change for work. By the time Sharon had directed her here, Laura was trembling from exhaustion, hunger and the most numbing case of stage fright she'd ever experienced.

Not exactly the best state when entering a room filled with noxious smoke.

"So this is your rabbit, eh, Alec?" The man's words slurred around the odious cigar clenched between his teeth. "Looks more like a scared little bunny to me. If you're counting on her to turn things around, she must be one hell of a trick." He snickered as if he'd said something clever.

One hell of a trick?

Blessed anger surged through her body and brought with it revitalizing strength. She didn't know what kind of game Alec had been playing, but it was over. Now.

Her gaze snapped to the older man's cigar. "How chivalrous of you not to smoke, Mr.... Parker, isn't it?" She'd seen too many publicity clippings not to recognize him.

His jaw dropped slightly, tilting the cigar.

Laura reached over and plucked the nasty thing out of his mouth, holding it between two fingertips. Wrinkling her nose, she searched the room for an ashtray. Finding none, she dropped the stub into Alec's unfinished coffee as if disposing of a bug.

Dusting off both hands with a grimace, Laura gave each man a long look. "Now then, let's get this straight. I am not, nor have I ever been, anybody's trick. I have never, in anyone's wildest imagination, been a scared little bunny."

She placed both palms on the table and leaned forward, focusing on the main culprit. "Apparently I have been naive, Mr. McDonald. I thought your assignment was the request of a mature professional. My mistake." The look on their faces was priceless, worth every sleepless hour. "But now that you've had your laugh, *gentlemen,* I'd like your attention for a few moments."

By God, they would either have the courtesy to listen to her presentation or watch her take it straight to a competitor! Laura pressed two fingertips on the bound proposal in front of her and shoved hard. It skidded across the table and was slap-stopped by a strong tanned hand.

I'll give you something to raise your eyebrow at, you rat. Just sit back and watch the show.

CHAPTER THREE

WITH DEADLY PRECISION, Laura shot off a round of statistics gathered from her research of three diverse Regency Hotels markets. She analyzed occupancy rates, gross operating room profits, competitive factors and guest demographics for each property, and supported the facts with graphs.

At first, her words were fueled by cold anger at everyone and everything conspiring against her career. Somewhere along the way, her genuine enthusiasm for the project took over.

She spoke directly to the man with the most at stake. "Unless the trend is reversed soon, Mr. Parker, you won't even be able to bail out by selling the company. No investor will touch the cash-eating monster Regency Hotels, Inc. has become in recent months."

Sam opened his coat and reached for a new cigar. The Havana was halfway to his mouth when he paused, looked questioningly at Laura and slowly returned it to his pocket.

Both of Alec's eyebrows shot upward.

"You seem to have made it your business to learn a lot about mine, young lady," Sam said. "Think you have the answer to saving my company? Not that it needs saving, by the way."

Was that a twinkle in his eyes? Laura found their sky blue directness appealing, now that they held no derision. She warmed another degree to the subject.

"I wouldn't presume to say I have the only answer. But I do strongly recommend that you change your target market. To women."

Alec's startled look turned speculative.

Sam snorted. "I already target women. Who do you think the flowers and soaps and fancy froufrou are for?"

"The wives and girlfriends of the *men* you target. The twenty percent of the population all your competitors want a piece of, too." She held up a hand to halt his protest. "Now I know you're a savvy businessman, but hear me out, please."

Laura poured herself a cup of coffee, sat down and prepared to jump in feetfirst. This time, she would bring her head along.

PRETENDING TO READ notes in his lap, Alec listened to Laura's impassioned husky voice. He was stunned, pure and simple. Tom had botched the presentation so thoroughly by showing the same tired unrevised concepts that Alec had figured the agency had nothing to lose by presenting her proposal. But damned if she wasn't putting on a show worthy of Siegfried and Roy, right down to creative concepts that blew him away.

How had she managed to put the thing together so quickly? It was impossible not to be impressed.

There was no trace of the impish tomboy now. In her place sat a no-nonsense businesswoman wearing a double-breasted navy jacket and slim gray skirt. Two days ago she wouldn't have caused so much as a speed bump in his swiftly passing gaze. But now...

He studied her from under lowered lids. Her braided hair was pulled back tightly with the ends tucked up—a crinkled swim cap glinting with fiery auburn highlights. She wore little makeup, and her skin was fine-pored and translucent. The fluorescent glare overhead was not kind to the faint purplish shadows beneath her almond-shaped eyes, though. She'd obviously had a rough night.

His ex-wife, Susan, used to camouflage her after-party fatigue with artfully applied cosmetics. This woman chose to steamroll over her exhaustion by sheer force of will. Even dead tired, Laura Hayes vibrated with more energy than any female he'd known.

What would it feel like to bury himself in all that exuberance?

Alec stiffened. Good Lord, what was he thinking? He'd always favored feminine petite beauties, not man-eating Amazons. Obviously his brain, goaded by that part of his anatomy with a mind of its own, fantasized using the material at hand. Still... the woman didn't have to act as if he were invisible, did she?

He frowned as Laura cited the tremendous increase of traveling women in the workforce and the fact that over ninety percent of vacation-destination decisions were made by women. She theorized that with many minor changes, but no major expenditures, Regency Hotels could become the preferred choice of an extremely loyal consumer group that was starved for "royal treatment."

The lowly copywriter had taken complete and absolute control of the meeting, Alec realized with a jolt. Unless he did something fast, she would leave him in the dust.

"The key to targeting women successfully is to seduce them with thoughtfulness," she continued in the definitive tone of an expert. "You can't imagine what a powerful attraction that is."

Alec grinned at Sam, man-to-man. "Funny, I've seduced my share of women over the years. But it wasn't my thoughtfulness they thanked me for."

Laura's golden eyes took on the look of a hissing cat's. "Must have been the twenty bucks you left on the nightstand."

Sam's whoop ricocheted off the walls. When at last he quieted, he wiped his eyes and glanced at his watch. "Holy jalapeños, it's almost happy hour." He sank back in his chair and looked from Laura to Alec, an odd expression on his craggy face. "What's all this Mister and Miz stuff? You two fight like you're married. Sure you don't have something going on the side?"

Alec gaped at Laura, her horrified expression no doubt a reflection of his own.

"Guess not," Sam said, chuckling. "How 'bout you two letting me buy you a beer? I know a place where the Corona's cold and the burgers are hot. We can talk some more about Laura's ideas there."

Reaching into his pocket, Alec pulled out a roll of Tums and peeled back the paper wrapping. He'd lost control all right. Of the meeting, and his whole sorry life. But by God he would get it back. Starting now.

He pushed away from the table and stood. "Last one there buys the first round."

LAURA TILTED her head back, swigged from a long-neck bottle and then plunked her drink down on the weathered picnic table. Thirty minutes ago she'd felt on top of the world at Sam's obvious interest in her proposal. Now here she sat on Bubba's outdoor patio, nursing a beer and growing irritation. She glared at Alec over her sweating bottle. Drat the man. Why had he accepted Sam's invitation before any decisions had been made? She'd had no choice but to tag along and protect her interests.

Sam lumbered up to the table clutching a red plastic basket and a frosty Corona. "Sure I can't interest either of you in a Buffalo Burger?"

They shook their heads in unison, Laura a bit more vigorously than Alec. She sniffed once and wrinkled her nose.

Sam grinned. "Don't knock it till you've tried it. I'd rather eat this than prime rib." He settled next to her and hovered over his basket of food like a mother bird over hatchlings.

Laura propped an elbow on the rough cedar and buried her chin in one palm. The outdoor speakers blared an Astros-Cubs game, its commentary droning like the speeding traffic visible on Loop 610. When Alec and Sam launched into a riveting discussion of baseball statistics, her lids drooped.

Lord she was tired—tired of getting the runaround and just plain bone weary. The sleepless night and constant worry over her family's well-being had caught up with her. She slumped lower. Her lids weighed ten pounds each. The warped table beckoned like a Beauty Rest mattress.

"I want this little lady in charge of my creative team, Alec," Sam said around a mouthful of food.

Laura's eyes popped open. She straightened. Alec looked like he'd just stepped in a cow patty and didn't know where to clean his foot.

Sam stuffed the last bite of burger into his mouth, washed it down with a lusty swallow of Corona and shifted on the bench to face both Laura and Alec. His baby blue eyes sharpened shrewdly. "You're lucky as a flea in a kennel she came along, son, and you know it. Now if you can just keep that snake-eyed Marsh character away from my account, we may still have a working relationship.''

Jubilation flowed through Laura, as reviving as caffeine. Alec had no choice left but to promote her now. She'd beaten him at his own game. Only...he didn't look beaten.

Alec drained the last of his beer with the air of a man about to take action. He thwacked the empty bottle down. ''Did you or did you not hire Harris, Bates and Whitman Advertising three months ago because of my track record?''

Sam beetled his brows. ''You know I did.''

''As I recall, you insisted I supervise your account before you signed our agency contract. What's the matter, Sam, don't you trust me anymore?''

The older man scrubbed a hand over his silver burr haircut. '' 'Course I do, Alec. You're the only reason I've stuck it out this long. Hell, my entire marketing department thinks you're God's gift to advertising, but...'' He trailed off uncertainly.

''But you've lost confidence in the rest of the agency, right? And I don't blame you.'' Alec toyed with his beer label a moment, then looked up with compelling earnestness. ''What if I were to tell you First National Bank has approved a generous line of credit for a new venture of mine? What if I said that venture would be up and running by the time you've come to the end of your ninety-day termination notice to Harris, Bates and Whitman? What if you knew that venture would make Regency Hotels its first priority? Think you could put your faith in *McDonald* Advertising?''

Laura's stomach sank. Had this ace been up his sleeve all along? She frantically called his bluff. ''I'd ask about the no-compete agreement he signed if I were you, Mr. Parker.''

Alec impaled her with a glance. "Being John Bates's son-in-law gave me certain privileges. I didn't sign anything." He focused back on Sam. "I've been planning this move for months, except the part about soliciting your business. I'd intended to leave the agency's existing accounts alone when I set up my own shop."

"What changed your mind?"

Raising a hand to block the setting sun, Alec squinted. "Tom's little stunt. I realized how much things have changed since John died. Integrity, professional courtesy—they're wasted on the present management. I'm neither legally nor morally obligated to give them my loyalty, Sam." His hand dropped. "I don't like how they operate, and I'm getting out—with or without your help."

Laura stared, fascinated in spite of herself. Lit by golden rays, his eyes shimmered as blue as Lake Travis on a cloudless day. He'd rolled his cuffs to midforearm and loosened his tie. A light breeze ruffled his gleaming black hair. Her mind struggled to match this man with the by-the-book, corporate stuffed shirt of yesterday.

As if reading her thoughts, Alec shifted his attention to her. A zap of pure energy zinged up and down her spine.

Sam cleared his throat. His twinkling gaze encompassed them both, then steadied on Alec. "Alec, you're a good man to have in my corner. I trust you with my budget, my marketing staff and my business strategy. But you couldn't come up with a good creative campaign if I held a knife to your zipper."

Alec visibly winced as Sam nodded toward Laura. She tensed.

"This girl's got great ideas and more goddamn balls than a Rockets' locker room. Just the kind of person I want on my team, Alec. Now you hire *her* to head up my creative team and I'll give your question serious consideration." He patted his shirt pocket, pulled out a cigar and matches, then lit up. Taking two deep puffs, he squinted through the smoke and awaited their reaction with obvious enjoyment.

Laura released a pent-up breath.

Alec was the first to recover. "Sam, please reconsider. This woman has no discipline, no self-control. She'll disrupt the entire office."

Laura threw him a poisonous glance. "Yes, Sam, have a heart. This man is a human robot. I can't be creative with him breathing down my—"

"That's my offer. Take it or leave it." Sam's expression hardened. "When I leave this table, my offer walks out with me. If I were you two, I'd come to some agreement real quick."

It occurred to Laura suddenly that the odds had shifted in her favor. That she had a golden opportunity to fulfill both her career goal and family obligation. And that, wonder of wonders, she held a royal flush.

Her heart racing with her thoughts, she kept her eyes on Sam. "I don't think I can work for Alec, Mr. Parker, but I'll consider working *with* him—at Hayes and McDonald Advertising."

Ignoring a strangled sound from across the table, she concentrated on Sam's admiring grin. "Those are my terms, if you're willing to accept them."

"Hell's bells, I like your style, girl! McDonald Advertising, Hayes and McDonald Advertising..." He shrugged a massive shoulder. "Makes no difference to me what's on the door, as long as you're inside. Guess it's up to you now, Alec. You can shake hands with your new partner and guarantee my business—or not. Either way, I'm firing Harris, Bates and Whitman Advertising tomorrow.''

Laura steeled herself to look at Alec. The lake blue eyes she'd admired earlier were the color of gunmetal now—and just as ominous.

I'll make you pay for this, those eyes promised as he slowly stretched out a hand.

She reached out and bypassed the fingertip grip he sought, sliding her palm to fit snugly against his. *Winner take all,* she silently answered.

In complete agreement, they shook hands.

''DAMN IT, Alec, have you lost your mind?'' Paul Whitman waved Alec's letter of resignation aloft and glared across the desk with milky blue eyes. His liver-spotted hand trembled before dropping to the gleaming wood. ''You can't just waltz out of here with our largest account. What would John think?''

Trust the last living partner of Harris, Bates and Whitman Advertising to try emotional blackmail. His manipulation made leaving the agency that much easier.

''John Bates is probably looking down and laughing his wings off right now. He left the door wide open for me to do this someday. In fact, I think he hoped I would,'' Alec said with a flash of insight.

Even after the divorce, his father-in-law had continued to treat him with respect and affection. Alec missed John infinitely more than his spoiled daughter. The perceptive businessman must have guessed Paul would exploit Alec to win accounts, then deny him adequate control. By waiving the standing no-compete agreement required of employees from midlevel management up, John had ingeniously protected his protégé's future interests.

Paul looked at Alec with basset-hound reproach. "To think we've harbored a traitor all these years. Disgraceful. Unethical."

"Like you cutting a deal with Sam Parker behind my back," Alec bit out. "Economax Lodges stuck with us through the shakiest year this agency ever had, Paul. They trusted us to follow through on the three-year plan we presented." He snagged Paul's darting glance with an accusing stare. "But you jilted that account like a bored lover when Regency Hotels crooked its little finger."

A dull flush crept up the old man's scrawny neck. His eyes blinked rapidly, then veered left to scan a track-lit wall filled with award plaques and certificates. He raised his sagging chin. "I did what I had to do, Alec. What you'll have to do, if you're still hell-bent on founding your own agency. You'll discover that soon enough."

Alec jumped to his feet, his only wish to get out now that he'd revealed his decision. "You'll have ninety days to turn over all art files and close out the billing, Paul. I know I can count on your professional cooperation during the transition." Alec paused, detecting a spiteful gleam in the CEO's eyes. "But if for some reason I don't receive it, I just might feel the need to solicit the other fifteen accounts I reeled in for this agency."

Leaving Paul's mouth working like a carp on a riverbank, Alec walked through the door without a single regret. He'd taken four steps down the hallway before relief made him lean against the wall.

Maintaining his composure at work the past few months had become increasingly hard. Living with Jason added pressure to his already strained self-control. Alec protected his son as best he could, but there were times he simply couldn't resist venturing near the bright, beautiful child—consequences be damned. If only he could trust his temper around the boy. If only...

Alec straightened and shook off his wistful thoughts. He couldn't change who he was. At least by regaining control of his professional life, he would strengthen command of his emotions at home. Laura wouldn't be a problem, once he'd talked with her.

Feeling lighter and more optimistic than he had in years, Alec headed back to his office. As usual, his secretary was hard at work. He would miss her, he realized with surprise.

"Good morning, Sharon. You're looking very well today."

She lifted startled brown eyes from the letter she'd been typing. "Th-thank you, Mr. McDonald." Fluttery fingers reached up to her iron gray coif, then drifted down to her matronly purple-flowered bosom. She clutched her strand of beads as if it were a rosary. "Are you feeling all right, sir?"

"Never better." He perched in companionable silence on the corner of her desk and noticed her empty ceramic mug. "Would you like some more coffee? I was about to get myself a cup."

She opened and closed her mouth, then shook her head.

"No? Well, when you finish that letter, I need you to run over to Human Resources and pick up something for me." He plucked a pencil and pad from beside the telephone, scribbled a quick note and ripped off the top sheet. "Give this to Mrs. Layton and tell her I need the file immediately please." He slipped off the desk and held out his hand.

Sharon stared as if he'd sprouted a wart on his nose, then snatched the note from his fingertips. What in God's name was wrong with the woman?

Twenty minutes later, all thoughts of her odd behavior fled when she handed him a large manila folder. He studied the tab labeled Laura J. Hayes and drew a deep breath. If he was stuck with a hand grenade like Laura for an indefinite amount of time, the more he knew about her the less likely he would accidentally pull the pin. Leaning back, he opened the file.

She was twenty-six, he learned with surprise. Her extraordinary confidence had fooled him into thinking her older, although her complexion should have clued him in. He found her guileless scrubbed innocence rather refreshing, actually. Especially after the hours he'd spent watching Susan preen in front of a mirror.

Tightening his mouth, Alec returned his focus to the file in his lap. If he'd ever doubted Laura's intelligence, which he hadn't, her résumé would have dispelled any questions on that score.

She'd received an academic scholarship to the University of Texas at Austin, graduating magna cum laude a full year early with a BS in advertising. It had taken three years, instead of the usual two, for her to earn her master's degree in marketing, but obviously not because of scholastic difficulties. She'd graduated in the top quarter of her class.

Past hobbies included intramural softball and singing with a rock band. He raised an eyebrow at that, then frowned at a series of complaints she'd filed against Tom Marsh. If Alec hadn't already resigned, he would get to the bottom of the creative director's antipathy toward her. As it was, she wouldn't have to worry about Tom any longer. Alec was a different story.

Sifting through the remaining papers, he was on the verge of closing the folder when a single sheet of elegant embossed stationery caught his eye. He pulled out the

letter of recommendation and noted its signature with a
sense of awe. No wonder Laura's proposal had been impressive. She'd studied under Professor Fisher, a world-
renowned authority on the subject of cultural trends and
life-style targeting.

Scanning the letter quickly, Alec's eyes widened at the
closing paragraph: "During several joint endeavors, I
have found Ms. Hayes to be a logical thinker, a self-
disciplined student and an even-tempered companion. In
short, an ideal partner."

An ideal partner.

The unfamiliar gurgling sensation swelled in Alec's
chest and filtered through his vocal chords in the form of
a deep rumbling chuckle. Giving in to the overriding impulse, he threw back his head and gave a great belly laugh
for the first time in seventeen years.

Just beyond his closed door, a ceramic mug crashed to
the floor.

LAURA SHOOK the empty can and stopped herself short.
Idiot. Like the coffee fairy would have visited her kitchen
between last night and this morning.

Thank heavens it was Saturday and she had the weekend to pull herself together. As Alec had guessed, her offer the day before of two weeks' notice had been flatly
rejected. She shuddered at the memory of Mr. Marsh's
hostile glare as she packed her personal supplies and de-
parted with cowardly haste.

Grabbing a box of tea bags from the pantry shelf, she
turned to her tiny stove and prayed the gas jet would ig-
nite without a match. For once the finicky burner coop-
erated. Setting the teakettle on it, she stepped back and
leaned against the opposite counter to watch for the first
feeble wisps of rising steam.

Three days ago her biggest professional challenge was writing a catchy Yellow Page headline. Yet Monday she was due at Alec's house bright and early to begin the daunting task of launching a new agency. Talk about sink or swim. She'd expected to have more time before—

Bang! Bang! Bang!

Laura jerked back, hitting her head against the cabinet door she'd left open. Darn efficiency apartment. No space, and no peace. The knocking on her neighbor's door came through loud and clear.

Pulling down a chipped mug, she dropped in a tea bag and poured steaming water over the fragrant leaves. Not as good as coffee, but at least it was caffeine. She shuffled into the bedroom cum living/dining room and sank into her only chair.

Bang! Bang! Bang! "Brenda Lee?"

Laura frowned at the sound of an angry male voice so close to her own front door. Why didn't her neighbor answer? Surely ten o'clock was late enough for Brenda Lee to be up, even if she had come home after two in the morning as usual. And awakened Laura as usual.

Sipping her tea, she snuggled more deeply between the chair's comforting overstuffed arms. Her older brother, Scott, had shown up with the orange plaid monstrosity in the back of his pickup four months ago, and she'd been thrilled. Every penny she earned went toward rent, student-loan payments and what she called her "guilt fund." If she was in a frivolous mood, she sometimes bought food.

There just wasn't enough left to spend on furniture. Lord knew if she had extra money, she wouldn't have forced a confrontation with Alec and be his partner now. Life had a funny way of—

Bang! Bang! Bang! "Brenda Lee. You open this door right now or I'm gonna bust it down!"

Laura straightened in alarm. Setting down her mug, she tiptoed to the door and fastened the chain lock, although from the sound of that voice it would be feeble protection at best. Why hadn't she installed a dead bolt and peephole like Scott had suggested?

Because he'd been domineeringly male about the whole thing, and I can't stand being treated like a helpless female.

"I mean it, Brenda Lee. I know you're in there. I saw your car."

Something about the man's surly voice made Laura break out in a cold sweat.

"Go away! I told you to leave me alone," answered a shaky female voice.

"Look, you little tease, I'm here to collect. You was friendly enough last night when I tipped you damn near my whole paycheck. *Now open this friggin' door and pay up!*"

Laura clutched her throat, then headed for the kitchen wall phone. This guy was dangerous.

"Go away, Jack, or I'll call the police!" her neighbor shouted.

A splintering crash rent the air, followed by a terrified scream. Laura's knees buckled. The woman needed help *now*.

Spotting her glove on the floor, Laura scooped up the softball tucked inside and fumbled with the chain latch on her door, cursing all the while until her clumsy fingers finally managed the task. She jerked the door open, stumbled outside and squinted against the sunlight.

The door adjacent to Laura's sagged open, two of its three hinges torn completely out of the shattered door frame. She peered through and froze at the sight of a huge brute grappling with a petite blonde. One of his hands held her two delicate wrists, while the other struggled with the zipper of his jeans.

"Keep still, bitch. Nobody comes on to Jack Brewster without paying up," he snarled, forcing the woman slowly toward a sofa.

Huge green eyes glittered with hate as the blonde threw back her head and spit in his face. He dropped her wrists and wiped his cheek.

"You shouldn't oughtta done that, Brenda Lee. Now I cain't be nice to you no more." Bunching his massive shoulders, he advanced toward her like an enraged bull. Terror replaced defiance in the blonde's eyes.

"Hey, pig!" Laura shouted, stepping through the doorway.

Jack spun around, his broad face incredulous, as Brenda Lee scuttled into the corner.

"You've got five minutes before the cops get here. I wouldn't advise touching her again." Laura's heartbeat reverberated in her ears. If only the softball she clutched were a gun!

Small bloodshot eyes the color of Brazos River mud inspected her body, then gleamed like a rat spotting cheese. He smiled, revealing yellow tobacco-stained teeth.

"Well, well, well. Looks like you got a friend who wants to join the party, Brenda Lee," he said, his gaze never leaving Laura. "Know what I think, lady? I think you're shittin' me. I think you never called no cops."

Like two gunslingers facing off, each waited for the other to move. Laura's fingers turned leather and laces to the correct position.

Jack's murky yellow eyes flickered. Laura wound back and let fly even as he lunged forward.

The ball smacked his left temple at fifty miles an hour. His eyes registered comical disbelief before rolling back in their sockets. Toppling forward, he hit the floor with a resounding thud.

In the silent aftermath, Laura trembled.

Brenda Lee crept forward, her curvaceous body outlined by a clinging silk nightgown. The picture of feminine distress, she knelt beside the felled giant, placed gentle fingertips against his throat and lifted a gaze stricken with emotion.

"Damn it to hell. The bastard's still alive." Rising, Brenda Lee bunched her nightgown, wiped her fingers on the silk and stepped forward well out of Jack's reach. Intelligence, humor and an iron core of strength radiated from her emerald green eyes.

Suddenly she grinned. Laura grinned back. A bubble of laughter escaped the blonde's slender throat. Laura snorted in return. Frayed nerves and aftershock did the rest.

They laughed until tears streamed down their faces. They laughed until they clung together for support. They laughed until a familiar voice thundered from the doorway.

"What the hell's going on here, Laura?"

CHAPTER FOUR

ALEC TOOK IN the splintered door frame, the huge man sprawled facedown on the floor and the two women laughing as if they might break into sobs at any minute.

"Answer me, damn it!" Fear harshened his voice.

They broke apart. Both wore nightclothes and identical expressions of surprise, but all similarity ended there.

The tiny blonde could have stepped off the pages of *Playboy* magazine. She had the lush curves and kittenish tousled look that made most men feel horny and protective at the same time. Alec gave her a cursory glance before turning to Laura and searching for signs of injury. She appeared shaken, but unharmed.

"Are you two okay?" he asked. When Laura nodded, he relaxed a bit, his gaze traveling head to toe in a second, more leisurely trip.

Laura's thick chestnut-hued ponytail fell to the middle of her back. A rumpled University of Texas T-shirt covered her to midthigh, revealing long shapely legs ending in fuzzy brown slippers shaped like Bevo, her alma mater's longhorn mascot. The horns protruding from her toes looked ridiculous, and endearing.

Despite the fact she could have stepped straight out of a sorority house, Alec's eyes returned to the decidedly interesting contours underneath the UT emblem.

The blonde studied him openly, making no move to cover the generous charms outlined by her pink nightgown. "He a friend of yours, honey?" she asked Laura.

"That's no friend, that's my partner." Laura's burlesque-style delivery earned a cheeky grin from the blonde.

Alec frowned and strode forward. "Are you going to tell me what happened, Laura, or do I have to wait for *him* to tell me?" He got down on one knee and felt the unconscious man's wrist. An ugly son of a bitch, he noted. A knot the size of an egg protruded from the guy's forehead, but his pulse beat strong and steady.

Alec rose and lifted an eyebrow at Laura.

"It was nothing very exciting, Alec. Jack here was trying to rape Brenda Lee. We persuaded him otherwise, that's all."

For all Laura's flippancy, the tight edge in her voice dissolved Alec's exasperation. He suppressed a startling urge to gather her in his arms.

Jack groaned.

Within seconds, Alec found himself sandwiched between two soft scantily clad females. He placed an arm around each woman's shoulders. "Are you sure he didn't hurt either of you?" When they nodded, the clamp around his lungs loosened. "Are the police on the way? You *have* called them, right?"

Laura raised her chin. "There wasn't time. He was breaking into Brenda Lee's apartment and...she screamed and...I had to do something fast." A shudder rippled through her slim body.

Yes, Laura being Laura, she would act impulsively—and courageously. He already knew that much about her. But to go up against the hulk on the floor...

It was all Alec could do to keep from kicking in the bastard's teeth.

Giving both women a last squeeze, he disengaged himself and moved into action. "Brenda Lee, call 911, then throw on a robe or something. This place will be crawling with cops soon." Brenda Lee nodded and disappeared into her bedroom. "Laura, find me something to tie him up with."

At his request for help, her dazed look vanished and she ran off. A door opened somewhere outside. Her apartment, he assumed.

Only minutes earlier, he'd been searching for apartment forty-six when laughter had slowed his steps. The shattered door frame of apartment forty-four had stopped his heart.

Just then Brenda Lee emerged from her bedroom, tying the sash of a floor-length silk robe. Edging around Jack, she walked into the kitchen and pulled down cups from the cabinet.

"They're on the way. Can I make you some coffee?"

He studied her over the freestanding island counter dividing the kitchen and living area. Not a sniffle in sight, praise the Lord. "That'd be great. Better make plenty."

The prone man didn't stir. Alec noted the oily hair, stained T-shirt and butt cleavage with disgust. The faded outline of a snuff can branded the denim of one back pocket. He moved closer, grimacing at the stench of stale beer and unwashed skin. Animal.

Loathing misted Alec's vision, curling his fingers into fists. He stared at Jack and saw another body crumpled on the floor, another man standing over it.

Quit your snivelin', boy. Your ma needs to know who's boss, an' it's my job to show her. Now, help me get her up.

Rising anger—hot, urgent and begging for release—mingled with twisting panic. Alec fought the tangled emotions. Hammered them down with the blunt force of reason. When he could see again, he remembered Brenda Lee. She watched him with an odd expression.

"Did you say something?" he managed.

"I asked how you like your coffee."

"Black." He flashed her a smile, a calculated facial movement that left his heart untouched.

She lost her wary expression and began fussing with the coffeemaker. Alec sighed with relief. Under control now, he resumed his study of the man on the floor. The creep looked strong as an ox.

"What did you hit him with, for God's sake?" he asked.

Brenda Lee stopped bustling and stared into space with an awed expression. "I thought I was a goner for sure. Jack was gonna haul back and hit me—I saw it in his eyes—then your friend yells from the doorway, holding a *softball* of all things. And I'm thinkin', Lordy, we're both gonna die, when she rears back and throws the thing so fast it's a blur." An admiring smile lit her face. "Damned if it wasn't just like David and Goliath."

Alec cocked a skeptical eyebrow.

Brenda Lee's smile vanished. "See for yourself," she challenged, pointing a finger. "The ball's right over there."

Alec's gaze followed her finger to a regulation softball resting benignly on the carpet. He hunkered down one more time next to Jack and pushed back a greasy lock of hair. Sure enough, the swollen lump bore a faint impression of crisscrossed laces. If Laura had missed, or hit any other part of the brute's body than his temple—

Alec cursed under his breath.

A door slammed nearby and Laura rushed into the apartment, holding out an assortment of items for his inspection. "I couldn't find any rope, but I thought maybe one of these would work."

He eyed the thick chain-link belt, spandex tights and oversize silk scarf, then chose the belt, knowing it would dig into Jack's skin. Planting a knee on the man's spine, Alec wrapped and tied the thick hairy wrists. Tight.

Ignoring Laura's amazed look, he stood and brushed off his khaki pants. "That was a stupid totally irresponsible thing to do, Laura. You were lucky as hell the ball hit him where it did."

Her eyes flared with indignation. She crossed her arms under her breasts. The movement pulled soft cotton taut and raised the hem of her T-shirt an inch. "Luck had absolutely nothing to do with it. I hit what I was aiming for."

If she wanted him to think she was Nolan Ryan, she'd damn well better put some clothes on.

Laura followed the direction of his gaze, blushed and dropped her arms. "I'm going to get changed. I'll be back in a minute," she mumbled.

Brenda Lee nodded to her fleeing back, then looked at Alec with a knowing grin. The distant wail of a police siren saved him from comment. He checked his watch. Jason had begged to be taken to Chuck E Cheese's for lunch, but this was an emergency. Mrs. Pennington would make him understand, Alec assured himself. It wasn't like he'd planned to miss lunch with Jason—not this time, anyway. The boy would probably get caught up in Nintendo and never even notice his absence.

As the siren grew louder, he walked to the doorway and leaned against the jamb, keeping one eye on Jack. The next hour was going to be exactly the kind of chaotic episode Alec hated. Served him right for deviating from his original plan to start an agency on his own. His "partner," it appeared, had a remarkable talent for disrupting both his peace of mind and the strategy he'd spent months developing.

Good thing he always carried a Plan B in his head.

LAURA SCANNED her cluttered apartment in dismay. Alec, who'd be through with the police any minute, had asked to speak with her privately. The thought of him seeing this mess galvanized her into action.

She grabbed the metal frame of her bed and heaved, watching the thin mattress fold into the innards of her sleeper-sofa. Stuffing sheet corners out of sight, she covered the evidence with orange-flowered cushions and scowled.

The man could at least have had the courtesy to call before arriving this morning. But no. Alec McDonald didn't answer to the same rules as the rest of modern society. Look at the way he'd taken charge when the police arrived, as if she couldn't speak for herself.

She rushed into the kitchen and began rinsing plates and glasses and loading them into the dishwasher. Strange how she'd lived here a year and never met Brenda Lee. Laura had learned some eye-opening facts after chatting with her neighbor during a lull in the excitement.

Apparently Brenda Lee had graduated two weeks ago from secretarial school, but wasn't having much luck finding a day job. She supported herself by waitressing nights at a "gentlemen's club," where Jack had been pestering her for weeks. She was fairly certain a jealous coworker had given Jack her home address.

Deep in thought, Laura held a glass under running water. She could see where Brenda Lee's face and body would turn some women pea green. Yet the vulnerability in her neighbor's eyes had spoken to Laura on a gut level. She knew what it felt like to be excluded. All her life, it had seemed as if women belonged to an exclusive club—one whose qualifications and bylaws eluded her.

Her upbringing had prepared her for the good-old-boys' club, instead.

Laura worried her lower lip as she loaded the last few plates. She had a feeling a friend might come in handy during the next few months. And maybe she ought to take a look at Brenda Lee's résumé, as well. She'd do it right after Alec left.

Slamming the dishwasher door, Laura moved back into the main room. An authoritative knock made her groan. Throwing a last wild look around, she moved toward the door and paused. The apartment wasn't dirty, just... crowded. If he didn't like it, tough toenails.

Flinging the door open, she caught her breath.

Alec stood with one arm high, his palm resting against the doorjamb. He looked rumpled, irritated and very masculine. The knit sleeve of his forest green shirt rode high on his raised arm. She stared at his formidable biceps and revised her opinion of indolent executives.

Dropping his hand, Alec swept past her without a word. Suddenly her apartment, which had only seemed small before, now felt tiny as a doll's house.

"Do come in, won't you?" Her voice dripped sarcasm.

Without ceremony, he plopped down on her sofa, stretched out his long legs and gave the room a thorough inspection.

"And do make yourself at home while you're at it." Laura wiped damp palms on her shorts. Her tacky little efficiency didn't reflect her personal style or taste, but he couldn't know that. She braced herself for his scorn.

"Thank God for garage sales and hand-me-downs, huh?" he said after a moment. "I never would've made it through school without them."

"You've got to be kidding." She crossed over to the plaid armchair and sank down, curling her Bevo slippers beneath her. "You mean you weren't *born* wearing a polo shirt and topsiders?"

Looking down at himself as if startled, his mouth twisted. "Not hardly. This apartment is the Hilton compared to the place I grew up in."

"Where was that?"

His gaze turned flat and bleak. "Hell."

Her eyelids fluttered, then steadied. "Then you should feel right at home working with me." There, he'd almost smiled. Pleasure scurried through her, as unexpected as it was strong.

He drew his legs in and sat up taller. "That's what I'm here to talk with you about. Our working together."

"Couldn't this have waited until Monday?"

"With a six-year-old bouncing off the walls at my house, I had the crazy notion your apartment would be a quieter place to talk. Call me stupid."

She was tempted. Oh, boy, was she tempted. "It's quiet now. So talk."

"I think we need to set the terms of our partnership straight. Our *temporary* partnership."

"Temporary?"

"That's right. We were forced into this arrangement against our wishes, and I'm suggesting a tolerable solution to the problem." He leaned forward and propped both forearms on his knees. "One year," he rapped out. "We work together one year, long enough to establish a full-service agency, as well as the new Regency Hotels campaign. Then we go our separate ways.''

Oh, Lord, not the drumrolls again. "And just who would 'go' with Regency Hotels?''

''I realize your creative strategy helped clench Sam's account, so I've given this a lot of thought. At the end of one year, I'd buy you out at fair market value, with your written agreement not to solicit existing clients. Then you'd be free to establish your own agency.''

He had it all planned, the jerk. He would use her until Sam grew dependent on the agency, then leave her to pick up the pieces of her life. She'd sung that song before, thank you.

Uncurling her legs, she mirrored his position. Nose to nose, they weren't more than two feet apart.

''Not a chance,'' she said.

''Look, Laura. I do not require, want or otherwise need a business partner to complicate my life. And let's be honest, you *are* gaining the benefit of my financial backing and business connections in this deal. You're obviously ambitious—hell, you went for my throat like a pit bull the other day. So what's the problem?''

He had her figured all wrong, but she wasn't about to drag her family's problems into this discussion.

Alec shoved a hand through his hair. ''We'll have a hard enough time sticking out the full year without killing each other. Our only hope is to have a light at the end of the tunnel.''

She shifted tactics. ''Sam would be mad as hell. Mad enough to fire you, maybe.''

''You leave Sam to me. I'm confident I'll find someone to fill your shoes when you leave.''

Her swift pang of hurt came out of nowhere. She looked down. Bevo smiled up from her slippers with disgusting cheerfulness. "Maybe I'll buy *you* out," she whispered.

Gentle fingers cupped her chin and lifted, forcing her to meet Alec's eyes. "With what? Face it, Laura, this is your best option. I promise you'll get a fair settlement. Enough to capitalize your own full-service agency for a year at least."

Or pull H & H Cattle Company out of debt once and for all, Laura silently added.

He released her chin and sat back. "Well? Is it a deal?"

The decision had been made long ago—the morning she'd left home vowing to make it up to her father and brother one day. Pride forced her to bargain at least a little. "I'll agree on one condition."

"Which is?"

"That I be an equal partner, with equal responsibility and input, until the day we split up."

Obviously smelling victory, Alec nodded.

"I'll hold you to that. In writing," she warned.

"I'll have the agreement drawn up by Tuesday."

She sighed. "Okay, then. I guess you have a deal."

Alec slapped his knee and smiled—the dazzling, dimpled, drop-dead gorgeous smile she'd waited for and envisioned ever since they'd met. Reality mocked her puny imagination.

God, she hated him.

MONDAY MORNING, Laura drove her old car through towering wrought-iron gates and parked in Alec's driveway. His two-story brick home looked even more imposing than she remembered. She unbuckled her seat belt and frowned.

Normally her memory for details never failed. But when Alec was near, everything else seemed to fade into the background. Disturbed at the realization, she grabbed her organizational notes, clambered out of the car and traipsed up the walkway. A small portico sheltered the front door, bounded on one side by a graceful potted fern and on the other by an ornamental iron bench. She sat on the cool metal and clutched her leather portfolio tighter. Her stomach rumbled from no breakfast and a bad case of the jitters.

Chicken. She had a perfect right to be here. If she turned wimpy now, she'd be wiping Alec's footprints off her back the rest of the year. Straightening her shoulders, she rose, faced the tall mahogany door and lifted the gleaming brass knocker.

The door swung open while her hand was still on the knocker, pulling her forward. She stumbled into a marble-floored entryway as a small human dynamo whizzed under her arm and out the door.

"Jason McDonald, you come back here right now," yelled a stern gravelly voice.

Still holding the knocker, Laura glanced across the foyer. A large woman with close-cropped gray hair marched toward the open door, her arms pumping. As she passed through, one down-swinging elbow caught Laura in the ribs, whirling her face first into the knocker.

"Ow-ow-ow!" Laura cupped her throbbing nose and turned to glare through a haze of involuntary tears.

"Don't make me come after you, Jason." The woman faced the street and crossed her arms, a pose that emphasized her narrow hips, thick waist and broad shoulders. Only the passing glimpse of a massive bosom negated the possibility she was a man.

Beyond the porch and midway down a bricked path to the curb, Jason paused and turned. He raised a thumb to each ear, wiggled his fingers and stuck out his tongue.

My sentiments exactly, Laura thought. From the moment she'd talked to Jason up in that tree, she'd felt drawn to the child. His beautiful eyes, so like his father's, except for a heart-wrenching hunger for attention, had aroused maternal instincts she hadn't even known were hibernating.

She frowned now as the marine-sergeant-in-drag uncrossed stocky arms and lowered a grizzled head. A glance at Jason's colorless face confirmed Laura's intense dislike of the woman.

Footsteps sounded on the marble floor behind her. "Laura! How long have you been here?" Alec joined her in the doorway.

His faded jeans were tight, his navy cable-knit sweater loose. Her stomach went bonkers, and not from lack of food.

She dragged her gaze back to Jason. "Not long."

Laura knew the exact moment the boy spotted his father. As if released from a snare, he turned and scampered down the path, his cherry red backpack bouncing against his white T-shirt and tiny denim-clad bottom.

Emitting an ugly grunt, the woman lurched forward.

"Is there a problem here, Mrs. Pennington?" Alec asked loudly.

She froze in midstep, turned around and sniffed. "Your boy stuck his tongue out at me again, Mr. McDonald. I've told you before he's got no respect for his elders. Ran off without finishing his breakfast, too." She clasped raw-boned hands over a shapeless cotton shift and pursed her mouth. "He'll be hungry by ten o'clock, mark my words."

Surely that wasn't satisfaction glittering in the woman's black eyes? Laura glanced up at Alec. The tender frustration on his lean face twisted her heart. Following his gaze, she located Jason sitting huddled on the front curb throwing pebbles into the street. He looked smaller than the canvas pack on his back.

Alec refocused on Mrs. Pennington. "I'll see that Jason gets on the school van safely this morning. You can return to your other duties now, thank you." He stepped outside and pulled Laura with him.

"Whatever you say, sir." Mrs. Pennington nodded in deference.

But there was nothing meek about the glaring look she gave Laura. The woman's ebony eyes gleamed with hostility. Laura glowered right back.

The minute Mrs. Pennington was out of earshot, Laura confronted Alec. "Why in the world did you hire that woman?"

He seemed startled. "Mrs. Pennington? She's an excellent housekeeper."

"Then she only takes care of the house? You have someone else who looks after Jason?"

"No, I didn't say that." His expression grew wary. "She generally sees Jason off in the morning and watches him when he gets home from school about three o'clock."

"Good grief, Alec. That dragon lady has no business taking care of children—"

The rumble of an engine interrupted Laura's lecture. A bright yellow van with Tanglewood Academy on the door pulled up curbside. The passenger door slid open, revealing small faces watching Jason with varying degrees of interest. A carrot-haired little girl smiled and patted an empty seat next to her.

Jason ducked his head, scrambled into the van and sat down. Reaching over to close the door, he looked at Alec as if to assure himself his father was still there. When his gaze shifted to Laura, his expression brightened with recognition. He waved once, a shy little movement that seemed uncertain of her reaction, then slid the door shut.

Suddenly finding it difficult to swallow, Laura waved back. She continued waving until the van drove out of sight. Feeling Alec's gaze, she dropped her arm. "That's a great kid you have there."

"I wouldn't know. He only shows me his worst side."

Laura swung around. Alec stood inches away, freshly shaved and sleepy-eyed. The intimate combination made her pulse leap. She stepped back.

"Before last week, I didn't even know you had a little boy."

"He lived with his mother overseas until two months ago. He's ... having a rough time adjusting to me."

After an awkward silence, she babbled the first platitude that came to mind. "Sharing time between divorced parents is hard on a child."

"Losing a mother in a car accident is harder."

Her mouth formed a silent *oh.*

He shrugged and stuffed both hands in his pockets. "Hey, don't feel too badly. The doctors said Susan was so full of gin she didn't feel a thing. And from what I can tell, Jason misses his nanny more than his mother's loving arms."

If he was trying to shock her, he failed. She'd seen the yearning look he'd sent his son. Right now, though, her sympathy rested with a little boy uprooted from all that was familiar.

"So whose loving arms hold him now? Certainly not the dragon lady's." She jerked her head to the door Mrs. Pennington had lumbered through moments earlier.

His jaw tightened. "Not that it's any of your business, but the last thing Jason wants is for me to hold him. He hates me."

Poor Jason. Poor Alec. Men didn't have a clue. "Of course he wants to be held. We all want to be held. Even a cold heartless SOB like you," she said, a teasing lilt in her voice. The man took himself much too seriously.

Amazement relaxed his scowl. "You are the most impertinent woman I've ever met. No wonder Jason likes you. You two have so much in common."

"Jason said he likes me?" She beamed.

His eyes thawed a bit more. "He didn't know girls could climb trees that good. To tell the truth, neither did I." He reached out and swiped a finger down her nose.

She flinched.

He leaned down and inspected her face. "You're hurt."

She caught the heady scent of soap, after-shave and clean male skin. Raising her portfolio, she hugged it to her chest. "It's nothing. I bumped my nose against the door knocker when Mrs. Pennington came out earlier."

Frowning, he gripped her shoulders and positioned her to face the morning sunlight.

Her heart lurched.

He raised one hand and cupped her chin, his index finger firm and slightly scratchy against the soft skin of her jaw, the pad of his thumb a gentle pressure beneath her lips.

Her mouth automatically parted in response.

He probed one side of her nose with gentle fingers. "Does this hurt?"

"N-no."

"How about this?" Feather soft, he grazed the opposite side.

Her stomach flip-flopped, making speech impossible. Wide-eyed, she shook her head, the action rubbing her sensitive lower lip against his thumb.

His fingers tightened. "I—" he cleared his throat "—I guess nothing's broken, then."

But he didn't release her chin. Instead, his other hand traced a gentle lazy path down her cheek, stopping at her lips. The sun blinded Laura to his expression, but she felt his increased tension nonetheless.

Her heart bludgeoned her rib cage as his head lowered, blocking the sun like an eclipse. His eyes, smoky blue and sleepier than ever, focused intently on her mouth.

Her lashes drifted down. Her breathing stopped.

His fingers fell away from her chin. "Come inside and I'll put some ice on that nose," he offered, his voice husky.

Her eyes jerked open. He'd moved back several feet and now avoided her gaze. "F-fine. Lead the way."

He turned with evident relief and headed through the door.

Idiot. Moron. Imbecile. Where was her brain? She had to work closely with this man for an entire year. His love-'em-and-leave-'em reputation had provided many an hour of gossip at the agency. Alec's withdrawal had been a blessing. Humiliating, but a blessing.

So why, then, did she feel like strangling someone?

How would she get through a year without strangling the man?

Laura paced the reception area of Blackburn Realty Corporation and fumed. Alec was late—after she'd broken every speed limit to get here on time, too. Her old car doing seventy miles an hour was comparable to the shuttle reentering earth's atmosphere. Only the shuttle probably shook less.

She crossed the plush carpet to a long sofa, plopped down and fussed with her skirt. Three days had passed since that almost kiss at Alec's doorway. Thank goodness it hadn't happened.

The first thing he'd done after leading her inside the house was stick a contract under her nose to sign. He must have dragged his lawyer off the tennis court on Sunday in order have the agreement ready and waiting Monday morning, instead of Tuesday as he'd promised.

With a curious mixture of emotions, she'd signed away any possibility of long-term commitment to Hayes and McDonald Advertising. The thought of paying off H & H Cattle Company's debts elated her. Yet so did the idea of developing an agency from the ground floor up.

How ironic that in her bid for personal creative freedom, she'd wound up chained to the most domineering, autocratic, *stubborn* man on earth. All the more reason to demand his respect and attention—on a strictly business level, of course. She wasn't a masochist.

Leaning forward, she pulled a copy of *Architectural Digest* from a chrome-and-glass coffee table and flipped the pages blindly. She'd give him five more minutes. Then she would insist Mr. Donelly show her prospective office space without the benefit of Alec's sage advice. They disagreed on almost everything, anyway.

"Would you care for some coffee now, Ms. Hayes?" the bored young secretary asked for the third time.

Laura smiled brightly and shook her head, then returned to the glossy pages as if engrossed. Mr. Donelly had his work cut out for him, poor man. She had argued with Alec for more than an hour about their future office site. He wanted to lease space somewhere inside Loop 610, believing central convenience and a prestigious location were worth the higher cost. Laura thought it absurd to pay top dollar for such intangibles. The quality of the agency's work would establish a good image, not the address on its letterhead.

She was much more concerned about employee reaction to the work environment, an issue her partner completely ignored.

The etched-glass entry door opened, and Alec swept into the sterile reception area, along with the scent of spring breezes and sandlewood cologne. He looked dark and commanding in designer charcoal slacks and a mist gray silk shirt.

The woman at the desk perked up like a poodle begging for table scraps. He tossed her a smile and strode toward Laura, oblivious to the receptionist's flustered gratitude.

"Sorry I'm late," he told Laura without a trace of apology in his voice. Dropping into a peach damask guest chair, he leaned forward, his tall powerful body obscuring the chair's delicate lines. "I was on the phone all morning with Harold Becker. *The* Harold Becker."

An underlying excitement darkened his eyes to near black. Women would have killed for his lashes, Laura thought resentfully.

"Did you hear what I said?"

She sighed. "I'm ignorant, not deaf, Alec. I'm afraid I don't know who this Becker person is."

Surprise, then smugness, crept across his face. "He's media director of the Spencer Group's Houston division. The corporate office is closing the southwest division in a month, but Harold hates living in New York. I sold him on the mental rush of building an agency from scratch. He'll be taking a slight pay cut, but he's agreed to work for McDonald and Hayes Advertising."

"Hayes and McDonald," Laura corrected automatically. "Let me get this straight. You hired a department head for our agency without consulting me?"

Alec frowned. "I hired a Madison Avenue pro who will lend credibility to an unknown hick-town agency. If I hadn't acted fast, he would have been snapped up by a competitor."

"Hick-town agency?" Her spine stiffened.

"That's not what *I* think, Laura. But like it or not, our industry still considers any agency outside New York strictly pedestrian. The more talent like Becker this city can attract and hold, the faster that prejudice will disappear."

His high-handed action made a distorted kind of sense, Laura admitted. But if he thought he could continue making decisions right and left . . .

"Mr. McDonald, so nice to meet you. My secretary said you'd arrived." A slender blond man not much older than Laura walked toward them, hand extended, his attention centered on Alec.

Alec rose and shook hands. "Donelly," he acknowledged with a curt nod. "I hope my requirements were not too limiting. I like to have several choices before making any decision."

Laura rose and faced the Realtor. "Mr. McDonald is big on having alternatives," she said wryly, holding out her hand. "I'm Laura Hayes—Mr. McDonald's business partner. He did mention that little detail, didn't he?"

Mr. Donelly flicked an uncertain glance at Alec before grasping her hand. "Of course. I'm sorry, Ms. Hayes, it must have slipped my mind. You'd have never been kept waiting, if I'd known you were so lovely." His smile could have graced a toothpaste ad.

"Our *commission* is lovely," she conceded, grinning as he focused more closely on her face.

"Please, call me David. And make no mistake, Laura. I know the difference between a commission and a lovely woman—" he squeezed her fingers gently "—as well as how to enjoy both to the fullest."

She pulled her hand away, hating the heat suffusing her face. It wasn't like he really meant it. Why couldn't she act cool and sophisticated? She peeked at Alec through her lashes.

He was watching the agent with peculiar intensity, as if willing him to look back. When David obliged, the two men exchanged a long enigmatic stare. Fifteen seconds into it Alec visibly relaxed.

David developed a tic in his left cheek.

"Am I missing something here?" Laura asked, irritated when neither man responded. Her foot tapped the carpet. "Can we possibly go now?"

The Realtor snapped out of his daze and smoothed his tie. "Certainly, Lau—er, Ms. Hayes. I've got five locations that would be perfect for your needs. My car is right outside. Ready, Mr. McDonald?"

"The sooner the better," Alec said.

Laura smiled happily and headed for the door. At last, something she and Alec agreed on. Surely that was a good sign.

CHAPTER FIVE

SILENCE REIGNED inside the parked car. Slumped behind the wheel, David bore little resemblance to the young man of collegiate good looks who'd flirted with her earlier, Laura observed.

His honey blond hair, fashionably tousled that morning, now tufted in unfashionable furrows where his fingers had plowed. The tic in his cheek had increased. He'd discarded his navy wool blazer long ago, since the Ford's air conditioner needed a shot of freon.

His Lincoln was in the shop, he'd explained, and this had been the last available loaner car. Laura carefully avoided looking toward the back seat. She heard movement, then felt a bump through the cushion against her spine.

"There's one place you haven't shown us, Donelly," Alec said, his tone surly. "You mentioned it to me over the phone, but I told you the location was unsuitable. Maybe I was a little premature."

The Realtor's gaze flew to the rearview mirror. "Which property was that?"

"I believe you said it was on Westheimer, just off the West Belt? An architectural firm had just moved out, and there were some rather odd features to contend with."

Comprehension and hope burgeoned on David's face. "Why yes, I'd almost forgotten." He started the engine and nosed the car out into the traffic, his jaw set with grim purpose.

Laura glanced from his white-knuckled grip on the steering wheel to Alec's pained expression, and decided to save her questions for later.

It wasn't her fault all five locations had been wrong. If Alec hadn't ignored every single one of her previous recommendations regarding a site, this wouldn't have been such a wild-goose chase. Lord knew where they were heading now.

David pointed out the thirty-story building from a half mile away. Its rose-tinted windows blushed against the azure sky. At the entrance, unpolished pink granite steps led up to an impressive welcoming arch.

As the Realtor parked in a visitor space, Laura glanced toward Alec again. He'd insisted on sitting in the back seat, despite her protests. "This is a gorgeous building, and so close to the Beltway we'd have access to all the freeways. I have a good feeling about this one."

Alec grunted from his jackknifed position.

Suppressing a smile, Laura hopped out of the car, turned and pushed her seat forward. Alec uncurled like a hermit crab from an outgrown shell. Hunched and groaning, he grabbed his lower back and straightened. "To hell with chivalry. I'm riding in front on the way back."

David faced the building, a militant gleam in his eyes, then smoothed his hair, tugged his sleeves and squared his shoulders. "Let's do it," he said, marching ahead without waiting to see if his clients followed.

Laura and Alec exchanged a startled glance, then hurried after him into the building.

The property manager appeared thrilled to see them, even though they were unannounced. She regaled them with a host of leasing benefits—none of which involved the actual space being shown—all the way up the elevator and down the hall.

Stopping at suite 1700, she inserted a key in the door and paused. "This is the last space available in the building. The previous tenants were a little ... avant-garde in their tastes. However, our staff architects have been briefed on the situation and are prepared to give the new tenants top priority." She took a deep breath and pushed the door open.

Alec, Laura and David filed into a large square room. No one spoke for a moment.

The first thing Laura noticed was the huge round hole in one wall. Well, not a hole, actually—the floor intersected the bottom—but it was round enough to be unlike any doorway she'd seen outside a Tom-and-Jerry cartoon. Tiptoeing forward, she passed through and peered back into the room. Alec was turning as if to leave.

"Wait," she called. "I want to see the rest."

Disgust, gratitude and surprise showed respectively on the faces of Alec, David and the manager. Laura flashed a smile at all three of them before spinning around to continue her journey.

The floor in the hallway, as well as in the front room, was covered with large matte black tiles. Round doorway openings beckoned her from both sides of the hall. She hurried forward and stepped through the first one to her right.

The tiles in this room were fire-engine red. She grinned in delight, scanning the floor-to-ceiling glass windows of one entire wall and reveling in the abundance of natural light. The room was huge and absolutely perfect for an art department.

She whirled around and nearly bumped into Alec as he walked through the door. He was still staring at the tile, mesmerized, when she brushed past him and entered the hallway, eager to complete her tour.

With each passing moment, Laura grew more and more excited. In addition to what she now thought of as the art room, there were ten modest-size offices, a small kitchen, two large storage closets and a bathroom. The tile floor of each room glowed in a different crayon color. She loved them all.

But the most exciting discovery in Laura's opinion crowned the end of the hall. She entered the vast circular room and stood at its center, awed by the tiled replica of a sun radiating beneath her feet. Rotating slowly, she imagined sitting beside Alec at a round conference table, neither greater nor lesser than her partner in the eyes of clients. Just . . . equal.

Determined to speak her mind, Laura walked back down the hall and into the entry room, where David and the property manager were pitching Alec fast and furious.

"It's a good compromise between your requirements and those of Ms. Hayes," David said, throwing his colleague a pleading look.

She picked up the cue. "We could have estimates on new carpet and conventional door frames in three days, a week tops."

Alec gave her a hard look. "That would knock up the square-footage price to inner-Loop rates. It's obvious why this space is empty. Your company will have to bite the bullet and absorb reconstruction costs if you ever want to lease it."

The property manager looked eager. "So let's talk."

Alec snorted. "Even if I wanted this...this—" he flung a hand at the round doorway "—this giant Swiss cheese you call an office, the reconstruction would take you at least a month. We can't wait that long."

Laura stepped forward. "May I speak with you, Alec?"

He turned, still glowering.

"Privately?" she added.

"We'll be in the hall if you need us," David said, looking relieved. He opened suite 1700's only door and slipped through, the property manager close on his heels.

When the door clicked shut, Laura gazed directly into Alec's eyes, letting her own excitement show. "I think we should lease this space, Alec. It's perfect."

He crossed his arms and raised an eyebrow. "Didn't you hear what I told them?"

Yes, Spock, I heard. "Very logical," she agreed with a grin.

"I don't know what's so funny. You've rejected every decent space we've looked at because of minor flaws. Yet now you're considering a place that would require extensive reconstruction. We can't afford to wait that long, Laura."

"Who said anything about reconstruction?"

When her meaning sank in, he shook his head. "No way. Our agency is not going to look like a day-care center. It would be bad for the image." He dropped his arms and headed for the door.

Laura stepped into his path and placed a palm on his chest. "No, it wouldn't. It would be great for the image. We're not a bank, Alec. We sell ideas...and imagination...and vision. Our agency headquarters should reflect that."

She searched his face for a sign of weakening. She wanted this space, but convincing Alec wouldn't be easy.

"When you give a presentation," she continued, "what gets the client excited? Facts and figures and research? Or razzle-dazzle, off-the-wall, how-did-they-think-of-that creative?"

As understanding filled his eyes, she clutched his shirt. "That property manager is desperate, Alec. No one will take the space as is, and reconstruction costs would jack the rent too high for the market. Just think of the deal she'd cut you for taking this space off her hands."

Laura paused, waiting for his business instincts to kick in. The minute his expression grew speculative, she pounced. "Give me a budget, a time frame and a little of your faith, Alec, and I'll give you an office to be proud of."

He reached up, covered her hand and pressed it against his chest. "You'd be putting heart and soul into a place you'll have to leave in a year. Are you sure you want to do that?" He squeezed her fingers gently. "Think hard, Laura, before you answer."

His palm felt warm, his heartbeat strong and steady. *You're playing with fire, Laura. Just stick to business, take your money and run.*

"It's just a job, Alec. I promise I won't get sentimental."

His expression cleared. "I must be crazy for agreeing to this, but okay, Laura. Give it your best shot." A predatory gleam appeared in his eyes. "I feel like doing a little negotiating. How about you?"

Laura stepped aside and opened the door, elation and fear sweeping through her as she waved him into the hall. Hand on the doorknob, she paused. Maybe a little private negotiating was in order for herself.

Please, Lord, if you help me keep my promise, I'll...I'll... What would be harder than resisting her

partner's appeal? *I'll never lose my temper with Alec
again.*

ALEC UNLOCKED the door, opened it just enough to slip
his arm through and flipped on a light switch. Only then
did he push his way into the room. After two weeks, the
early-morning ritual still gave him a charge.

Ten track lights beamed with concentrated focus on a
rectangular section of wall featuring the words Hayes and
McDonald Advertising. The letters had been custom-cut
from the same black tile as the floor, their matte finish
contrasting against a background of gleaming red tiles.

Laura had given herself top billing, but he could hardly
complain. She'd bartered her creative services to a tile
craftsman in need of a brochure. Otherwise the sign would
have cost a fortune. And it certainly made an impressive
statement.

He set his briefcase on the floor and circled the room,
turning on overhead lights and a squat black table lamp
drizzled in red glaze. His approving gaze swept the
grouping of gray leather furniture. He particularly liked
the contemporary area rug bordered in red. Laura had
picked it up for a fraction of its original cost at a designer showroom auction.

A cluttered spray of magazines on the coffee table
caught his eye. Frowning, he sat on the couch and began
arranging the periodicals in a neat row.

True to her word, Laura had performed miracles within
a very modest budget. Susan had spent twice that amount
furnishing his study years ago, and that hadn't even included the fees of an interior designer. Not that he'd
minded. He realized now his ex-wife had symbolized his
personal triumph over poverty. No doubt he would have

indulged her all the way to bankruptcy court, if she'd valued her wedding vows half as much as his money.

Alec pulled a roll of antacids out of his pocket and popped one in his mouth. He had everything, including himself, under control. He really did—despite having an impulsive partner and a rebellious child to deal with. Years of practice had made restraint second nature to him.

Rising, he crossed over to the sleek black reception desk and plucked several messages from his slot. With characteristic irreverence, Brenda Lee had noted that a "very rude stockbroker" wanted him to return an "earthshakingly important" call. Alec rolled his eyes and stuffed the pink slip into his pocket.

It wasn't enough that Laura had saved Brenda Lee's ass. No, his partner had gone and hired the former cocktail waitress as office manager. Propping his hip against the desk, he sifted through his remaining messages. Nothing earthshaking in the bunch. His thoughts drifted to Laura.

Apparently when she took on a friendship, she assumed responsibility for that person's happiness. Such unprofessional blind loyalty annoyed him—almost as much as the wistful pangs he tried to ignore.

In all fairness, Brenda Lee handled the job with skill and finesse. He pulled the pink slip from his pocket, reread her message and snorted. If she would just curb her tongue and dress properly, he would consider the agency lucky—

"What kind of message did she leave this time?" Laura's husky voice spoke from behind.

Alec spun around. She stood ten feet in front of the door, an amused gleam in her eyes. He unclenched his fists.

"How do you *do* that?"

"Do what?"

"Open a door and walk on tile without making a sound?"

Her golden eyes grew mysterious, her smile self-satisfied. As she crossed to the reception desk, slim and graceful in a sweeping navy blue skirt and tailored white blouse, she reminded him once more of a cat.

"I can walk through a loft of hay without making a rustle, so this is a piece of cake." She glanced down at her red leather flats. "I'd never pull it off wearing shoes like Brenda Lee's."

Her words conjured a sudden image of long shapely legs in spiked heels. Only the legs weren't Brenda Lee's. Damn his imagination, anyway.

"Alec?" Eyes puzzled, Laura laid her hand on his sleeve.

His senses leapt to attention at her gentle touch. He jerked his arm away, then glanced at his watch. "It's almost eight. I need to get some calls made before things get crazy."

"Sure. No problem." Her eyelids fluttered and dropped—but not before he'd seen her wounded look.

Well, hell. Alec grabbed his briefcase and fled the room. Hitting his office at top speed, he let out a pent-up breath. Like it or not, Laura was his business partner for one year. He'd better settle down and stop this schoolboy fantasizing before he screwed things up completely.

Pulling a fresh legal pad from his desk drawer, he jotted down notes for the staff meeting. After a few minutes, his pencil slowed. Laura's face stared back from the lined yellow paper in a series of expressions. Outrage. Fury. Impudence. Delight.

The corners of his mouth lifted. As he'd guessed at their first meeting, her golden brown eyes and wide sensitive mouth revealed exactly what she was feeling *when* she was feeling it. She wasn't the least bit afraid of him, a fact that pleased him on a gut-deep level he refused to analyze.

More and more, he'd been wondering what those eyes might look like in the throes of passion. He shifted uncomfortably in his chair. If she ever suspected her effect on him...

Alec grimaced at the power it would give her. Power she could and no doubt would use to gain control of the agency and his peace of mind. For all her refreshing candor, she was ambitious. Hell, she'd be a fool not to take advantage of his weakness. And Laura Hayes was no fool.

The sound of high heels tapping toward his office announced Brenda Lee's arrival. She stepped through the door bearing a steaming cup of coffee in one hand.

Today she wore a bright red scoop-neck dress in some clingy material that stopped well short of her knees. The same getup on another woman might have seemed a bit inappropriate for the office. On Brenda Lee, it bordered on being scandalous.

"Who died, boss? Harold, maybe?" she asked on a hopeful note.

Alec smiled in spite of himself. Brenda Lee had taken an instant dislike to his media director and vice versa. "He wouldn't give you the pleasure, I'm afraid."

She clicked across the floor in red spiked heels at least four inches high. "Oh, well, tomorrow's another day." Setting his coffee mug on the desk, she sat uninvited in one of his two guest chairs. "Don't get used to this service, Mr. McDonald. I just needed an excuse to see you in private and say thank you."

"Thank you?"

"Yeah, you remember. Those two words people say when you've done something nice for them?"

Actually, he couldn't remember the last time someone had thanked him for anything. It was a sobering thought.

"Don't play dumb now," she continued. "Laura told me how you picked me over the other candidates for this job, knowing I was having a hard time changing careers and all."

He kept his expression blank. "Laura told you that?"

She leaned forward and grabbed the edge of his desk. "Oh, please don't be mad at her. She said you wouldn't want me to know. But I couldn't let you think I don't appreciate your kindness. I...I've waited a long time for this kind of job."

A remnant of chivalry kept him from asking why no one had hired her before now.

Her green eyes sparkling with unshed tears, she lifted her chin. "I'm not dumb. I graduated top of the class at Thompson's Institute of Business Technology. But the men who interviewed me would take one look at me and either think I was stupid or want to get in my pa—" She bit her lip and blushed. "Well, you know what I mean."

Alec could guess. A surprising surge of anger at those faceless men welled up out of nowhere. He looked Brenda Lee in the eye. "I don't know why you'd thank me for making a smart business decision. I expected you to do an exceptional job, and you haven't disappointed me. Now, why don't you go start earning your salary?"

Brenda Lee straightened her spine, pride replacing her embarrassment. "Yes, sir, boss, sir." Tossing her shoulder-length blond hair, she rose and walked, hips swaying, toward the door.

He waited for his body's response. Nothing. What the hell was wrong with him?

Just before she stepped into the hall, Brenda Lee turned. "Don't tell Laura I told you what she said, okay, Mr. McDonald? She'd feel real bad."

Alec lifted an eyebrow. "Yes, I imagine she would. Don't worry. It'll be our secret."

As she headed down the hallway, Alec rolled his pencil back and forth across the yellow pad. Laura had to stop undermining his authority. As it was, he walked a thin tightrope. One inch to the left or right, and at best, he'd fall on his face before the business community and become one more entrepreneurial failure. At worst, he'd snap and...

Shuddering, he snatched up the pencil and threw it across the room. The last thing he needed was more secrets in his life. Just what other little surprises did Laura have in store for him?

"I THINK WE SHOULD HIRE Sharon Barnes for the job." Laura scanned the small core staff of Hayes and McDonald Advertising, and waited.

Surprise, Alec thought, closing his eyes. When he opened them, four pair of eyes, not including Brenda Lee's, stared back from a scattered semicircle. Until a reasonably priced conference table could be located, staff meetings were held in the agency's reception area.

"Sharon is a wonderful personal secretary, Laura, but she wouldn't have the faintest idea what to do as traffic manager," Alec said, holding on to his patience.

Harold pushed up his round wire-rimmed glasses and cleared his throat. "This Barnes woman is a secretary, Alec?"

"That's right. A damn good one, I'll admit. She worked for me at Harris, Bates and Whitman."

"All the more reason you should think twice before hiring her," the media director said. "Old loyalties die hard, you know."

A loud "harrumph!" sounded from the reception desk across the room. When Harold shot Brenda Lee a lethal look, she gave him a saccharine smile and wiggled her fingers.

"That's exactly my point," Laura stated. "Sharon was completely devoted to you, Alec. To her, *you* were the agency, no matter what the name on the door said. She kept track of nine jillion details at once without blinking an eye. Making sure our departments produce on schedule would be child's play for her."

Alec ground his teeth. Laura was doing it again, damn it. Questioning his judgment in front of the staff. "Even if we did make an offer, she'd never leave her present job so close to her retirement and risk jeopardizing her pension. That would be extremely foolish."

Three male heads nodded in agreement.

Laura met Brenda Lee's sympathetic gaze before turning back to Alec. "*Ask* her before you assume. Women are loyal creatures at heart. Give her the chance to prove it."

Loyal creatures, bull. He knew better. "We'll discuss it later, Laura."

"But Al—"

"*Later.*" He deliberately turned from her flushed face to the man seated next to her. "How's that new scanner program working out, Steve?"

The young art director's shy brown eyes lit up. "I haven't quite mastered the calibration procedure yet, but I can already see it's light-years ahead of what we used at Unicorn Designs. Man, you should see the photo I converted using diffusion dithering. It more than holds its own against a mezzotint. I can run and get it if you'd like."

Alec smiled but shook his head, aware of Laura's stony expression all the while he pretended interest in the scanner's virtues. When his gaze slid past her to the controller, she turned her head—as if she couldn't bear to look at him.

Well, hell. "Jim, I'd like to show Sam a sample run of our billing breakdown tomorrow," Alec rapped out. "Is that possible?"

The chronically stoop-shouldered man snapped to military attention. "Shouldn't be any problem. I'll print out a few test runs today just to make sure. And I need to talk to you about a glitch in the payroll system when you have time."

Steve spoke up. "I have some questions about that *Host and Travel Index* ad layout you wanted. Could I stop by your office later?"

"Alec, if we don't approve this first-quarter radio buy soon, the rates will go up," Harold added.

Feeling his tension ease, Alec allowed himself to look at Laura. She sat remote and still, staring somewhere over his left shoulder. "We haven't heard from you yet, Laura. Weren't you researching snack suppliers for the coffee bar? Can you give us the status?"

Laura lifted her nose and regarded him as if he were raw sewage. With queenly dignity, she stood and raked each man with a scathing glance. "Gentlemen—" her tone mocked the term "—this meeting is adjourned."

"Hallelujah," muttered a feminine voice in the distance.

"Alec, may I see you in the conference room for a moment?" Laura's eyes were dull.

Well, damn it to hell! He rose, conscious of the curious gazes of his staff. "You heard the lady. Meeting adjourned."

Laura was halfway to the conference room, head held high, when he entered the hallway. His long strides ate up the distance until he dogged her heels. He found himself wishing she'd undo her hair. She always wore it up in that braid thing. Hanging free, it would be long and wavy.

She stopped suddenly. Alec rammed against her back, momentum plunging his face into the crown of her head. Soft as spun silk, her hair smelled of lavender, and Laura. He jerked back.

"Must you follow me so closely?" she said through her teeth.

"Sorry." He followed at a respectable distance when she started forward again. Her back was ramrod straight as she stepped into the empty conference room.

As usual, the circular space made him uncomfortable. "Let's go into my office, where we can sit and talk like civilized people."

She whirled around and crossed her arms. "Civilized? *You* want to be civilized? You'll have to crawl out of the cave first."

Tension coiled his muscles. He rubbed his neck. "I don't know what you're talking about."

"I'm talking—" she stabbed an accusing finger toward the hall "—about that fiasco you staged a minute ago. Don't you *ever* treat me like a fluffhead again, in public or private, is that understood?"

Anger lifted its ugly head and hissed a warning. He broke out in a cold sweat. "I'm sorry if I offended y—"

"Don't patronize me, damn it! You had every intention of offending me. That way everyone knows just where I stand in the pecking order around here, right, partner?''

A fine mist of red edged his vision now. His breathing grew labored. "For God's sake, lower your voice. This room echoes."

She paced the floor. "So what are you afraid of, Alec? That they'll hear the truth? That you're so insecure the thought of losing authority scares you to death? That sharing power with a woman threatens your masculinity?" She stopped a foot away and dropped her voice to a whisper. "That being in control is so important you think nothing of humiliating me to gain it?"

Something in her anguished tone reached through the mist and tugged. Alec concentrated hard on Laura's eyes, wincing at the hurt she couldn't conceal. Searching for appropriate words, he watched her trembling lips tighten, her wounded expression harden.

She lifted her chin. "We're *equal* partners, Alec. That was the agreement. I don't know why that terrifies you, but if you can't deal with me, say so now. I'll make sure Sam doesn't penalize you when I leave."

In his entire adult life, no one had ever suspected his fear. Yet this woman had penetrated his guard in a matter of weeks. He felt both violated and relieved. And more vulnerable than any time since enduring, as a frightened sixteen-year-old, his father's parting, hate-filled glance.

He drew an unsteady breath. "I've tried to deal with you, Laura. I just don't seem to know how."

She searched his eyes for a long moment, her own softening by degrees. Her wide mouth relaxed, then twitched. "Somebody once told me you were a smart *pompous* bigot. You can learn."

Even as he cursed himself for a fool, his spirits lifted. He reached out and stroked her cheek, marveling at its velvety softness. Her saucy smirk faded into wide-eyed expectancy.

"Ah, Laura. What am I going to do with you?" God help him, he knew what he *wanted* to do with her. He dropped his hand with a sigh. "I've depended on myself too many years to change overnight. But I'll try. That's all I can promise. Can you live with those terms?" he asked, knowing he'd never agree if the situation was reversed.

When she nodded, the last of Alec's tension slipped away.

He sensed they'd crossed a barrier, which would make working together much easier for Laura in the future. As for him, there was only one thing certain after the crazy promise he'd made.

He was in for sheer hell.

CHAPTER SIX

LAURA STOOD in front of the bathroom medicine cabinet and looked from her mirrored image to the magazine photo she'd taped in one corner. Hopeless. Worse than hopeless.

Her unruly hair looked no closer to matching the model's than when she'd started fussing with it an hour ago. No big surprise. She'd always been better with a curry-comb than a brush.

While other young girls had experimented with their hair and makeup, Laura had helped with ranch chores or tagged behind Scott and his buddies. Finally Maria, the ranch housekeeper, had taught Laura how to weave the tangled mess into a simple braid. Later, she'd graduated to a more complex French braid. The style was neat, pro-fessional . . . and boring as oatmeal.

"Aarrgh!" Ripping the glamorous photo from the mirror, she quickly braided and pinned her hair as usual. Sam was coming by the agency this morning to meet his new account team for the first time. She hated to aggra-vate Alec by being late. They'd been getting along so well lately.

Uncapping a shiny gold tube, she leaned forward and dabbed her mouth with the exact wine red shade as her new suit. Great. Now her pale skin looked ghastly. This was definitely not her color, despite what the saleslady said. She'd be lucky to get through the day without a wooden stake being plunged through her heart. With a final despairing glance in the mirror, she tossed the lipstick in her purse and slammed out the door.

During the crawling drive up Westheimer, Laura's mind wandered to Alec. A fascinating puzzle. The complete opposite of Michael Slade, the last man who'd possessed her thoughts so thoroughly. Whereas Michael had constantly sought new thrills, Alec worshiped control, was terrified, in fact, of stepping outside conventional boundaries of behavior. His vulnerability attracted her as much as his potent masculinity.

Their relationship had undergone a subtle change since their showdown last week in the conference room. She felt less defensive about her inexperience. He treated her with the completely impersonal, strictly professional respect of an equal.

Be careful what you wish for, kiddo. You just might get it. Her father's familiar advice tugged at her heart. As a teenager, she'd hated his trite warnings to curb her natural impulsiveness. Funny how often his advice popped into her head as an adult. If only she'd acknowledged his wisdom while growing up.

Fighting her sudden melancholy, she flipped on the radio. Although she'd quit Michael's band four years ago with a severely damaged ego, her love of music had survived intact. Soon she was humming, then singing along with a popular ballad. When the upbeat melody ended, her office building glittered ahead like a reflection of her happier mood.

Walking through the lobby five minutes later, she stiffened at the sound of a low wolf whistle. A curl of pungent cigar smoke tickled her nose. She splayed a hand on one hip and turned. "Sam Parker, don't you know that's not acceptable these days? You could get yourself slapped with a harassment lawsuit."

The reprobate grinned around his cigar stub and rocked back on his heels. "Laura Hayes, don't you know you look prettier'n a fresh-picked rose this morning? You wouldn't spoil an old fart's fun now, would you?"

"I'll let it pass this time." She patted his stocky pin-striped shoulder and nudged him toward the elevators. "Come on up. You're early, but at least you aren't a *day* early."

Alec had told her about the surprise visit that had led to their present partnership. Heaven help them both if Sam didn't like what he saw today. By the time she pushed open the agency's door, her smile felt cast in plaster.

"Welcome to Hayes and McDonald Advertising," she said, waving Sam inside.

From behind the reception desk, Brenda Lee's eyes widened. Rising, she arched a questioning brow at Laura.

"Sam, this is our office manager, Brenda Lee Wilson." Laura noted the older man's sweeping head-to-toe survey. Thank goodness her friend was wearing the conservative black skirt and cream silk shell Laura had made a point of admiring last week.

Sam reached out and shook Brenda Lee's hand a tad longer than necessary. "If I'd known you were here, hon, I would have come around sooner."

Brenda Lee extracted her hand with a cool smile. "Two hours early is quite sufficient, Mr. Parker. If you'll have a seat, I'll tell Mr. McDonald you're here."

The subtle reprimand and professional greeting would have been beyond Brenda Lee's capability three weeks ago. As the petite blonde disappeared down the hall, Laura knew she'd just witnessed an imitation of herself. And by God, it *was* the sincerest form of flattery.

"What are you grinning at, Laura?" asked Sam. "Can't a man say anything nice to a woman these days without getting his head snapped off?"

"I warned you, didn't I? Besides, what are you doing flirting with her? I thought I was your fresh-picked rose." She heaved a maidenly sigh. "How quickly they forget."

Sam chuckled. "You, my dear, are impossible to forget."

At the sound of approaching footsteps, they both turned. Alec emerged from the hallway wearing a tailored black suit. "Isn't that right, Alec?" Sam asked.

"Isn't what right?" His teeth flashed white against bronzed skin. A lock of ebony hair grazed his forehead.

"That Laura is impossible to forget."

Turning his head, Alec examined her with amused tolerance.

I love your eyes, Laura thought with stunning force.

His cobalt gaze flickered, steadied and simmered with something that made her knees tremble. "Impossible," he agreed.

"This place is damned impressive," Sam said, capturing Alec's attention. "When do I see the rest?"

"How about now? You're so early there might even be some coffee left. Come on, we'll give you the ten-cent tour."

Laura released her breath slowly. "Be there in a minute, Alec. You two go on." He nodded and led Sam down the hallway.

She slumped against the reception desk. Dumb move, ogling her partner like an infatuated groupie. After all, the man was human. Or close enough to respond like one, anyway. She'd be a fool to read anything into his look of intense male speculation. In less than a year she was outa here. And "temporary" partnerships, as Michael had taught her years ago, were best left platonic.

She shook off her painful thoughts and caught up with the men as they were leaving the art room. Alec continued down the hall, introducing Sam to various employees. Content for once to let her partner take the lead, she swelled with pride at their staff's concise reports and genuine enthusiasm.

Harold Becker's office represented the biggest hurdle of the morning. He and Alec had spent days compiling competitive media expenditures as backup for presenting a suggested increase over last year's media budget. Sam's approval would guarantee the advertising reach and frequency necessary to launch a new strategy. Anything less would jeopardize the campaign's effectiveness.

Alec halted before Harold's doorway. "Go on in, Sam. I need to grab something from my office." He nodded once at Laura and strode down the hall.

When Sam entered, Harold rose from behind his desk, looking very Madison Avenue with his precision haircut, wire-rimmed glasses and double-breasted gray suit. Laura lingered in the doorway, curious to watch him in action.

"It's a pleasure to see you again, Mr. Parker," Harold said, shaking Sam's hand. "You may not remember, but we met five months ago when the Spencer Group gave you a spec presentation."

Sam cocked his head. "No offense, son, but you pitchmen all look alike after a while. What was your angle on the account?"

"We recommended an extensive direct-marketing program."

"Now I remember. Your 'recommended' budget gave me nightmares for weeks."

Harold laughed good-naturedly. As the two men sat down and reminisced, Laura wondered what could be keeping Alec. She slipped away and walked down the hall, slowing at the sound of soft swearing. Poking her head inside Alec's door, she gasped.

Papers littered his desk as if tossed before an oscillating fan to land at will. Drawers, file cabinets and his briefcase gaped open, their contents scattered willy-nilly. Slamming a drawer, Alec looked up.

"It's not here."

"What's not here?"

"Our budget recommendation. It's not here. I took it home last night and made some revisions on my personal computer. Even reprinted the damn thing, so I wouldn't have to do it this morning. Only...I forgot to lock my briefcase."

She hesitated. "Is that significant?"

"To Jason, my briefcase is Pandora's box." He slumped in his chair and stared bleakly into space.

Laura rallied. "Well, look, it's not a disaster. Where's your backup disk?"

"Same place as the hard copy, probably. Wherever Jason hid them."

Uh-oh. "How long would it take you to recreate your corrections here at the office?"

Alec's mouth tightened. "It took me four hours last night, but I could probably get it down to three in a pinch."

"How about if you and Harold talk Sam through the preliminary rationale, while I run to your house and pick up the report. Is Mrs. Pennington there?"

"I doubt it. She was leaving to do some personal errands right after Jason left for school." He glanced at his watch. "About thirty minutes ago." He waited, sullen, yet expectant.

"Okay, okay. No problem. Just give me your house key, and I'll tear the place apart until I find the hard copy. Any idea where Jason might have put it?"

A spark of hope lit Alec's eyes. "Try his room first. Under the fire engine in his closet. That's where I found my wallet last week," he said dryly, extracting a key ring from his pocket. Selecting one key, he extended it toward her. The others fell in a dancing jingle. "Go ahead and take my truck. The square key next to this one opens the back kitchen door."

Laura made a swipe for the ring, her hand closing over warm fingers and cool metal. Their gazes locked. Awareness crackled between them. Still gripping the key, he focused on her mouth. "Thanks, Laura."

His gaze slid lower, lower, lower...then slowly back up to her eyes, gaining voltage as it traveled.

"New suit?"

Lost in his thousand-watt gaze, she nodded.

"I like it," he said, relinquishing his hold.

The keys dropped and clattered onto the desk. Cheeks burning, she picked them up and backed away. "Th-thanks. I'll go as fast as I can." Ducking her head, she fled the office.

The drive passed in a blur, obscured by more vivid images. *He likes my new suit.* Pulling into Alec's driveway, she glimpsed her dreamy smile in the rearview mirror.

What a dork. She'd better get her mind on the job. If she found the report in Jason's room, she could be back on the road in minutes and salvage the meeting.

Yanking the key from the ignition, she scrambled out and slammed the truck door. The house stood silent. And cold, despite the redbrick shimmering in the rising heat.

Shaking off the fanciful thought, Laura slipped through the backyard gate and rounded the corner. The shaded flagstone patio was lovely. Did Alec sip his morning coffee out here? No, not a chance. He'd gulp a cup on his way to the office. Pity.

Continuing toward the back door, she inserted the square key and pushed with her shoulder. The door soundlessly swung open. She bustled into the shadowed room, kicked the door shut and waited for her eyes to adjust. Where was the light switch? She needed to get mov—

A high keening moan in the distance raised the hairs on the back of her neck. It was a sound of terror. A distress call. A signal from a child in trouble.

Oh, God. Oh, God...

I'M NOT AFRAID of the dark. There's nothin' in here. Nothin' breathin' behind me with big sharp teeth. Nanny Howard said there's no such thing as monsters, and she wouldn't lie. I'm not scared. I'm not...

Jason hugged his shins more tightly and ground his face into his knees. The bony pressure felt good against his puffy eyes.

His dad wouldn't cry. His dad would turn around and grab the monster and kill it! If Jason had his ninja sword, he'd kill it, too. Then he'd chop his way out of the dark and kill *her*. Well, maybe not kill. But he'd beat up her mean ugly face, so she'd go away and never come back.

The thought made him feel better. He scooted his bottom a little to one side and made a face at the tingling feeling. *She* didn't think he could sit his butt still for two seconds, but he'd been here longer than that. Way longer.

He'd missed the school van again. He should've climbed his tree right away, instead of trying to snitch a

few cookies. But he'd gotten so hungry last time waiting
for his dad.

She'd caught him sneaking out of the pantry. Before he
could run away, she'd dragged him by the ear and closed
him in the dark so he could think long and hard about
what a bad little boy he was. If he sat quiet until she got
good and ready to let him out, maybe, just maybe, she
wouldn't tell his father what a horrible brat he was.

Mean old witch!

He'd stuck his tongue out so she wouldn't know how
scared he was. He sort of wished he hadn't done that now.
I'm not afraid of the dark.

If he'd made it to his tree, maybe his dad would've
brought that nice lady Laura home again. Jason squeezed
his eyes shut hard until he could see her face.

She was pretty. Not don't-touch-my-hair pretty like his
mom had been. But pretty like…Joey's new puppy down
the street. Laura had eyes like Biscuit's, warm and
friendly and goldish brown in the sunlight. She'd tickled
his leg and smiled at him with her whole face, not just her
teeth—like she didn't think he was a brat at all. She could
climb real good, too—for a girl. Jason almost smiled
against his knees. Almost.

She sure was nice. He bet if he hugged her, she wouldn't
care if he messed up her hair or the gunk on her face.

He tightened his arms and rubbed one cheek against his
knees. His chest ached on the inside, like it was bruised or
something. *I won't think about hugging. I won't think
about bein' alone. I won't think about the dark.*

Nobody wanted him. Not his mom, who'd left him with
Nanny Howard to go to heaven. Not Nanny Howard,
who'd sent him away to his dad's. Not his dad, who'd left
him with the witch to go to work. Nobody.

Except the thing behind him.

Jason could hear it breathing, feel its big, bulgy eyes staring at his back. He had to be quiet. She wouldn't let him out if he made a noise. Fear rose in his throat. He stuffed a fist into his mouth. The muffled, high moan seeped around his knuckles and filled the dark.

EVERY MATERNAL CELL in Laura's body strained toward the sound. The cry faded into eerie silence.

She cocked her head and listened. If she charged into an unknown situation recklessly, she might do Jason more harm than good. Slipping off her pumps, she crept across the tiles, her gaze scanning the shadowed breakfast nook as she passed. Pans and utensils hung like bats in ghostly silhouette. Surfaces gleamed and winked. Not a bogey-man in sight.

In the kitchen.

Pausing at the entrance to the vast living room, she heard the faint drone of a television coming from upstairs. She crossed white carpet to the marble foyer. Alec's front door appeared bolted from the inside. Was that good or bad? She swung around and faced a sweeping staircase.

With each step, the frenzied noises of a popular game show jangled her nerves. At the top stair, she hesitated. A large open area to the right held a pool table and wet bar. Nothing else. She turned left.

Three doors lined the hallway. Two were closed. The last one stood cracked open, emitting the unmistakable squawks of a TV. Her heart racing, she tiptoed forward and peered through the gap.

A chest of drawers and protruding bed frame flickered in blue-green light. Splayed feet encased in sturdy black shoes stretched out from a chair beyond the bed. She'd seen those shoes before.

Laura pushed the door wide, allowing light to spill from the hall into the bedroom. Mrs. Pennington sat slumped in a rocking chair facing the television, her eyes closed and head lolling to one side. Something about her utter stillness and slack mouth warned Laura this wasn't a simple nap.

Alarmed, she swept past the rocker to the window and yanked open the heavy floral draperie. Sunlight flooded over Mrs. Pennington's sagging face, sallow but for the red veins webbing her prominent nose. Rehearsing CPR techniques in her mind, Laura bent over to search for signs of a stroke. Fetid whiskey-fumed breath sent her reeling backward.

The woman was sauced!

Dear God, where was Jason?

Laura whirled around and switched off the television. "Jason? Where are you?" Her voice echoed in the silence.

Mrs. Pennington groaned. Laura threw her a furious glance before running into the hallway.

"Jason, it's Laura. Please answer me."

A small sound caught her attention. She strained to pinpoint its location. There it was again—a choked pitiful sob coming from the other end of the house. She rushed toward the empty games room. The crying strengthened in volume.

"That's right, Jason. Nice and loud, so I can find you."

Tracking his voice to the east wall, she flung open a series of cabinet doors containing stereo equipment, CDs and games.

"Laura?" Jason croaked.

Her head snapped to the right. "Say something else, honey, so I can find you." She approached a large bar, complete with brass foot rail and dozens of bottles against a mirrored back wall.

"It's so d-dark."

There. Laura ran around an oak countertop and crouched on the floor. A side wall papered in wine-and-forest-green pheasants revealed a cleverly concealed door, about three by four feet, papered in the same pattern. She grabbed a brass knob and pulled.

Damn! A small part of her had clung to the hope he'd just been hiding. "I'm here, honey. Do you know where the key is?"

"*She* has it."

"Mrs. Pennington locked you in here?" Laura's nostrils flared. "Hang on another minute, and I'll get you out." She started to rise.

"Wait."

At his panicked tone, Laura knelt back down. "Don't worry about Mrs. Pennington. She's not going to hurt you, I promise. Let me get the k—"

"Wait! She's a witch!"

Laura leaned her forehead against the cabinet and squeezed her eyes shut. What kind of woman would do this to a child? She forced the anger from her voice. "I know, sweetheart. But you're safe now. I'll be right back, I prom—"

"*Waaait!*" His anguished panting breaths could be heard through the wood barrier. "She'll get mad at you for helpin' me. You gotta go."

Laura blinked.

His breathing slowed. He sniffed hard. "I'm okay, Laura, honest. I won't cry anymore."

Stunned, she sat back on her heels. He was worried about her safety, not his own. Swallowing thickly, she narrowed her eyes.

That woman is dead meat.

"I'll be right back," Laura repeated, rising to march down the hallway and into the last bedroom.

Mrs. Pennington sat hunched forward in the rocker, her eyes and forehead cupped in both hands. The neck of a whiskey bottle peeked out from under the ivory dust ruffle near her feet.

"Where's the key?" Laura demanded.

Lifting the heel of one palm, Mrs. Pennington delivered a hostile bloodshot glare before deliberately covering her eye again.

Laura charged the rocker and grabbed a thick wrist in each of her hands. The housekeeper was built like a linebacker, but Laura's younger athletic muscles were fueled by fury.

She pried Mrs. Pennington's hands apart and leaned forward. "Listen to me, woman, and you listen good. Either you tell me where that key is *now,* or I won't just see that you never work near children again, I'll file criminal charges with the police! Just try to get *any* job with a record, lady."

Head weaving, the housekeeper sneered. "The boysh a crybaby, thash what. Lucky I didn' take a shtrap to hish back."

Laura thought of the six-year-old "crybaby" who'd exhibited more courage and chivalry than any grown man she'd known. Very slowly, she increased the pressure of her hold on each wrist. "Did you know, Mrs. Pennington, that it's very common for drunks to accidentally injure themselves?" She felt a savage glee as the woman pulled and jerked to no avail. Laura's viselike grip twisted in a wrestling maneuver she'd learned from Scott. "For instance, if a woman your age tried to break a fall with her hands, she could fracture her wrists."

Fear sobered as nothing else could. Mrs. Pennington flung her head back. "You're crazy. Let me go!"

"Where's the key?" Laura looked long and deep into the other woman's eyes, hiding none of her rage.

Mrs. Pennington blanched. "In the top chest drawer. Under the handkerchiefs," she whispered.

Laura found the small key with no difficulty, thank heavens. At the doorway she paused and turned. "Pack your things. *Now*. There'll be a cab out front in thirty minutes."

Mrs. Pennington slumped forward, a pitiful drunken old woman.

A woman who'd locked a small child in a storage cabinet, Laura reminded herself.

Running back to the bar, she slipped behind the counter. "I'm back, Jason. Just a minute and I'll have you out of there." How long had he been locked inside? Hands shaking, she inserted the key and pulled open the door.

Jason sat huddled in a space the size of a small doghouse. He squinted against the light, his pale cheeks tracked with tears, his swollen eyes searching her face.

"You okay?" he whispered.

His concern was her undoing. Laura reached inside, grabbed his hands and pulled. He flew into her lap, wrapping thin little arms around her neck and burying his face in her shoulder. She rocked him and crooned words of comfort, treasuring the feel of his warm sturdy body. Long soothing minutes passed.

When Laura finally moved to get up, Jason clung to her torso like a tree frog. She relaxed again and stroked his hair. "Jason, sweetheart, I've got to call your father now and let him know you're all right." *And tell him to re-*

schedule the meeting with Sam. "Have you had any breakfast, yet?"

The boy shook his head, the action burrowing his face deeper into her shoulder. Laura struggled to keep her voice light. "Let's go see what we can rustle up for you to eat while I make the call."

She eased him off her lap, stood up and stretched out a hand. As his small palm slipped into hers, Laura knew Jason McDonald had slipped just as firmly into her heart. She accepted his trust and all accompanying responsibilities without question. He needed love, and she had plenty to spare. Especially for such a brave dear little boy.

Laura led Jason to the pantry, then settled him at the breakfast table with a glass of milk and a plate of Oreos. There was a time for good nutrition, and this wasn't it. As she walked to the kitchen phone, he rewarded her with a chocolate-toothed grin.

Shaking her head at the resiliency of children, she picked up the receiver and dialed the office. There was so much to say—and so much to hear. How could this nightmare have happened in the first place? She would try and withhold judgment about Alec's negligence until she'd heard his explanation.

But for his future health, it had better be a damn good one.

CHAPTER SEVEN

ALEC BROODED over his glass of beer, oblivious to the crowd of uptown professionals sharing the restaurant bar where he waited. Sam wasn't due for another ten minutes. Alec hoped like hell he could salvage yesterday's fiasco.

After Laura had called with her shocking report on his housekeeper, he'd charged out of the office without a word. He'd reached the parking garage before remembering Laura had borrowed his truck.

When he'd finally pulled up at his house in Harold's Jaguar, Alec had already flayed himself bloody for not checking Mrs. Pennington's falsified references personally. His ex-wife had been an indifferent mother at best. Yet Susan at her worst wasn't as bad as that monster he'd unknowingly hired.

He sipped his beer, wishing he could chase it down with whiskey. Maybe then he could forget the tongue-lashing Laura had given him.

To her credit, she'd allowed him a chance to explain his irresponsibility. But hell, it was so...complicated. He didn't know north from south anymore. Only one thing was clear.

He loved his son. Always had, from the moment those tiny day-old fingers had fisted around his thumb and clogged his throat with emotion. He'd stared into unfocused blue eyes and sworn to be worthy of such complete innocence and trust. And for two years he'd kept his promise.

Bad seeds grow weeds, boy. You're just like me, and not a goddamn thing'll change that. Blood will tell, wait and see.

Would he never get his old man's sneering voice out of his head?

A red-jacketed bartender picked up Alec's water-beaded glass, wiped the ring underneath and set it back down on the bar. "Like another beer, sir?"

Alec shook his head and pulled the glass toward him, nursing his last few sips. He'd proved Pop right, after all. And two-year-old Jason had been snatched from Alec's life to be raised by nannies, while Susan traveled the world's glamour circuit. Monte Carlo, Paris, Acapulco—wherever the hottest celebrity house party led her. Her tour had ended three months ago on an autobahn at 110 miles an hour. A fitting end. Fast and dramatic, like the woman herself. Alec snorted into his glass before draining the final golden inch.

He'd mourned his father-in-law's death six months ago far more than Susan's. Some thought it odd that his relationship with John had remained friendly even after the divorce. But Alec's mentor had loved Susan unconditionally—not blindly. Her excesses and emotionalism had made Alec's own rigid control seem admirable in John's eyes.

A brunette two bar stools away tossed her hair. Recrossed her legs. Laughed too loud. He knew the routine. If he looked her in the eye, she'd close in like a black widow spider.

He shifted toward a bank of harmless ferns and checked his watch. Three minutes left. Three minutes to get his mind on Regency Hotels and off Jason's haunted expression.

I'm sorry, son. I thought I was protecting you.

After Susan's death, authorities had returned Jason to Alec in the States. There'd been no other living relatives. No other choice. And damn his selfish soul, he'd been glad.

Fate had dropped Jason back into Alec's life for some cosmic reason. Not daring to push his luck, he'd supplied a room full of toys, a closet full of clothes and had kept his distance. Distance was the key to appeasing the gods, he'd determined. As long as he avoided Jason, the boy would be safe—and allowed to stay. So far the strategy had worked.

But suppose, just suppose, Laura was right? What if Jason truly was reaching out for love and affection with his acts of rebellion? Alec couldn't relate. He and his mom had tiptoed around Pop as if he was nitroglycerin. Hell, pulling stunts to get his attention would have been suicidal.

Alec straightened his spine and pressed a fist into his lower back. Lord, what a mess. He didn't like tempting fate, but he sure as hell wouldn't risk another Mrs. Pennington. He didn't know beans about being a father, but he'd watched his share of reruns. If Bill Cosby could do it, so could he.

After all, how hard could raising a six-year-old be?

SAM PLOWED his way across the posh restaurant bar, leaving a wake of grumbling patrons behind. Were all these people waiting for tables? He couldn't see why. Ten to one this place wouldn't know a Corona from sparkling water.

Glimpsing a sultry brunette through the crowd, he perked up. She did great things for a bar stool. And she wanted someone sitting to her right to notice.

Without looking, Sam knew he'd found Alec. Yep, there he sat, scowling into his empty beer glass. Damned if he didn't attract women like ants to a picnic, and there wasn't one sweet thing about him. In fact, there was a darkness in him, a dangerous edge that glinted once in a while. A man's secrets were his own. But Sam wondered just the same.

Customers stood yacking in groups, sucking up gossip as fast as the complimentary wine they sipped. Sam used the opportunity to observe Alec unawares.

Tall, fit, handsome without working at it, he was a man's man. And sharp as a scalpel. For the first time in two years Sam felt excited about his future. The nagging tugs of dissatisfaction, the sense he was missing something important in life, had faded to an occasional twinge.

He'd taken a huge risk backing Hayes and McDonald Advertising, but from everything he'd seen yesterday, despite the interrupted meeting, his company was in talented and capable hands. If he wasn't due in Dallas this afternoon, he would have enjoyed returning to the agency and continuing discussions there. His account team was dynamite.

Together, they were going to bend over and moon the hospitality industry, particularly the smug leaders who'd predicted Regency's downfall. Sam mentally rubbed his hands together. He'd be the first to drop his pants.

Alec shifted on his stool, allowing Sam a clear view of his face. Something was eating the guy up inside. Had Alec's son taken a turn for the worse since Sam had called yesterday evening?

Compassion bloomed in his chest. Approaching the brooding figure, he slapped Alec on the back.

"If I wanted to eat lunch across from a sourpuss, I'd have invited my second wife."

Alec swiveled and broke into a grin. "Right on time, Sam. Thanks for fighting this crowd." He slid off the stool and extended his hand.

Sam pumped it once and held on. "How's your boy?"

Sam had always wanted kids, had tried and failed with each wife. The fact that children were often taken for granted, and sometimes abused, infuriated him.

"Just fine, I think. We're going, that is, I'm going to arrange a few sessions with a child psychologist, just to be safe."

Releasing Alec's hand, Sam nodded. "Sounds sensible." Times sure had changed. People were learning to confront their dirt, not hide it. "Which talk-show host gave you that idea?"

"Are you kidding? Laura could give Oprah lessons. Come on. Let's go see where we stand on the waiting list." Alec picked up a briefcase from the floor and strode forward.

Fascinated, Sam watched the crowd part before the younger man like the Red Sea. Not a soul grumbled. He followed as Alec broke into the hostess's charmed inner circle and grasped the podium with one hand.

"Excuse me, miss. Is there a table ready yet for McDonald?"

The pretty young woman glanced up from her seating chart and blinked twice.

"Party of two?" he added, flashing a deep dimple and strong white teeth.

Sam snorted.

The hostess blushed and lowered her head. "Let me check for you, sir." Recovering her poise, she ran a finger down the waiting list, consulted her seating chart and looked up with a coy smile. "Perfect timing, Mr. McDonald. A table *just* opened up. If you'll follow me, please."

Chuckling, Sam shook his head and obeyed Alec's beckoning nod.

The hostess seated them at a window table, then handed out leather-bound menus. "If there's anything I can do for you gentlemen, please let me know," she invited, looking straight at Alec.

After she'd swished away, Sam leaned back, cocked his head and smirked.

"What?" Alec asked.

Sam rolled his eyes.

"What?"

"You had that little girl wishing you were on the menu, Alec. And the pisser is, you don't even like women."

Alec's eyebrow shot up.

"Don't get me wrong. I can spot a soprano a mile away, and you're definitely a bass. It's just that, well, you don't seem to *like* women, if you know what I mean."

From Alec's resigned sigh, apparently he did. "I enjoy women. Isn't that enough?"

The poor schmo was serious. "Depends on your expectations, I guess." Sam unfurled his napkin and smoothed the cloth in his lap. "Now me, I enjoyed the hell out of my second and third wives before things got ugly. But I *liked* my first wife more than anyone I've ever met before or since." His voice softened in memory. "Jenny and I were high school sweethearts. She put me through college. Fact is, if it hadn't been for her, I never would have founded Regency Hotels. When she died..."

When she died, he'd almost swallowed the bottle of pain pills by her empty bedside. Jenny had stopped him. The lovely healthy Jenny of old. She'd sat right down on the bed and told him his grief was holding her back. That she'd be waiting on the other side when the time was right for him to join her. She'd held him through the night, and in the morning she was gone.

He'd never told anyone.

Sam glanced up, cleared his throat and frowned. "Jenny was a damn good partner—in business and in life. I'd give everything I own to find another woman like her, son. The right partner can turn the shit life throws you into fertilizer. After you've had that, simply enjoying a woman isn't enough. Not nearly enough."

Suddenly self-conscious, he opened his menu and studied the blurred print. Alec followed suit, a thoughtful expression on his face.

A waiter, dressed in a kelly green polo shirt and white cotton drawstring pants, approached the table. "Hi. My name is Bob and I'll be serving you today. We have several specials not on the menu you might be interested in." Without waiting for a response, the young man launched into a list of complicated entrées, glancing at crib notes throughout the recitation.

During the entrée de la salmon topped with crab, Sam leaned forward. "Say, Bob?" he interrupted.

The young man stiffened. "Yes, sir?"

"Save it for your next customer and bring me a burger, rare, with a side of onion rings. And a cold beer, Corona if you've got it." He folded his menu and handed it to the waiter. "Think your chef can handle that?"

Bob relaxed and turned into a regular kid. "I don't know about him, but that's the first thing somebody's ordered I can remember. It's my first day here. And believe me, I've taken college courses that aren't this hard." Clutching his cheat notes, he turned to Alec. "What can I get you, sir?"

With a what-the-hell shrug, Alec extended his menu. "I'll have the same as my friend. But make my burger medium rare."

Bob beamed. "Yes, sir. I'll turn those orders in right now."

As the waiter hustled off, Alec opened his briefcase, pulled out a thick sheaf of papers and slid the agency's recommended media budget between Sam's fork and knife. "This is self-explanatory, but I'll try to recap the high points."

Throughout their simple meal, Sam listened to a thorough analysis of why a twenty percent increase over last year's budget was vital to the success of the new campaign. The total figure screamed from the last page like his controller gone berserk. He could manage it—barely. But it'd be close.

After the final dish had been cleared, Alec gave Sam a hard level look. "You know first-year startup costs for a new hotel far exceed the second and third year of operation. The same holds true for launching a new marketing strategy."

"I know, I know." Sam opened his coat, reached for a cigar, then stopped. Pushing a breath through his teeth, he glared at the surrounding tables. Damned no-smoking law. He'd like to take away these yuppies' after-meal coffee and see how they reacted.

"If you maintain status quo, you'll continue to lose revenue. I know you don't want to sell, Sam. This strategy is the best chance you have of retaining ownership."

If the strategy fails, I'll be ruined financially.

The unspoken words hovered between them like the lingering smell of onion rings. Gridlock. Sam felt every one of his sixty-three years.

Alec rapped his fingertips once on the table and leaned forward as if he'd made a decision. His eyes held sympathy, but no compromise. "You've taken a great many risks in your career, Sam, especially in the beginning. What would Jenny advise you to do in this situation?"

Sam's mind jerked. Jenny? Jenny had encouraged him to leave the docks and use his brain for a living. Jenny had forced him to write his first business plan and present it to a banker. Jenny had listened to his dreams with shining eyes and died before the dreams had come true.

Very slowly, his gaze refocused on Alec, who looked as if he was holding his breath. Confidence swept away Sam's doubts, energizing his smile. "Jenny would say go for it, as if you didn't know. All right, you sneaky bastard. You've got your budget."

His smile faded. "Now make us famous."

GOOD LORD, look at the time. Eight o'clock already.

Alec lowered his wrist and scanned the unfinished paperwork on his desk. A week had passed since Mrs. Pennington's departure and his decision to practice the role of father. If he intended to read Jason a bedtime story as promised, this stuff would have to wait until tomorrow. He reached for the phone and dialed home. On the fourth ring, someone picked up.

"McDonald residence, Ronald's not home," Jason shouted, competing against a TV blaring in the background.

"And he'd better not come back, is that understood, young man?"

"Yes, Dad," Jason answered meekly. "When are you comin' home?"

Alec glanced at his desk and rubbed his neck. "Soon. Have you eaten yet?"

"Mrs. Polk made meat loaf..." His voice trailed off, as if he'd been distracted.

"What are you watching?"

"*E.T.*"

"Is it Halloween yet?" His son had watched the scene a hundred times. Spielberg's magic still held strong.

"Yeah, and the mom is taking pictures. She thinks her little girl is the ghost." Jason giggled. "Look under the sheet!" he bellowed, his head turned away from the receiver.

Mrs. Polk confiscated the phone, her voice calm and strong. "Mr. McDonald? Not to worry. Jason's been bathed and fed. And as you can tell, he's happily watching a movie now."

"I should wrap things up and get out of here soon. But it will probably be an hour before I make it home. Is that okay?"

"Take your time," she assured him. "We'll be fine."

"Thank you, Mrs. Polk. Tell Jason I'll read him a story when I get there."

"Will do, Mr. McDonald. Bye now."

Relieved, Alec hung up and sank back in his chair. Mrs. Polk worked at Jason's school library. Asking if she would like to earn extra income in the evenings had been an inspired impulse on Alec's part. Both she and Jason were delighted with the arrangement.

Restless, Alec stood up and stretched. He'd been parked on his butt all afternoon and had barely scratched the surface of his workload. At this rate, he'd not only fail as a business owner, he'd get soft, too. Especially if he kept eating burgers and onion rings for lunch.

Unknotting his tie, he yanked it off and opened the top button of his dress shirt, realizing he'd never performed this entirely natural sequence at Harris, Bates and Whitman Advertising. If only Tom Marsh and the other sticklers for formality could see him now.

Smiling, Alec reached down and unfastened his second button.

That business at the restaurant last week had been awkward, to say the least. After he'd paid the bill, he and Sam had almost reached the door when Alec had felt the unmistakable prickle of someone's stare. He'd turned— and met the hostile glare of his former creative director.

Tom had been sitting with Charles Ritten, president of Golden Door Hotels and an old friend of Sam's. One thing led to another, and they'd all wound up drinking coffee together. Very civil, very nineties. Very boring.

Then Charles had cited Tom's exceptional creative work as the deciding factor in choosing Harris, Bates and Whitman as his agency of record. Alec shook his head and began sorting the papers on his desk into neat stacks. Go figure.

Oh, well, if Tom had found a source of inspiration, who was Alec to begrudge him? Maybe it would heal the man's bruised ego after losing Regency Hotels.

Tossing his tie and jacket over one shoulder, Alec stepped into the hall. The place was too quiet. He missed the hum of activity, the bursts of laughter, that filled his daylight hours. The hours when Laura circulated throughout the office.

He shook off the thought and headed toward the lunchroom. Brenda Lee had lectured him about leaving the coffeemaker on the last time she'd scrubbed the charred remains from a previous day's pot.

Glancing into each office he passed, Alec registered small details. Harold's desk looked meticulous, and Sharon still needed a fax machine. He'd have to ask Brenda Lee about that tomorrow. The closer he got to Laura's office the stronger his sense of awareness grew. He slowed, paused and ran unsteady fingers through his hair.

Hell, he thought she'd already left. Every self-preservation instinct he possessed told him to turn around and go home. Fast.

Something even more powerful and basic drove him forward.

When Alec stepped inside Laura's doorway, she looked up from writing on a legal pad and smiled. A pleasant warmth burst in his chest and spread rapidly downward. He slipped the coat from his shoulder, draped it strategically over his forearm and leaned back against the wall.

"It's getting late. Security leaves at seven, you know."

"I know. But this TV concept is finally coming along and I hate to stop." Laura rolled her shoulders and grimaced. "I've been hunched over so long my back muscles are killing me." She threw down her pencil and rubbed her neck with both hands. The voluminous blue silk blouse she wore pulled taut against her arched chest.

For an instant, each breast was revealed in exquisite detail, from the pattern of her lace bra to the condition of her nipples.

They were hard.

His body reacted in kind, surging against his clothing. *Damn.* He looked away, sensing when she dropped her arms.

"You look...stressed. Why don't you go home, Alec?"

"Yeah, I think I will. Come on and I'll walk you out."

She fiddled with her legal pad. "No, you go ahead. I need to finish this script."

He scowled. "It can wait until tomorrow, Laura. I don't like you being here all by yourself."

"I'll lock the door when you leave."

She was so damned independent, so stubborn sometimes. "What about walking to the car? Anyone could hide in that garage and surprise you."

Her eyes gleamed with amusement, although she never actually smiled. "I'm a big girl, Alec. If it makes you feel better, Scott taught me some basic self-defense maneuvers before I left for college. I promise I'll be careful walking to the car."

Overconfidence got people killed. Longing to wipe the patronizing smirk off her face, he lowered his voice. "So, you think you can handle an attack from a man?"

She looked startled, then wary. "I think I can take care of myself, yes."

He straightened from the wall to his full height, enjoying the sudden flare of uncertainty in her eyes. "What if the man was rather large. Say... about my size?" He stepped toward her desk and dropped his jacket and tie into a guest chair.

"What's with the games, Alec? What are you trying to prove?" Her tilted cat's eyes glittered in anger now.

"You're the one making unbelievable claims, Laura. Care to prove you're not just bragging?" He noted she sat perched on the edge of her chair as if prepared to leap at his slightest move. For just an instant, he considered abandoning the lesson.

Then he caught a whiff of her elusive lavender scent.

Laura erupted from the chair. Anticipating her direction, he rounded the desk. Their eyes met, hers wide, his narrowed.

Whirling, she grasped her chair and shoved. He stopped the rolling weapon with his shins and flung it aside, his eyes never leaving hers. She was agile, but no match for his long legs. Two tremendous leaps brought him close. Clamping an arm around her waist, he swept her toward him like a pile of poker chips.

"Let me go, you meat head!" she yelled.

A heel connected with his kneecap. An elbow slammed into his ribs. A small hand grabbed a fistful of hair and pulled until his eyes watered. If he didn't stop her soon she'd hurt herself—or him.

He half lifted, half dragged her to a side wall. She'd break her fool nose against the plaster if she kept struggling.

"For God's sake, Laura, calm down."

"Go to hell!"

In one neat motion, he spun her around to face him and pressed her against the wall with his body. She went completely, blessedly still.

Bracing a hand on either side of her head, he looked down into honey gold eyes wide with shock.

"Ready to cry uncle, now?" he asked, wishing he could snatch the juvenile words back.

Predictably Laura renewed her struggles. He pressed even closer, restraining her slim body by the sheer bulk of his own. His breathing stilled. His eyes closed.

The breasts he'd admired earlier were soft and yielding against his chest. The legs he'd deemed worthy of a Las Vegas show girl branded his thighs with heat. The hair he'd imagined flowing loose whispered against his chin. He buried his nose in the fragrant strands, inhaled deeply and groaned.

Laura squirmed, whether in anger or fear he never knew, for her action wedged his throbbing erection exactly where nature intended. He fought for command of his traitorous body.

She was right. He was behaving like a meat head. Worse, like the greenest adolescent, instead of a man who'd enjoyed many attractive women in his life. A man who *always* stayed in control.

He raised his head and looked down to apologize. Laura's eyes were huge and filled with dazed confusion. Her combination of innocence and sensuality had driven him crazy for weeks.

"If I say I'm sorry and promise to let you go, will you cry uncle?" he whispered.

She nodded, her pulse throbbing visibly below each delicate ear.

"I'm sorry." He lifted a hand off the wall and encircled her pale slender throat from pulse point to pulse point. "Now you say uncle."

The heartbeat under his fingertips fluttered like moth wings. The eyes beneath his searching gaze grew heavy-lidded and sultry with arousal.

"Uncle," she breathed, her lips remaining slightly parted.

His ears roared. His senses filled with soft curves and perfumed skin and small panting breaths. His body clamored to take what she offered—whether she realized her invitation or not. He shouldn't. Dear God, it would be stupid as hell.

But if he didn't taste her *now,* he'd die.

At the sight of his descending head, her eyes grew wider. Her full lips trembled. "You promised to let me go."

"I lied," he growled.

CHAPTER EIGHT

LAURA CLAMPED her lips together and cursed her weakness. He'd made his point. Must he strip her of all pride?

Warm breath tickled her ear. She shivered and cocked her head. Then he was trailing quick, nibbling kisses down her throat.

"So sweet," Alec murmured against her throbbing jugular vein.

If he stepped back, she would collapse like a Slinky toy. Michael had *never* inspired such melting heat.

"So stubborn," Alec whispered, dragging his mouth across her jaw and upward. "So soft," he crooned, turning his face and rubbing his own bristled cheek against her smooth one. She relished the abrasion even as she winced.

"So sensitive," he added, chuckling deep in his chest.

Laura's mouth curved upward. His unexpected gentleness disarmed her far more than a show of physical strength. He'd given her mixed signals for weeks. Was he really attracted to her, or just challenged? If only she was more experienced.

Her clenched hands, trapped between their tightly pressed bodies, splayed against his chest. At the slight movement, Alec's entire body tensed. Surely he wasn't reacting to her touch? Her eyes closed at the thought.

Instantly his lips dropped warm intimate kisses from one trembling eyelid to the other. "So beautiful," he breathed.

Everything in Laura froze. She wasn't beautiful, not by a long shot. Oh God, this was all a cruel joke. How could she be so naive? Afraid of what she would see, Laura lifted her gaze.

His eyes flared like jets on a gas stove. She stared, mesmerized by their unmistakable hunger. Her hands stirred against his chest. Incredibly, the flame's intensity leapt up a notch.

She could feel his heart pounding nearly as hard as her own. Intoxicated at the implication, she slid her hands up his chest. Alec's head fell back, the action parting his unbuttoned shirt to reveal a wedge of tanned skin sprinkled with black hair. Dark against the white cotton. Unequivocally masculine. She reached for the nape of his neck. As her fingers threaded through the thick raven's-wing curls, she sighed. Glorious. Better than glorious.

Drawn irresistibly to his strong bronze throat, she leaned forward and touched the tip of her tongue to his skin.

Alec's head snapped up, his nostrils flaring. He seemed larger, more powerful suddenly, like Scott's prize stallion just before covering a mare. His smoldering eyes focused on her mouth. Oh, God, she'd been told she wasn't a good kisser. What if—

His lips smothered the thought.

They were warm and smooth. Firmer than hers, but not the carved marble she'd expected. They brushed, hovered, then brushed again, as if waiting for her to do something. Remembering her earlier success, she touched her tongue to his mouth.

He reacted explosively, plunging his tongue between her lips and exploring her mouth as if charting a new world. His hands slid down her waist, clasped at the small of her back and pulled.

She nearly fainted. All feeling, all concentration and every ounce of blood in her body pooled in one location. The ache throbbed for release. Demanded release. Lost in a sensual haze, she rose up and down on tiptoe and stroked Alec's body with her own.

Emitting a low rumble, Alec covered her breast with one hand and kneaded gently. Was that whimper coming from her? Uncaring, she engaged his tongue in a wild dueling match, fencing more frantically as his fingers plucked and teased her nipple through a layer of silk and lace. She needed . . . needed . . . needed . . .

Alec ripped his mouth from hers, rested his chin on her head and took deep ragged breaths.

Bereft without his kiss, Laura stirred. "What—"

"Shh!" He stepped back.

Her knees buckled, jolting her into awareness. Then she heard it, too. The rattle of wheels rolling across tiles. Dear Lord, the cleaning crew would be here any minute.

She stiffened her spine, tugged down her skirt and smoothed her blouse, avoiding Alec's eyes all the while. Memory of the past few minutes came back in searing detail. Her cheeks burned. She'd practically raped the man.

"Laura?"

What must he think of her? Never a coward, she turned. "Yes?"

He looked disheveled, frustrated—and impossibly handsome.

"About what just happened. I had no business letting things get so out of hand. Of all the dumb, asinine…" He stabbed his fingers through the curls she'd caressed earlier. The cleaning cart rattled closer. "Hell," he muttered.

So much for sweet nothings in her ear.

Her chin came up. "Don't worry about it, Alec. I take full responsibility for my actions. Like I told you before, I'm a big girl." She walked over to get her purse from under the desk. Straightening, she added, "I can take care of myself."

Liar, her heart screamed.

A middle-aged woman carrying a mop and bucket walked past the door, starting in surprise. "Oh... Excuse me." She bobbed her head in apology.

"We were just leaving," Laura explained, turning to Alec. "I'll take you up on that offer to walk me to my car—if the offer's still good, that is."

He started to say something, clamped his mouth shut and nodded.

"Fine. After you, then." With a calmness deserving an Oscar, she waved him through the door.

If it killed her, she would be adult about this. As sophisticated as his other women. Never, under any circumstances, would she reveal he'd knocked her world right off its axis.

LAURA AWOKE to a sunbeam spotlighting her eyes. She groped for a pillow and plopped it over her face.

Darn those crummy miniblinds. If they'd fitted properly, she'd still be with Alec in her favorite hideaway on the ranch, a tree house built high in a towering oak. He'd still be kissing her while those delicious feelings curled her toes....

Her eyes popped open. She flung the pillow aside. Scrambling upright in bed, she hugged her shins and groaned. Two weeks had passed since Alec's kiss, and the memory still haunted and mortified her. They were barely past the midpoint in completing the Regency campaign, else she'd be tempted to call in sick tomorrow. He could

play King of the Monday Staff Meeting with her blessing.

How *could* she have been so wanton that night? Seeing
him at work the next day had been the most awkward, no,
the second-most awkward experience of her life. Alec had
acted cool and detached, or she would never have managed. But several times since then, she'd caught him
looking at her *that way*. When his expression cleared seconds later, she'd questioned her sanity.

Laura slid her legs down, punched her pillow, then
hugged it to her chest. Damn the man! Until becoming
Alec's partner, she'd pretty much accepted her low li-
bido, and even lower sex appeal, as a fact of life. Thanks
to him, she didn't know herself anymore.

Maybe if her mother had lived...

Laura buried her nose in the comforting yield of goose
feathers and sighed. No sense wondering what if. She
couldn't change who she was or what she'd done. Guilt
was lousy for concentration. Almost as lousy as desire.

If she didn't settle down and focus on something besides gorgeous blue eyes, her half of the agency wouldn't
be worth a fall calf at a spring auction. Then she'd never
be able to send money home. Or open her own agency—
the one place in the world she was sure to fit in.

Releasing the pillow, she slid from the bed and made
her way to the kitchen. Drat. She'd forgotten to buy coffee again. A knock on the door jolted her heart like a cattle prod. Would that sound ever stop making her nervous?

"Who is it?" she called.

"Land shark. Open up before I drop all this stuff."

Smiling at the honeyed drawl, Laura unlatched the
chain and pulled the door wide. Brenda Lee stood holding a tray loaded with coffeepot, cups and a massive pile
of doughnuts. She looked young, carefree and beautiful

in faded cutoffs and a blue shirt tied at the waist. *Elly May Clampett, eat your heart out.*

"Mornin' sugar. Ready for a little flab and gab?" Without waiting for an answer, she breezed past Laura and bumped her shins against the metal mattress frame.

Laura shut the door. "Wait a minute and I'll get that out of your way."

"Oh, don't bother. This'll make a great table." Brenda Lee lowered her tray to the middle of the bed, flipped off her thong sandals and scrambled up to sit cross-legged. She patted the mattress beside her. "Sit down and rest your merits awhile."

Laura obeyed, shaking her head at the tray. "I can't believe you did this. How'd you know I was out of coffee?"

Her neighbor poured out two cups and slanted her a wry look. "You've been borrowing mine for the past week, goose. You've got it worse than I thought."

"Got what?"

Rolling her eyes but declining to comment, Brenda Lee leaned over the tray and wriggled her nose. "There's nothing like a good pigout to make a girl feel better. Let's see now. We've got chocolate-covered, lemon-filled, apple-filled and, in case you're on a diet, plain old glazed. Name your poison."

"*Brenda Lee.* This is total obscene gluttony."

Her friend turned, eyes wide and hand poised above a gooey chocolate ring. "Sure it is, honey. That's what makes it fun. Besides, you could use a little fattening up."

Laura concentrated suddenly on adding sugar and cream to her coffee.

"What did I say?" Brenda Lee asked.

"Nothing."

"It's not nothing. You should see your face."

"Okay it's something. But it's really stupid."

"That crack about fattening you up?" Grabbing both of Laura's hands, Brenda Lee squeezed. "Laura Hayes, I meant that as a *compliment*. Why, I'd sell my soul to the devil for a figure like yours."

Laura managed something between a snort and a shaky laugh. "Yeah, right. Why look like a Greek goddess when you could look like Gumby?"

"You're joking, aren't you?" Anxious green eyes peered into Laura's. "My God, you're serious! Where'd you get an idea like that?"

"Daddy longlegs, Twiggy, pencil legs—I've heard 'em all." She took a sip of coffee and looked away.

"But you must have been just a kid when they called you those names."

"Actually, no. In elementary school I could beat the tar out of every kid there, and they knew it. But in junior high, when every other girl filled out and I just grew tall..."

Skinny and flat-chested, she'd felt like an alien in the midst of her own sex. Starting her period, getting her first training bra, all the rites of passage usually handled by mothers were awkward memories for her. She'd muddled through with the aid of a school nurse and a trip to K Mart.

"Aw, hon, that's rough." Brenda Lee released Laura's hands and plucked a chocolate doughnut off the tray. "But what about high school? If you looked like you do now, the boys must have been falling all over you by then."

She *seemed* serious. Choosing a filled doughnut, Laura settled back against the pillows and spoke between bites.

"I went out on exactly two dates in high school, both in my sophomore year. I was totally inexperienced, so when they started groping, it caught me off guard. Both those guys walked around with cracked ribs for a couple of weeks, thanks to me.''

"Naw. Get outa town.''

Laura grinned around a mouthful of lemon filling. "Yup. I wasn't very good at verbal self-defense back then. I had a much more literal education.'' She sipped her coffee. "Anyway, after those two dates, I never got asked out again. And the nicknames...changed.''

Brenda Lee stopped chewing and raised a delicate blond brow.

Laura sighed. "Ice queen, dyke, lesbo—''

"Idiots!'' Brenda Lee spat. "Ignorant jerks.''

Wide-eyed, Laura crammed the remaining two bites of doughnut into her mouth.

"Do men *ever* think with the head on their shoulders, instead of the one between their legs?''

Laura choked. Gasping for air, she grabbed a napkin and held it to her mouth, forcing herself to swallow.

Brenda Lee administered several blows to Laura's back. "Oh, hell, now I've gone and shocked you. It's just that I had a few nicknames of my own in high school, all because I kind of overblossomed in my freshman year.''

Laura raised her head.

"Slut seemed to be the favorite, but white trash was a close second.''

"That's terrible.''

Popping the last bite of pastry into her mouth, Brenda Lee swallowed and shrugged. "My school was smack-dab in the middle of Atlanta's richest neighborhood. The difference from where I got on the bus and where I got off was...'' She swallowed hard, her eyes reflecting remembered pain. "There wasn't a bit of truth to any of the rumors about me, but the reputation stuck just the same.''

Making a sympathetic sound, Laura wondered once again at the cruelty of young people.

Brenda Lee licked five chocolate-dipped fingertips clean before looking up. "Twelve years old or sixty, there's no meaner snake alive than a jealous woman or a man who's been rejected. I'm a lot happier since I quit worrying about either one of them."

Laura imagined the warm generous girl Brenda Lee must have been and the spite she'd endured for the sin of being born beautiful—and built. "Idiots! Ignorant jerks!" she snapped.

Suddenly they were both laughing. Laura felt wonderful, as if confiding hurtful memories had somehow exorcized her pain. Was this what it felt like to have a girlfriend? For the first time she conceded her male-dominated upbringing might have been a trifle limiting.

Brenda Lee drew both legs up, hugged her ankles and propped a rounded chin on her knees. "Okay, so high school sucked the big one for both of us. Please don't tell me college wasn't wonderful. I always wished I'd gone."

Laura smiled at her wistful tone. "It was wonderful. I loved the ranch, but there was so much more I wanted to see and experience. Other students hated to study, but I loved my classes."

"Beauty and brains, all in one package. You must have beaten the men off with a stick."

Irritation pricked sharp. "I wish you'd quit saying that. It's embarrassing."

"What'd I say now?"

"Once and for all, I am not beautiful, I have never had to beat men off with a stick, and what's more, I'm not...normal."

"Not normal?"

She'd been the one to start this true-confessions thing, after all. Laura took a deep breath. "I've never... I can't respond in... you know, in bed."

Brenda Lee raised her chin, eyeing Laura with interest. "Bullcorn," she said.

Perversely angry, Laura gathered up the tray, slid off the mattress and padded into the kitchen. Setting the tray down with a clatter, she called out, "How would you know?"

A grunt was her only answer.

Laura stepped around the dividing wall. Brenda Lee had folded the mattress up and was heaving the frame into the sofa. Task accomplished, she straightened, blew a few blond wisps of hair out of her eyes and crossed her arms.

"Anyone who can defend a woman like me, or tell off a man like Alec McDonald, or light up at the mention of a little boy like Jason—sugar, that's a woman with *passion*."

She walked over to a stack of flowered cushions and carried three back to the sofa. Her voice jerked as she punched them into place. "If you've been cold in bed, blame the heating pad, not yourself. The way I figure, you probably haven't plugged in all that many, anyway. Am I right, hon?"

Laura could only nod at the outrageous question.

Brenda Lee smirked. "Thought so. You find the right heating pad and you'll set off every smoke alarm in the building, I promise."

The image of Alec pressing her against the wall made Laura blush. And ache. Grateful that Brenda Lee had bent down for another armful of cushions, Laura rushed over and split the load, helping her plump and arrange in companionable silence. At last both women sat down and turned to each other.

Brenda Lee frowned. "I don't know how you got this fool notion you aren't attractive to men, but I suspect that's the reason you haven't been beating them off with a stick."

Aha! "That's what I've been trying to tell you."

"No darlin', men don't think you're unattractive—*you* do. You're sending off No Trespassing signals to any man who comes close." She leaned back and cocked her head. "If you ever started making the most of what God blessed you with...whoooee! Things would get mighty interesting at the office."

At the office? "God *blessed* me with hopeless hair and stilt legs."

Brenda Lee reached over and pulled out Laura's ponytail clip. A full minute passed before she spoke. "Laura, you fool. Women pay salons hundreds of dollars for waves like these. Why do you hide this awesome hair?"

Laura raised her chin.

"And what's this about stilt legs?" Brenda Lee hooted, stretching out a perfectly proportioned—but petite—leg for inspection. "I look like one of those troll dolls sitting next to a Barbie doll, and you have the nerve to complain. Come on, gimme a flaw I can sink my teeth into."

Laughing at the absurd comparison, Laura obliged. "I'll give you two. My eyes are downright weird, and my mouth's too wide."

Brenda Lee shooed off the assessment with a wave. "Your eyes are unusual, not weird. Actually, exotic is a better word. But I agree your mouth is too wide." She held up a palm. "I didn't say you were a conventional beauty, Laura. Alec would be bored to tears with that, anyway." Her gaze swept Laura from head to toe and gleamed. "What I could do with such raw material boggles the mind. We'll have to do something about this."

Alec again. Was she so transparent? Laura opened her mouth to protest, gasping when the front door flew open and banged against the inner wall. Brenda Lee yelped.

A tall man stood frowning in the doorway, his black Stetson, jeans, boots and white Western shirt setting off his rangy body to advantage.

"Damn it, Laura. Haven't you put that dead bolt in yet?"

"Scott!" With a joyful smile, Laura catapulted from the couch and into her brother's arms.

ALEC KILLED the Chevy's engine, cutting off Reba's sassy twang in midsong. The chopped notes echoed in the silent parking garage.

Pretty damn sad when a man spent Sunday at the office, instead of with his son. He rubbed his neck, remembering his flippant thought about following in Bill Cosby's fatherly footsteps.

Determined to become more involved with Jason, Alec had learned six-year-old boys were a unique life form. They fed on activity, growing cranky and bored without a steady stream of stimulation. Steady, as in constant.

Alec had played video games, answered endless questions, visited the Houston Livestock Show and Rodeo, filled three coloring books, visited the zoo, erected an entire Lego city and almost lost his temper more times than he could count during the past few weeks.

He'd fallen asleep in the middle of reading The Berenstain Bears' *Too Much Junk Food* last night. Saturday night, for cryin' out loud. Now there was a picture for *Forbes* magazine.

Waking up next to Jason's curled body this morning had filled Alec with tenderness—and dread. His son knew just which buttons to push when it came to testing his patience. So he'd called Mrs. Polk and made up an excuse about needing to work a few hours today. Pretty damn sad.

Alec closed his eyes as Pop's voice rang in his head.

You wanna hit me, don't you, boy? It's in your blood. Go on, do it. See what it feels like to be a man.

God, what was happening to him? Buried memories were unearthing right and left, foul and decayed after years of festering.

He scrubbed his face with both palms and opened bleary eyes. Everything would be okay, he assured himself. The control he'd spent years shoring up would withstand the stress. Laura's kiss two weeks ago had registered off the Richter scale. If he could make it through that without cracking...

Alec stopped rationalizing and admitted the truth. He wanted Laura Hayes. Wanted her so much his teeth ached. If he hadn't heard the cleaning cart that night, he would have taken her right there against the wall. His *temporary* business partner, for God's sake. Talk about shooting himself in the foot.

Underneath that independent spirit lurked a passion most men only fantasized about. Now that he'd kissed her, it would be damn near impossible to resist another taste. But he'd do it.

His iron control had already sustained severe damage. Spending more time with Jason would weaken it even more. Laura's passion could very well be the quake that blasted his restraint straight to hell.

He'd already been there, thank you. He wasn't going back.

Resolved, Alec locked the truck and headed for his office. Five minutes later, he stretched out his key toward suite 1700 and paused. The door, which should have been locked, stood ajar. Probably just a maid mopping those endless tile floors. Just the same, with computer equipment a prime theft target these days, he'd better make sure.

Pushing the door open, he crept across the floor, grateful he'd worn his running shoes. The murmur of voices drew him toward the hallway. A woman's rich contralto escalated his heart rate. An answering deep rumble raised his blood pressure to match. What was Laura doing at the office on Sunday afternoon?

And who the hell was she doing it with?

CHAPTER NINE

CLENCHING HIS FISTS, Alec headed toward the voices.

"I'm so glad you came. You always seem to know when I need you. I . . . I've really missed you." Laura's admission drifted down the hall.

Alec froze in midstep.

"I've missed you, too, Laura. It wouldn't hurt you to visit *me,* you know."

"Oh, Scott, you know how Dad is."

Scott. Laura's brother. The air flowed back into Alec's lungs.

"He'd try and talk me into staying," Laura continued. "We'd only end up fighting."

"I know. That's why I didn't call you right away. The doctors agreed stress of any kind should be avoided. Laura . . ." He paused, as if struggling for words.

"Oh, my God!"

"Calm down, he's doing just fine. It was a mild heart attack, nothing life-threatening. You can call him at the hospital and hear for yourself. Pete's there now. Dad's being released tomorrow."

"When . . . ? Where did . . . ?"

"Last night in the barn. I'd made his favorite dinner— spaghetti. When he didn't come in, I got nervous. He'd been stacking bales, stubborn fool. I told him I'd get around to it when I could." Air hissed through teeth. "You remember how it is, Laura. There's always a fence down, or a pump that goes out, or a calf tangled in wire. I can't be everywhere at once."

"It wasn't your fault. You're doing the work of three men, as it is, plus the cooking. If anyone's to blame, it's me!"

Her anguish reached into the hallway and pulled Alec forward. He stopped at the sound of a chair scraping and the rustle of clothing. For the life of him, he couldn't back away.

"Hey, hey...it's okay, runt. Don't tear yourself up over this. You're doing your share. Those checks you've been sending have really helped."

Laura snorted. "A spit in the ocean, and you know it. I wish I could send more. Can you hire another hand while Dad's laid up?" Her voice sounded distorted, as if muffled by a chest.

"I... We had to let Bill and Hank go two weeks ago. Pete won't leave of course, but God knows when he'll see his wages." Weariness and frustration vibrated in each word.

Laura moaned. "Are things that bad?"

Scott's silence spoke volumes.

"You haven't... Oh, Scott, you haven't sold Twister?"

"No, I haven't sold him."

"Promise?"

"I've never lied to you, runt."

"Liar," she said, a smile in her voice.

Alec relaxed and inched backward.

"But unless a miracle happens by mid-June, I may have to sell him," Scott added.

"So soon?"

"The bank has given us two extensions already. The loan committee won't approve a third—can't even say I blame them."

"I'm coming home," Laura stated. "I've been selfish to stay away this long."

"No! Absolutely not." His voice gentled. "I'm impressed as hell with this place, Laura. You've got a good thing going here. A chance to build a solid future doing something you love. And you really do love it, don't you?"

"Yes."

If he hadn't been straining to hear, Alec might have missed her quiet reply.

"Then don't be a martyr. Your coming home wouldn't change the company's profit-and-loss statement. But it *would* screw up a dream you've had since undergraduate school."

"But, Scott—"

"No buts. There's only one thing I want you to do for me."

"What? Anything."

"Put this agency on the map, runt. Show the world *everything* is bigger and better in Texas."

Alec could almost see Scott grinning. He sounded like a man worth knowing. A man who probably wouldn't be caught dead eavesdropping.

Giving brother and sister the privacy they deserved, Alec turned and crept back down the hall. He'd known about H & H Cattle Company, but just general stuff. Certainly nothing about its financial difficulties. With this new knowledge, his buy-out offer to Laura took on a whole new meaning.

Easing out the front door, he left it cracked open and headed for the elevators. It would be just like Laura to take personal responsibility for her family's problems. She was obviously filled with guilt for not helping more. Much as he'd like to dismiss his sudden compassion, he couldn't. If there was one thing he understood, it was guilt.

Maybe Jason would like to go out for pizza later. Suddenly Alec couldn't wait to get home.

JASON WAS PERCHED on the edge of his bottom-bunk bed, one high-top sneaker resting on Alec's thigh.

"But *why can't* we ask her, Dad?"

Alec tensed at the underlying whine—a sure signal of trouble ahead. He finished tying a neon orange shoelace and sat back on his heels.

"Because most people like to rest on Sunday evening, and Chuck E Cheese's is not exactly a restful place."

"It is so res'ful. All she has to do is sit at a table and watch the show. How tired can she get doin' that?"

"I think Laura's brother is visiting her this weekend. Let's wait and ask her another time. Have you combed your hair today, son?" At Jason's guilty flush, Alec dug a comb from his pocket and set to work.

"Her brother can come, too. I don't mind. *Please,* Dad, can we call her?"

"I said no, Jason. We'll ask her another time, I promise."

The bright blond head jerked back, leaving Alec's hand suspended in air.

"You promise. You promise," Jason mimicked bitterly. "All you do is make promises, but you never keep 'em!" He pulled up his legs and scrambled deep into the bunk-bed shadows like a wounded animal.

Alec counted to ten. Every time he was alone with the boy, there was a major confrontation. He half rose, intending to go read the Sunday paper and the hell with it. Jason's accusing eyes glinted from the shadows.

Sighing, Alec ducked his head and sat on the mattress. "What promises have I broken?"

"Lots."

"Name one."

The child thrust out his lower lip in a startlingly familiar gesture. His resemblance to Susan was uncanny sometimes. And why not? She'd had the mannerisms and maturity of a six-year-old.

Alec cocked an eyebrow. "Well?"

"You . . . you promised to read me a bedtime story the night Mrs. Polk stayed late, and you didn't." He lowered his chin and picked at the rubber tread of one sneaker. "I knew you wouldn't."

That damned night again. The night Alec had kissed Laura. It seemed destined to haunt him in more ways than one.

"You were asleep in front of the TV when I came home, Jason. I carried you into your room and tucked you into bed."

Jason's fingers stilled. "I thought Mrs. Polk carried me."

Alec hadn't let her. He'd savored the excuse to cradle the sleeping child against his heart.

"No, I did."

A pleased little smile crossed Jason's face before he looked up. "You could've woke me."

"Mmm. Let's see now." Alec rubbed his jaw. "You wanted me to wake you up so I could read you a story so you could fall asleep. Is that right?"

Jason thought a moment, then grinned sheepishly.

Alec reached out and tousled the hair he'd just combed, his palm sliding down to cuddle the boy's cheek. Oh, the luxury, the soul-deep joy, of simply touching his son.

Jason leaned into the caress. "I guess we can call Laura another time, Dad."

His throat working, Alec looked into solemn blue eyes wise beyond their years. "You win, buddy. Let's look up Laura's number and give her a call," he heard himself say.

As Jason let out a war whoop, Alec mentally shrugged. No sense punishing his son because he didn't trust himself with Laura. Chuck E Cheese's was hardly conducive to a romantic interlude. Chances were, she'd bring her brother along, anyway. Surely he could keep his hands off her under those conditions.

He'd have to play dumb about Scott's visit, Alec reminded himself on the way to the phone. Laura's pride would suffer if she knew he'd overheard about H & H Cattle Company's financial troubles.

By the time Alec dialed her number, he'd convinced himself an outing was just what she needed to take her mind off problems for a while. If his heart sped up as the phone rang...well, he just hoped she wouldn't disappoint Jason, that was all.

LAURA'S HEART RACED as Scott parked in front of the popular family pizza parlor and cut the engine of his battered pickup. Before he could unlatch the door, she placed a hand on his arm. Tawny eyes, so like her own, questioned her from under a curving black felt brim. Scott only removed his Stetson for weddings and funerals.

"Yeah, runt?"

Laura hesitated, unsure how to start. "Be extra nice to Jason now. He's had a rough time of it and deserves a little spoiling."

"Guess I'll leave my switch in the truck then." He threw her a disgusted look. "Since when have I ever been mean to a kid, Laura? What's the deal?"

"Nothing," she said too quickly. "I think he's pretty special, that's all. And...and when you meet Alec, lay off giving him the third degree, okay?" Her skittering gaze glanced off Scott and quickly returned. "Get that smirk off your face, Scott Hayes, before I scratch it off!"

"Oh-ho. So that's how the wind blows. I gather Jason isn't the only guy you think is special."

Laura dug her nails into the worn vinyl seat. "Alec is my business partner, Scott, and a damn good one, too. When you leave tomorrow, I have to stick around and face him at the office. I'll thank you to remember that."

Scott swept off his hat and clutched it against his heart, revealing thick brown hair burnished with gold. "I'm crushed. My own sister is afraid I'll embarrass her."

"I'm *afraid* you'll get all macho and protective on me and embarrass *yourself*. I haven't forgotten what you did to Greg Taylor for insulting me at the Dairy Queen."

Laura had walked into the crowded teen hangout searching for a friendly face. Fate had sent Scott walking out of the rest room just as Greg called out, "Hey, everybody, it's Butch."

Her brother tilted his head back, a cocky reminiscent grin on his lean face.

Laura punched him in the arm. "I thought Mary Beth was gonna faint in her french fries when Greg's nose bled like a stuck pig's. You started the biggest brawl in Luling's history."

Scott's grin widened. "I did, didn't I?" He eyed Laura with interest. "Ol' Greg would shit a brick if he could see you now. Mary Beth's big as a heifer, and you're, well, damned if you're not just like Mama."

Laura blinked rapidly, unable to speak for a moment. She only knew their tall striking mother from family photographs. But Scott had been twelve when Patricia

Hayes had succumbed to cancer, and he'd clearly adored her.

Straightening, Scott plunked on his hat, tugged the brim down and chucked her under the chin. "Don't worry, runt. I'll behave. Now let's go meet these paragons of manhood before I change my mind."

Laura slid out of the cab and smoothed her jeans. She hadn't wanted to alert Scott by changing clothes after Alec had called, but now she wished she had.

After countless washings, her jeans were old, worn and very tight. And her faded T-shirt clung much more snugly than the shirts she usually wore. She hadn't braided her unruly hair, either, but had simply clipped it back in a low ponytail.

Disgusted with herself, Laura tossed her head. Why should she care what Alec thought, anyway? She was here to see Jason.

"Earth to Laura. Come in, please, Laura," Scott called from where he stood, holding the restaurant door open. Grant Hayes believed in old-fashioned courtly manners and had taught his son well.

Laura jogged toward him, tugging Scott's hat brim over his knowing grin as she passed through. Five steps inside the door she stopped. And stared.

Mechanical and computerized games of every kind lined the cavernous space, each one glowing or blinking garishly in the dim light. Bells, whistles, clangs, pops and simulated warfare noises competed with dozens of laughing shrieking children bouncing from game to game like human pinballs. The noise was deafening.

Dazed, Laura looked over her shoulder at Scott and shared a wide-eyed look of amazement.

"Do you see them anywhere?" he shouted.

She frowned and shook her head, searching the room for a blond child. Boys seemed to be the dominant sex here, ranging in age from one to twelve. Even though there were countless parents shepherding their children, she saw no sign of Alec.

Laura was turning to consult Scott when a flash of orange caught her eye. She pinpointed the source and smiled in delight.

Jason barreled straight toward her, dodging moving children and a stationary space rocket with the agility of a Heisman Trophy winner. He launched into a bear hug at full speed, sending Laura staggering backward a few steps.

"Hi, Laura! Where've you been? I've been waitin' and waitin'."

Laura looked down into the upturned face glowing with happiness and felt her insides go buttery. What woman could resist a welcome like that?

"Sorry, honey, we were running a little late. Where's your dad?"

"He's orderin' a pizza. The line's real long."

She squeezed him briefly, then pulled back and spun him around. "I want you to meet someone special. Jason, this is my brother, Scott."

Scott stepped forward and extended his hand with grave politeness. "Hello, Jason. Any boy who can climb a thirty-foot tree is someone I want to meet."

Jason puffed out his chest as he shook her brother's hand.

Thank you, Scott.

"I got a cowboy hat like yours," Jason said, gazing at Scott's Stetson with an awed expression. "I wore it to the rodeo with my dad. He's got a hat, too, only he doesn't wear it much 'cause it makes his head itch."

"Hats'll do that sometimes," Scott solemnly agreed.

Jason stuck one hand in the pocket of his baggy stone-washed jeans, duplicating Scott's stance. "Are you a real cowboy or a fake one?"

"Depends on what you mean by fake, I guess." Obviously struggling to keep a straight face, Scott threw Laura a wild glance for help.

She crossed her arms and grinned.

"Fake is when you put on a hat and boots for fun and walk around eatin' sausage on a stick and lookin' at the cows and tractors and stuff," Jason explained. "Dad says we're fake. He says real cowboys put on a hat and boots for *work*, not fun."

"I guess you'd say I'm a real cowboy then."

As the two continued talking, Laura discreetly searched the room. Where did one order pizza in this madhouse, anyway? Her gaze roved, passing over and discarding a series of harried fathers before landing on a tall broad-shouldered figure with midnight hair.

Her heart banged like sneakers in a dryer.

Alec stood near the back wall, fists on hips. He wore threadbare jeans and a purple-and-white baseball jersey, snug in the shoulders and loose at the waist. The curves and bulges of his wide stance were the stuff of women's fantasies.

Laura had no time to hide her thoughts before Alec saw her. All movement and noise ceased.

I remember our kiss, her gaze told him. *I remember how you felt and tasted.*

Alec's eyes flared. A hot sizzling current leapt between them and held, making it impossible for her to look away.

"Hey, Dad!" Jason yelled. "Look who's here!"

Suddenly she was being pulled by a small determined hand toward those electric blue eyes. Only when Jason stopped did Laura realize he'd dragged her brother along, too.

"Guess what, Dad? Scott's a real cowboy, just like in the movies!"

"Just like in the movies, huh?" Alec exchanged an amused look with Scott. The two men shook hands. "Thanks for coming, Scott. I know this is not exactly on your itinerary of fun things to do." He shot Laura a wry glance. "Or yours, either."

As Scott picked up the conversational ball, Jason tugged on Laura's arm. She bent down.

"What's eye-ten...eye-ten-er..." Jason struggled with the word.

"Itinerary? That means a schedule or plan for the day."

"Oh." He frowned and looked away.

"What's wrong, Jason?"

He shrugged and shook his head.

Laura dropped on one knee, oblivious to the men who'd stopped talking. She smoothed back the silken blond waterfall that had fallen to the tip of his nose. "What is it, sweetie? Tell me."

Her endearment seemed to break his control. "You don't wanna be here. I'm not in your plan for the day," he said in a choked whisper. His crystalline blue eyes glistened with unshed tears.

Horrified, she pulled the boy into her arms for a long fierce hug. He returned it with surprising strength.

"Jason McDonald, there's no one else on earth I'd rather be with today than you," she said, completely sincere. "We *all* want to be here, silly, or we wouldn't have come. You're a very special little boy, and we love you. Understand?"

Jason sniffed against her shoulder.

"Understand?" She ran her hands lightly down his ribs, smiling to herself when he flinched. "Better say you understand, Jason, or the tickle monster's gonna get you."

As Laura wiggled her fingertips over the squirming child, a single gurgle erupted. Then another. Until finally he became a writhing ball of giggles.

"I un'erstan'!" Jason shouted at last, collapsing on the floor and panting like an exhausted puppy. Amid the general pandemonium, no one even looked twice at the sprawled child.

Laura smiled. "There's a rumor this place has a band. Is that true?"

Jason lifted his head, his eyes shining. "Yeah. It's really cool, Laura. There's bears and dogs and they sing and play music. Only they don't really sing, 'cause they're *robots*."

Scrambling to his feet, he reached out his hand. "Wanna go see it?"

"You bet."

With Jason's help she lurched to a standing position, then glanced at Alec. His eyes were dark with some powerful emotion.

Self-conscious, she walked toward her brother and slid an arm around his waist. Scott looked down at her in surprise, then back up at Alec. As a slow enigmatic grin spread across his handsome face, Laura pinched him in the ribs.

Scott chuckled and squeezed her close, lowering his head to her ear. "Like I said, Laura," he whispered. "Just like Mama."

ALEC SCANNED the accounting "laundry list" on his desk for the third time. They were halfway through May already, and no matter how he looked at it, the bottom line was the same.

Hayes and McDonald had to bring in more accounts. Fast. Putting all their eggs in the Regency Hotels basket was not only risky, it was damned stupid.

The Regency campaign was going well, but nothing was guaranteed in this business. As long as advertising agencies made an easy scapegoat for poor company performance, the only protection was an ongoing business-development program.

Thumbing through his business-card file, he stopped at the *S* tab. Sanders Development Corporation. Smiling, he pulled out the foil-embossed card and flicked it absently beneath his chin. Jerry Sanders's master-planned communities were just the steady advertisers Alec was looking for. Income from collateral materials alone would pay the rent for a year.

And Jerry liked to work with women, Alec remembered. Laura was more than a match for the real-estate mogul's demanding personality. He'd take her with him on his first call...

Alec threw down the business card in disgust. He had to stop thinking and planning as if Laura was more than a temporary partner. He'd be cutting his professional throat to include her in active solicitation of new accounts. Clients would balk or, worse, defect, when she left in less than a year. But damn it all, she didn't make it easy to exclude her from his plans.

Laura took their agreement to be equal partners very seriously. Anybody else with a guaranteed buy-out in her contract would have coasted through the year doing as little as possible. But Laura worked harder than any woman, or man, he'd ever known. She was tireless, cheerful, imaginative...

And sexy as hell.

When he'd first spotted her yesterday evening at Chuck E Cheese's, he'd nearly leapt out of his skin. In tight jeans and a snug T-shirt, her body had drawn the gaze of every father in the place. But her gaze had been on him. Molten gold. If Jason hadn't broken the moment, Alec would have incinerated where he stood.

It was easy to see why his son adored her. She'd transformed a potentially traumatic moment into one of happy laughter. Seeing them together, he'd thought what a good mother she would make.

Alec swiveled to stare out the window. He felt like throwing his chair through the glass pane. He felt like getting drunk, picking a fight and slamming a few heads together. He felt like burying himself in Laura's lithe, lovely body.

He groaned, his fingers tightening on the armrest. Lust and anger really were just a heartbeat apart like some people said. And if he couldn't control the first, how in God's name could he hope to curb the second?

A small sound in his doorway alerted him to someone's presence. "What is it?" he barked, his back to the intruder.

"Uh... everyone's waiting for you out front, Mr. McDonald. Do you want us to begin the staff meeting without you?"

Alec spun around and met Sharon's worried brown eyes. Old loyalties did die hard, as Harold had said. His former secretary remained attuned to his needs and moods.

He forced himself to soften his expression. "No, that won't be necessary. I'll be right there."

Sharon nodded in relief and slipped away.

Grabbing the list and a notepad, he headed for the reception area. Laura had been right. Sharon made a damn good traffic manager. Few consumers realized how many hands were involved in the production of the simplest ad. If one pair of hands fumbled because of a missed deadline, it jeopardized the quality and timeliness of an entire agency's work.

Alec entered the reception area and frowned. He was proud of the team at Hayes and McDonald Advertising. They deserved a more professional environment for staff meetings.

Laura looked up from the sofa with a welcoming smile. He crushed his blossoming pleasure.

"How are you coming along with the acquisition of a conference table, Laura?" he asked, sitting in his usual spot.

Idle conversation ceased as six startled faces turned his way. Normally he would have opened the meeting with a recap of last week's progress.

Laura recovered quickly. "I haven't spent a lot of time on it lately. With the campaign breaking in three weeks..."

"I seem to remember your promising me, and I quote, an office I could be proud of." Lifting an eyebrow, he scanned the men and women, several perched on chairs dragged from their own offices. "What if a prospective client walked in right now? How do you think I'd feel?"

Two spots of color appeared in Laura's cheeks. "Like an arrogant insensitive jackass?"

Someone snorted. Several people chuckled.

He watched her eyes turn the cloudy amber of stirred honey and knew he'd hurt her. And he'd done it on purpose, out of pure sexual frustration.

"I believe 'pompous bigot' is the correct term," Alec said, holding her gaze. *I'm sorry. Forgive me?*

You were a total jerk, but. . . okay, her eyes answered.

The room had fallen quiet. Good Lord, they all thought he'd lost his mind. He could see it in their faces.

"How about starting this meeting over?" he addressed the group. "Harold, let's hear from you first. Were you able to lock in that booth at the convention in San Francisco?"

Harold pushed up his glasses and straightened. "Just barely. The booking agent swore there was no room left on the floor. Then he tried to stick us in an annex reserved for spillover booking. I had to remind him we were sponsoring their general welcome party before he'd thaw out. . ."

Alec's mind wandered as Harold reported his success. The meeting was back on track, with everyone jotting notes and asking questions. He glanced at Laura and caught her eye.

Watch yourself, her look said as clearly as if she'd spoken.

He nodded and winked.

Much later, after the meeting adjourned, Alec realized he'd never winked before in his life—and hated people who did.

LAURA GLANCED at her watch and sighed. No way could she make it until noon without food.

She'd come in early again without eating breakfast. And after the staff meeting, hunger had been the farthest thing from her mind. She'd retreated to her office and tackled the outdoor-board copy due next week. But her brain refused to cooperate.

She couldn't believe that stunt Alec had pulled! He hadn't acted so . . . pompous since her first weeks with the agency.

She hadn't even had the satisfaction of staying mad. Nothing had prepared her for catching Alec's hard uncompromising face in a boyish wink. It made him appear years younger and, well, cute. For a moment he'd seemed lighthearted—free of the turmoil she so often sensed beneath the cold businessman.

Propping an elbow on the desk, she leaned her head in her hand. *Fool,* for wanting to chase away his shadows and make him happy. Especially since the situation was out of her control. He'd made things very clear since their devastating kiss. He didn't want a personal relationship. And Lord knew she was having a hard enough time with their business one.

An odd gurgling sound erupted from her stomach, so loud she laughed. Brenda Lee usually took an early lunch. Maybe she'd like some company.

Grabbing her purse, Laura walked toward the reception area. Shouting voices eddied down the hall as she approached. What in the world . . . ? She stopped, caught between embarrassment and curiosity. Not that the arguing couple noticed.

"Are you capable of following directions, Miss Wilson, or is that too much to ask?" Harold stood toe-to-toe with Brenda Lee, his neck craned forward and his glasses fogged.

"I followed your damn directions, Mr. Becker, and nearly got my ear chewed off for my trouble." Brenda Lee's fluffy blond head barely reached Harold's chin, but what she lacked in stature, she more than made up for in fight.

"I did *not* ask you to tell Miss Bowers I was canceling lunch for someone more important," he said through his teeth. "I asked you to tell her something pressing came up. There's an enormous difference in semantics, one I assume they didn't teach you at . . . what was it you said? Thompson's Institute of Technology?" His tone oozed contempt.

"*Business* technology," Brenda Lee corrected, lifting her pert nose.

"How careless of me to forget such an illustrious institution. And to think I went to Harvard, instead."

Tie askew and hair rumpled, he seemed halfway human to Laura for the first time. Too bad he was such a jerk.

Brenda Lee narrowed her eyes. "Are you or are you not going to 'do lunch' with the publisher of *Departure* magazine?"

"Yes, but—"

"And would you say he's a pretty important guy for you to soft-soap?"

"Soft-soap?"

"Brownnose, suck up to, kiss ass—"

"I get the picture, Miss Wilson." He sniffed. "Although I wouldn't put it so crudely—"

"Answer the question, damn it!"

Harold blinked down into Brenda Lee's snapping emerald eyes. For a moment, he appeared to lose his concentration.

She jabbed a finger at his chest. "Well?"

He took a startled step backward. "Yes. He's an important person for me to know."

"Then don't spout off your fancy Harvard college talk as if you're better than me, big shot." She jabbed his chest again, stepping forward as he moved back. "Because the fact is, you wanted me to lie to your girlfriend for you—'' jab ''—and that purely stinks—'' jab ''—no matter *what* words you use!''

She'd backed him up against the wall! Laura's rising laughter died as she noticed Brenda Lee's expression. After a tense moment, the blonde flung herself away from Harold and walked to her desk. She looked close to tears.

Laura stepped into the room. ''Ready to go to lunch now, Brenda Lee?'' she asked, pretending not to notice her friend's dazed confusion. Walking to the reception desk, Laura located Brenda Lee's purse tucked in a drawer and turned to Harold.

''We might be a while, because we're running by Office Depot on the way back to check out getting a fax machine for Sharon's office.'' Placing an arm around Brenda Lee's shoulders, Laura walked to the agency entrance.

''Wait a minute,'' Harold protested, glancing at the switchboard. ''Who'll answer the phones?''

Laura opened the door, prodded Brenda Lee through and looked back at the bewildered executive. ''How about you? It's an easy system. Anyone with an ounce of practical common sense could operate—''

She stopped and hit her forehead with the heel of her palm. ''Oops, how silly of me. For a minute I forgot. You went to Harvard.''

CHAPTER TEN

"FOR THE LAST TIME, you are not going to get fired." Laura reached over the basket of tostada chips and patted Brenda Lee's hand.

"But I screamed at an officer of the company. And I...I..."

"Backed him up against a wall? I know. I saw the whole thing."

Covering her flushed face with both hands, Brenda Lee moaned. "I'll never be able to face him again."

"Snap out of it, Brenda Lee. What's gotten into you? Harold's the one who'll be embarrassed. He acted like a pig, and you put him right in the sty where he belongs. I was s-so p-proud." Laura dabbed her eyes with a napkin.

Brenda Lee peeked between her fingers and grinned. "I did give him hell, didn't I?"

"Abso-damn-lutely." Laura raised her frozen margarita and sang the first stanza of "I Am Woman."

Heads swiveled at nearby tables.

"She missed her medication this morning," Brenda Lee explained.

"Hail to the new queen of put-downs. I relinquish my crown."

Sweeping up her matching drink, Brenda Lee clinked Laura's glass. "I'm not worthy, Your Highness. I'll never be as bitchy as you."

Choking on a laugh, Laura lowered her glass and blotted her chin. "You know, Brenda Lee, I actually ate and drank like a civilized person before I met you."

"But you didn't have nearly as much fun."

"You're right. I didn't."

They exchanged a warm understanding look.

Brenda Lee dunked a chip in hot sauce. "I didn't know you could sing, Laura. You're really good. Loud, but good. Are you in a choir or something?"

"Nope. Used to sing in a rock band, though. Schizophrenic played the top clubs in Austin while I was in school. Hey, watch that chip! Picante's hard to wash out."

"A rock band? No way. Somebody snatched the Laura I know. Did you wake up in a pod this morning by any chance?"

"Surprised? So were a lot of other people when the leader hired me." Especially her. "It was good money until the group broke up."

"I can't get over this. You, in a rock band. God, don't you miss the excitement?"

Laura sipped her drink. Then sipped again. She'd thought she would die from missing Michael that first year. The pain had eventually dulled, but the scar was deep. She shrugged with studied nonchalance.

"I've got all the excitement I can handle trying to pull off the Regency campaign. Now, enough about me. I've got to know one thing before it kills me." Propping her elbows on the table, she leaned forward. "Did you really misunderstand what Harold asked you to tell that woman on the phone?"

Brenda Lee stopped chewing and averted her gaze.

"I didn't think so," said Laura. "Want to tell me why you did it?"

"Oh, Laura, I don't know what came over me. When he asked me to do his dirty work, I should have said no, but I couldn't. It's the first time he's ever asked me a favor, you know? But then, when I heard that woman's voice..." Brenda Lee's brows met in a fierce line. "She's the rudest, most stuck-up person I've ever talked to. And she's all wrong for Harold."

"And, um, you know who's right for him?"

The blush creeping up her friend's neck spoke for itself.

"I see." Laura pulled on her straw and sighed. "A fine pair we are."

Brenda Lee looked startled, then triumphant. She slapped her palm on the table. "I knew it! Thank goodness you came to your senses. Watching you and Alec sniff at each other through a fence has been frustrating as hell."

Laura didn't pretend to misunderstand. "*You're* frustrated? I'm sick to death of that fence. I just don't know how to get through it. Or if I should even try."

Amazed at how easily the words came, she straightened and flagged down a passing waiter. No sense killing a good buzz. "Two frozen margaritas, please. With salt."

"Are you serious?"

"I like salt."

"No, about getting through that fence."

Laura didn't like the evangelical gleam in those big green eyes. She backpedaled. "Let's not get carried away now. Tequila has a way of doing my talking for me."

Brenda Lee shook a pink lacquered nail. "Oh, no you don't. You're not squirming out of this on a technicality—I've got evidence. You confessed plain as day. You're sick of the fence—and I'm going to help you get rid of it. Case closed."

Their waiter arrived, removing two empty glasses and setting down replacements. "Can I get you ladies anything else?"

"A good lawyer maybe?" Laura asked.

"Nothing right now, thank you," Brenda Lee said sweetly. The minute his back was turned, her eyes narrowed. "Very funny. Just don't plan anything for Saturday. We're going shopping."

Clutching the stem of her glass, Laura adopted a reasoning tone. "I can't afford to go shopping. Besides, there's not a thing wrong with my clothes."

"Not if you're Whistler's mother."

"I beg your pardon?"

"Don't go getting all huffy. She's a classy old broad. But covering up your body from head to toe is a crime."

"Oh, give me a break."

"See? That's exactly what I mean. I'm tired of hearing you put yourself down. It's time you accept the fact you're a beautiful woman and make the most of it."

Laura sipped her drink and glared, feeling a twinge of belated sympathy for Harold. "But—"

"Don't tell me you can't afford to give yourself a treat, either. You live like a spartan. You've got to have a little stashed away."

She did. But it wasn't for clothes.

"So get that gloomy look off your face, because by the time I'm finished, you won't have to worry about getting through that fence. Alec will kick the damn thing down!"

Somewhere deep inside, an embryo of hope fluttered to life. Grabbing her straw, Laura ducked her head and didn't lift it until she heard the sputter of air.

Brenda Lee frowned. "Aren't you going to say something?"

I'm scared. What if I make a fool of myself?

"Well?"

"Oh, waiter?" Laura called, lifting a weaving finger. "One more margarita, please."

"I'LL GET YOU for this, Brenda Lee," Laura grumbled seconds before a steamy towel swathed her face.

Pleasant experience, ha! So far, her muscles had been pounded like cheap meat. The hair had been ripped from her legs like plucked feathers. Being cooked alive was the last insult.

"Quit whining and let Marilyn do her job," Brenda Lee called from across the salon. "No pain, no gain."

I'll give you pain, Laura thought, forced into silence by the gentle pressure of hands on the towel. Why she'd agreed to a beauty make-over before the shopping trip she would never know. No, that wasn't quite true.

Damn those margaritas at lunch.

"There, that should be long enough." The beautician unwrapped the moist cloth and stooped to inspect Laura's pores.

"Are you finished?" Laura asked. "Or do you like your clients well-done?"

Chuckling, the red-haired owner of A Beautiful Experience patted Laura's arm. "Just one more thing before we start your makeup session. Don't worry, you should love this."

"What is it?" Laura eyed the aqua-colored bottle suspiciously.

"Rejuvenating skin toner." Marilyn splashed a generous amount of fluid onto a cotton pad and wiped industriously.

Gasping, Laura shoved Marilyn's hand away. "Rejuvenating? That stuff'd wake the dead!"

Behind a small table across the room, Brenda Lee stood up and smiled at her manicurist. "Thanks, Janie. I'll settle up before I leave." Fingers splayed, she walked to Marilyn's side and blew on each long crimson fingernail before giving Laura a level look.

"Sugar, I know you're uncomfortable with all this fussing, but remember our deal. Today *I'm* the boss. And as of right now you're on probation."

"What'd I do?"

Brenda Lee nodded toward the hovering beautician. "Marilyn here squeezed you in as a favor to me, and you're acting like a spoiled brat. Do you want that fence we talked about knocked down or don't you?"

Laura stared at her Keds for a long moment. She *had* been acting terrible. But as usual, the more awkward she felt, the sharper her tongue had grown. Marilyn didn't deserve such treatment.

"I'm sorry," Laura addressed both women. "I'll try to have a better attitude from now on."

Brenda Lee beamed like a proud parent. "That's more like it. Now comes the really fun part. Marilyn is a magician with makeup."

Emboldened, the plump beautician cupped Laura's chin and turned her face toward a high-wattage lamp on the counter. "Such lovely skin. And those eyes! I'm looking forward to this, Brenda Lee."

"What did I tell you? And that's without a speck of makeup. I've been dying to see what some earth tones will do for her."

"And the purples, too, I think, but only for evening. Can you imagine violet against her golden eyes? Stunning."

Fascinated, Laura listened to the women analyze her features and discuss cosmetics like military strategists.

Come to think of it, maybe she was preparing for battle. A battle against Alec's stubborn self-control. If only she had more skill using standard female weapons.

"Ready?" Marilyn asked, pulling out a pink plastic tackle box from under the counter.

Helpless as a hooked trout, Laura nodded. Brenda Lee settled on a nearby stool to watch.

"We'll start with foundation. Your skin has a touch of yellow. A little Pink Bisque should take care of that." Marilyn opened her box, revealing an array of eye shadows, lipsticks, brushes and mysterious bottles.

Laura swallowed hard.

For the next hour, Marilyn dabbed, stroked, dusted and lined, allowing Laura only tantalizing glimpses of herself in the mirror. Once, a client wandered over and exclaimed, stirring Laura's curiosity.

"No, no, hold still!" Marilyn scolded, lip pencil poised in the air. She glanced behind her shoulder. "She's ruined the line. I'll have to start over."

Brenda Lee sent Laura a withering look. "I'm sorry, Marilyn. Remember, she's never done this before. I appreciate your patience."

After that, Laura sat still as a lizard on a rock.

When Marilyn unbraided Laura's hair and called a colleague over for consultation, she didn't even peek. She was playing dress-up for the first time in her life and enjoying every minute of it. If they wanted to surprise her with the final results, okay by her. Maybe that was one of the rules.

Wearing a Mona Lisa smile, Brenda Lee blocked the mirror while Laura watched clumps of chestnut hair drift to the floor. Good Lord, what had she gotten herself into? She hated her uncontrollable hair, true, but parting with it put a different perspective on things. Visions of outlandish, MTV hairstyles flashed in her mind as rapidly as Marilyn's snipping scissors.

At last Marilyn plunked scissors and comb in a jar of alcohol, stepped back and cocked her head. "Shake your hair for me, Laura."

Laura shook, feeling ridiculous.

"Hey, guys," Marilyn called to the salon in general. "Check this out!"

She grabbed the vinyl seat back and spun Laura's chair to face the gathering employees and clients. No one said a word.

Laura's stomach fell.

Then everyone spoke at once. "She's gorgeous!" said Janie, the manicurist. "Just like Julia Roberts," agreed the shampoo girl, sighing. "Do my hair like *hers*," Mrs. Bernstein ordered Kevin, her hairstylist. Noting the woman's chin-length bob, Laura panicked.

"Lord have mercy, girl." Brenda Lee circled to the front of Laura's chair and grinned. "As my uncle Homer used to tell me, 'You clean up real good.' Just look at yourself, honey." She whirled the chair and shooed Marilyn out of the way.

Laura stared at the stranger in the mirror.

The young woman's thick chestnut hair fell from a side part to brush the tops of her shoulders. The rippling waves, at once a little wild and terribly chic, framed a creamy oval face. Large almond-shaped eyes—a mysterious smoky amber color—stared back at Laura in dazed wonder. And the woman's mouth...

Laura leaned forward and squinted. "How did you do that, Marilyn?"

"Which 'that' do you mean?" the beautician asked, her expression smug.

"My mouth. How did you make it look so...normal?"

An old friend by now, Marilyn shoved Laura's shoulder. "Shame on you. You've got a great mouth."

"But you've made it look smaller," Laura insisted. "Show me what you did."

Marilyn devoted the next twenty minutes to explaining color and application techniques so Laura could duplicate the day's efforts at home. In the manner of a true convert, she listened, enthralled, and determined to practice what was preached.

At one o'clock, Laura gathered up the cosmetics she'd purchased, followed Brenda Lee to the shop's exit and waved goodbye.

"Knock 'em dead, Laura," Janie called.

"Let us know what happens," Kevin added.

Marilyn rushed up and shoved a bulging plastic bag into Laura's arms. "I tossed a few samples together for you to take home. I get so many, you know."

Eyes misting, Laura smiled. "You've been so kind. I don't know how to thank you."

Marilyn patted her arm. "Just tell everybody where you spent the morning, dear. You're a walking billboard for A Beautiful Experience. And if you forget anything I taught you, feel free to call. I haven't had so much fun in years."

Amen, Laura thought. The past few hours had unlocked something deep inside she hadn't even known existed. She felt invincible. Womanly. And oddly at peace with herself.

Smiling, she turned to Brenda Lee. The day wasn't over yet.

"Come on, *boss.* We've got some shopping to do."

SAM AIMED his remote control at the big-screen television and switched channels in rapid succession. Bowling, golf, "Flipper," commercial, commercial, "Wheel Of Fortune," Gary Cooper... They'd colorized "Sergeant York," the bastards. Why couldn't Turner leave the classics alone?

He clicked off the TV and tossed the remote onto the couch beside him. Picking up a stack of rumpled newspapers, he searched for articles he might have missed the first time around. Slim pickings. When he caught himself reading the obituaries, Sam snapped the section closed with a grunt. Tomorrow would be better. Sunday's issue was good for at least a half day's read.

He rubbed a hand down his bristled jaw and considered going out. Willie G's served fresh crawfish and cold draft at the bar. Hollis appreciated a good tip and always threw an extra dozen in Sam's order, more than he could eat by himself. He straightened hopefully. Maybe Alec would be up for some mudbugs and a brew. They could meet...

No, Alec had a young boy's needs to think of, not some lonely old coot's.

Sam stared at the blank TV screen and wished it were Monday. The grandfather clock ticked, ticked, ticked. He and Jenny had bought the antique when his first hotel had sold at a forty-percent profit. They'd been high on the hog, secure in a bright future together. Regency Hotels had been just a gleam in their eyes back then. Shortly after, he'd watched hers grow dull with pain. *Jenny, are you still waiting for me?*

The clock ticked on, in no hurry to reunite Sam with his soul mate.

He rose and looked through the sliding glass door. Long ago he'd imagined children splashing in his turquoise pool. Now he paid a service good money to maintain its glassy untouched perfection. Just as he paid others to tend his blooming landscape, cook his meals and see to his laundry. He had no hobbies or domestic skills. During the frantic years of building his hotel chain, he'd scoffed at Vicki's gardening, Marian's bridge club.

God, no wonder they'd divorced him. He'd been a blind ass. They were remarried with grandkids now, while he lived in a house with more bedrooms than friends or family to fill them.

Regency Hotels would regain market share. Or not. Either way, the world would keep turning. His pool would stay glassy. He would remain alone.

Sam scratched his rumbling stomach, the movement drawing attention to his reflection in the glass. God he looked old! Turning quickly away, he walked to the kitchen and rummaged in the refrigerator. He could feed himself, damn it. He wasn't ready for a nursing home, yet. Dragging out vegetables and plastic containers, he piled them on the counter and took stock.

What would Mrs. Kelch do now? Surely the woman used a cookbook now and then? He found a whole stack of them next to the phone. Pulling out the largest, he began flipping pages. He'd always loved hanging around hotel kitchens. Over the years, he'd rubbed elbows with some of the finest chefs in the country. The terms in this cookbook weren't completely unfamiliar.

A pleasant sense of challenge straightened his shoulders. There was no denying he'd made his lonely bed and deserved to lie in it. But since when had he taken *anything* lying down?

THE PHONE! Laura unlocked her apartment and staggered inside. *Please don't hang up.* Dropping an armload of shopping bags onto the floor, she ran to the kitchen.

"Hello?" she answered, a bit breathless.

"Hi, Laura! It's me, Jason!"

Laura massaged her ear and smiled. "Hi, Jason. What a nice surprise."

"Where you been all day? I called you a hunnerd times. We want to know—"

A voice rumbled in the background, followed by Jason's muted protest.

"Jason? Oh, Jason?" Laura prompted.

"Dad says I shouldn't ask where you were 'cause it's rude. Am I bein' rude, Laura?"

"Not at all. I was out shopping."

"Oh. Dad thought maybe you were at the office, 'cause you go there sometimes on weekends. We called there, too."

Interesting. "Well, now that I'm home, what is it you want to know?"

"Um . . ." Loud, heavy breathing.

"Don't hold the phone so close to your mouth, honey."

Silence.

"Jason?"

"Can-you-go-to-the-baseball-game-with-us-tonight?" he blurted. "The Astros are playin' the Braves. We have an extra ticket and Dad said I could ask anyone I wanted."

Laura felt a warm rush of pleasure. "I'm flattered, Jason."

"Does that mean you can't go?" he wailed.

Realizing her mistake, she laughed. "No, honey. Flattered means I'm proud and happy. Are you sure you don't want to ask one of your friends?"

"I did. You. What's the matter? Don'tcha like baseball?" Before Laura could answer, he sweetened the offer. "Dad says we can get hot dogs."

Laura thought of the long-anticipated steak she'd pulled from the freezer that morning. The one she would eat by herself. Maybe it was still frozen.

"I love baseball . . . and hot dogs. As long as your dad says it's okay, I'd love to go to the game with you."

"Yesss! Wha—? Oh, hold on a minute. He wants to talk to you."

Laura's heartbeat tripled as she listened to the fumbling exchange.

"Laura? It's Alec." The deep-timbred voice vibrated up her spine.

"Hi," she croaked.

"The game starts at seven-thirty, but we should give ourselves an hour to get to the Dome and park. Can you be ready at six-thirty? We'll swing by and pick you up."

"Your house is a lot closer to the Dome than mine. Why don't I drive over and we'll take one car from there?" She glanced at her watch. "I can be there by six-forty."

"Well . . . I guess that does make sense." He sounded uneasy. "You know, Laura, if you already had plans or something, don't feel like you have to do this for my sake."

Laura's pleasure dimmed. "Quite frankly, you never entered into the decision. I enjoy being with Jason."

Alec hesitated. "Right. See you at six-forty, then." Click.

Goodbye to you, too, grouch. Laura hung up and sighed.

She would not let Alec's coolness dampen her spirits. She had a new hairstyle, dazzling new clothes and a whole new outlook—thanks to Brenda Lee.

In the bathroom, she stripped, rummaged under the cabinet for a complimentary hotel shower cap and slipped

it on before stepping into the shower. She wasn't taking
any chances on ruining Marilyn's handiwork.

The pulsating needles of hot water felt wonderful
against her weary neck and shoulders. What a day! If
having her hair and face done had been fun, shopping had
been the ultimate blast.

She and Brenda Lee had hit Westwood Mall first to pick
up a few shorts and tops, then headed for Loehmann's
loaded for bear. The endless racks of discount designer
wear had yielded several treasures.

Laura had spotted the royal blue Buscati suit amidst a
row of drab counterparts. The long body-hugging jacket
and short flippy skirt were professional, but far from
conservative. And the color did amazing things for her
hair.

She reached for a bar of soap and lathered, thinking of
next week's schedule and planning what to wear. In addition to the suit, she'd bought two new dresses. Then
Brenda Lee had remembered Sam Parker's promise to
hold "one hell of a kickoff party" for the Regency Hotels campaign. They'd headed for the evening-dress section like giddy teenagers shopping for the prom.

She smiled at the thought of Harold Becker. The poor
man wouldn't have a chance once he saw Brenda Lee in
black chiffon. Cutting off the water, Laura stepped out,
toweled off and dusted with lavender-scented talcum
powder. She didn't dare let herself think about her own
purchase. Loehmann's didn't allow returns.

Walking to her dresser, she pulled out panties and bra,
then headed for the abandoned shopping bags. Sometime during the day, her desire to breach Alec's defenses
had strengthened. She sensed the darkness awaiting her,
but also the promise of pleasure such as she'd never
known. And Laura wanted to know it. Wanted, too, a

chance to lighten the heart of a stern, impossibly demanding, undeniably *good* man.

She was no stranger to challenge. She'd always worked, competed and fought for what she wanted as aggressively as a man. But this would be the ultimate test of her courage.

Because now, for the first time in her life, she would fight as a woman.

ALEC SAT FORWARD in the stadium seat as if focused on the game's action. In reality, his mind still reeled.

When he'd opened his door to Laura earlier, shock had wiped the welcoming smile off his face. It hadn't come back, either, despite Jason's puzzled glances at the adults he sat between. Alec knew he was being irrational, but damn it, *why the hell had she gone and changed?*

The prim-haired, scrubbed-face, innocent partner of old had robbed him of sleep more nights than one. This new Laura—the wavy-haired, sophisticated, sensual creature lounging with her feet propped on the empty seat ahead—oh, God, this new Laura could strip him of his sanity if he wasn't careful.

Why the *hell* had she gone and changed?

Alec tugged down the bill of his baseball cap, shielding the direction of his gaze. Those legs. He ground his teeth and looked away. Slowly, helplessly, he looked back. Those long sleek legs had felt like warm satin when he'd tapped them on his way to the aisle. Laura had met his eyes with a startled look, then dropped her feet to the floor and let him pass.

But as soon as he'd returned with the hot dogs, up those legs had gone, as distracting as a triple play.

Her moss green shorts were modest by most standards. So why did he imagine those legs wrapped around his waist as he—

Alec groaned, thankful for the shortstop's brilliant fielding and the crowd's instant booing displeasure. Shifting in search of a comfortable position, he scowled. There was only one thing that would give him relief. Changing positions didn't do it.

He glanced down at his son. Like Alec, Jason wore a navy Astros cap. But his blue eyes sparkled with excitement, and his mustard-stained mouth grinned, whereas Alec felt decidedly antisocial at the moment.

Wallowing in a blue funk, he ignored the crack of a bat and collective gasp from their section of the mezzanine. Everyone around him jumped up and reached for the foul ball. Head flung back, Laura strained forward and lifted her arms, pagan as a Viking ship's prow.

Muttering a curse, he jerked off his cap and dropped it over his lap.

Two rows ahead, a teenaged boy caught the ball and raised his trophy for all to see. Laura laughed good-naturedly and glanced at Alec, her smile fading, then, oh, so slowly, reappearing in a different form. Gentle, mysterious, filled with tantalizing promise.

His testosterone level hit the sky boxes. And she knew it, damn her.

A small hand shook his shoulder. "Does that guy get to keep the ball, Dad?" Jason asked, his expression envious.

"He caught it, fair and square." Jason thrust out his lower lip and flounced down in his seat along with the rest of the disappointed souvenir hunters.

"They're selling autographed balls next to the concession stand. I'll try and get you one before the game is over," Alec promised.

Jason's eyes widened. He fisted one hand and drew his elbow sharply into his waist.

"Yesss!"

Over the boy's head, Alec met Laura's amused grin and felt an answering tug at his mouth. This was Jason's first visit to the Astrodome, and his excitement was contagious.

Alec had to admit the facility was an incredible place— especially since it was the first sports dome ever built. Over the years he'd sat from field box to sky box, and every seat offered a clear view of the infield action. Roving vendors, scoreboard antics and blessed air-conditioning kept fans comfortable and entertained. He sat back and decided to enjoy the spectacle.

By the seventh-inning stretch, he'd relaxed enough to invite Laura along while he bought the coveted autographed ball for Jason.

His son reached for it in awe. "Read me some of the names, Laura," he pleaded, holding the stitched rawhide in front of her nose.

"Well, let's see. There's Nolan Ryan—"

Jason lowered the ball. "I wanna be a pitcher when I grow up."

"Tomorrow's Sunday. Why don't you get your dad to throw a few practice balls with you?" she suggested, giving Alec a pointed look.

He'd planned on pouring over the final Regency Hotels media schedule all day tomorrow.

"Naw," Jason spoke directly to Laura. "He won't have time to play with me. He's gotta work so we can pay the bills."

Maybe the schedule could wait. Maybe he could manage both. "Who says I can't play ball with you? I used to have a pretty mean curve in high school. But that's a hard pitch to learn. We'll have to start with the basics first," Alec warned.

"You mean it, Dad?" At his father's nod, Jason hopped in a circle, then threw his arms around Alec's waist.

His heart contracted, then he felt an upsurge of happiness. He patted the small back awkwardly. Sensing Laura's gaze, he looked up and basked in her soft approval.

Refusing to name the emotion filling his chest, Alec disengaged himself and cleared his throat. "Anyone want to leave now?"

"Nooo!" Jason wailed.

Laura feigned outrage. "And miss the Astros rally? Not a chance."

"Last one back to their seat is a rotten egg," Jason yelled, racing off in the direction they'd come.

Within seconds, he was swallowed up by the milling crowd.

CHAPTER ELEVEN

ONE MINUTE Jason was in sight, the next he wasn't.

Don't panic, Alec cautioned himself. He moved forward at a normal pace, expecting to glimpse the small bobbing Astros cap any second. Laura fanned out parallel and they wove through the throng of people heading back to their seats.

Wait'll he caught up with the kid. Man, would he give Jason an earful. Alec walked a little faster, searching the concourse ahead at child level. In this mob, he could pass right by his son and not know it. Would Jason have enough sense to stop at their section entrance and wait? Would he even remember what section their seats were in?

Speeding up to a half jog, his pulse a half-step faster, Alec scanned each inset ramp he passed. He hadn't shown Jason the correct entrance sign or given him a ticket stub. What if he entered the wrong section? Would he ask a stranger for help?

Oh, God.

Breaking into a full jog, Alec spotted their entrance several sections ahead. His stomach rose in his throat, then plummeted to his toes. No little boy stood waiting against the wall. Where the hell was he?

Alec headed down the steps to check their seats. Empty. Ripping off his cap, he wiped his clammy brow with a shirtsleeve.

I should have talked with Jason about safety. I should have told him what to do if we got separated. I should have been a better father.

He ran back to the concourse and looked both directions. Across the crowd, Laura caught his eye and mouthed, "Jason?" He shook his head and pointed to the right. Face pale and expression grim, she nodded her understanding. Alec took off to the left.

He checked the bathroom, the row of vendor carts, the concession stands—searching, searching...

With every passing second, his heart thudded louder, his inner voice screamed no, this couldn't be happening. Stories of children kidnapped from shopping malls and amusement parks flashed in his mind, complete with heartbreaking endings.

He'd only taken his eyes off Jason for an instant. How could he have disappeared into thin air?

Memory ripped through Alec's fear. He stopped and braced one hand against the wall, a solid link with the present while the past overwhelmed him.

He was seven years old, standing outside a bar in the cold and dark. His pop had told him to stay put, but hunger tore at his belly. He dug out the twenty-five cents hidden in his shoe and went in search of a candy bar. Within five minutes of wandering the seedy red-light district, he was lost.

Hours later a gruff cop delivered him, trembling and years wiser, to his mama just as she got home from her night shift at Denny's. Mama had held him close and cried. His old man hadn't staggered home until dawn.

Like father, like son.

Alec shuddered at the prophecy. He beat back the crawling horror and forced himself to think. He would have to contact security. Surely there were procedures in place for this kind of situation. Surely someone would notice and help a lost, or struggling, little boy. Surely—

"Dad!" Jason darted around a shuffling old man, sidestepped a lanky teen and pounded forward into Alec's waiting arms.

Sweet Mary, the relief! It buckled Alec's knees and left him shaking and dizzy. He treasured the feel of Jason's small quivering body, then pulled back.

"Don't *ever* run off like that again, Jason, especially in a crowd like this. Do you understand?"

Eyes welling with tears, Jason nodded. Laura raced up with a glad cry.

Alec shot her a warning glance. "Don't look at her, son. Look at me when I'm talking to you. Do you have any idea how worried I was? Or what could have happened to you?"

Laura shifted from foot to foot.

"Next time we go someplace, first thing we'll do is pick a spot we can both remember," Alec said, ignoring the sound of Laura clearing her throat. "Then, if for some reason we get separated or if you can't find me, you're to go immediately to the place we agreed on and not move." He ignored Laura's heavy sigh. "Even if you have to wait for a long time, stay there and I promise I'll come get you for.... For God's sake, Laura, what is it?"

She stopped tapping her toe, uncrossed her arms and placed a hand over her chest with wide-eyed affront.

"Excuse me? I was just minding my own business. But as long as you asked, why don't we go back to our seats? We all had a good scare. Everybody's sorry. Now let's put it behind us and enjoy the rest of the game."

He glanced down at Jason's whipped-puppy expression. During their moment of reunion, he'd clung like a suction cup. He wasn't likely to run off again anytime soon.

Just to make sure, Alec leveled a stern look. "You promise to hold my hand?"

"Yes, sir."

"All right. Let's go back to our seats."

Five minutes later, the Astros began a heroic comeback. By the bottom of the ninth, the score was tied seven to seven. The inevitable organ flourish sounded the battle call. Alec leaned forward right along with thirty thousand fevered fans.

"Charge!" he yelled, as the team's power hitter stepped up to the plate.

Whack!

Everyone in the crowd surged to their feet. The Braves' left fielder pumped full speed back...back...then slammed into the wall as the ball sailed over his reaching glove into the bleachers.

All hell broke loose in the Astrodome.

"Home run! Home run! We won!" Jason screamed, jumping up and down and clutching whatever parts of Alec and Laura's clothing were within reach.

People poured out of their seats and into the aisles. It was a long walk to the parking lot. A long *crowded* walk. Alec planted a restraining hand on Jason's shoulder and leaned down to speak in his ear.

"Don't rush off. Now get your drinking cup. Yes, you get to keep it. Put your ball inside and I'll carry them for you."

Face stricken, Jason searched near his feet.

"Jaason," Alec said on a groan.

His son raised panicked eyes. "I just had it, Dad. What'd you do with it?"

"What did *I* do with it? You haven't had that ball one hour and you've already lost it."

Alec glanced toward Laura for support and found her five seats down the row, bending over to look beneath the seats. His gaze lingered on her round bottom, then darted away as she straightened.

"Found it!" She held the autographed baseball aloft. "How about I put it in my purse until we get to the car?"

Jason beamed. "Thanks, Laura."

"Stay close," Alec warned, prodding them both into the jostling boisterous stream of fans attempting to leave the stadium. He saw Laura grab Jason's hand and experienced a fierce surge of protectiveness.

Shouldering his way forward, he reached down and captured Laura's palm. She seemed startled, then relieved.

"Keep holding Jason," he commanded. She nodded once and threaded her slender fingers through his.

Alec took the lead, using his bulk to forge an opening through the crowd, trusting Laura to tow Jason in her wake. Her hand felt good and right in his—just as the knowledge she held Jason's hand felt good and right.

They reached the ramp and headed down the steep slope, forming a human chain as the crowd opened up. Jason giggled at their gravity-induced walk.

Once on even ground, Alec released Laura's hand. Ignoring an odd sense of loss, he stopped and got his bearings. He'd parked the car a good quarter mile away. Jason would never make it on his own by the looks of his drooping eyelids.

Reaching down, Alec hoisted the delighted child onto his shoulders, grabbed Jason's shins and set a quick pace for Laura to follow across the lot.

Long ago, watching other children ride on their father's shoulders, Alec had fought pangs of envy. Judging from the way his son squealed, it must be as much fun as he'd always imagined.

Moments later he slid Jason down to stand beside the sleek Lexus. As Alec dug into his pocket for the keys, Laura moved up and smoothed Jason's hair. The boy turned and buried his face in her stomach. She stroked his back in lazy circles. *Lucky kid.*

Alec unlocked the doors and motioned for the two to get in. His son fell asleep in the back seat before they'd left the parking lot. He and Laura talked about the game for several minutes, then lapsed into an easy silence that lasted all the way home. Pulling into his driveway, he cut the engine, acutely aware of the enclosed intimacy of man, woman and sleeping child.

The kind of intimacy a family shared.

A delicate trace of lavender teased his nostrils. He turned and studied Laura's pensive expression in the dim light filtering from the lamps on his porch.

"What are you thinking about?"

"I was remembering the first time I sat in this driveway with you. You'd just issued an impossible challenge, and I was scared to death."

"Could've fooled me. In fact, I remember thinking you were the most brazen woman I'd ever met."

"The story of my life. Just once I'd like to meet a man who..."

Her blush intrigued him. Suddenly it was very important she finish. "A man who what?"

She shrugged. "Who thought I was nice or fun or...or even just pretty." This last came out as a whisper.

He stared at the arresting features that made other women seem bland by comparison. Where was her brazen confidence now? "You are nice. And fun. But you're far from pretty."

Her lashes swept down.

He reached out and cupped her stubborn elegant jaw. "You're a knockout, Laura. A definite ten."

Their gazes held. The moment stretched. He'd only meant to soothe her wounded pride. Not fill her eyes with wonder and...something else. A need that quickened his heartbeat. An emotion he dared not acknowledge for fear of having to reject it.

"I'm the first man to tell you that, aren't I?" Even before she nodded, he knew it was true. A part of him ached for her, but an overwhelmingly larger part rejoiced in the blindness of his gender. Another possibility struck him hard.

"My God," he breathed, absently rubbing his thumb against her jaw. "You've never been with a man, have you?"

Her eyes widened, but she didn't confirm his statement. He released her chin as if burned.

"I'm twenty-six, Alec, what did you expect?"

Alec stiffened, feeling ridiculous. "You don't owe me an explanation. I shouldn't have said—"

"Michael had a band," she interrupted, her eyes sending a message he couldn't decipher. "You know, the kind that plays fraternity parties and local clubs? He'd advertised for a female singer, and I was sick of waiting tables, so I tried out. Michael... I don't know, dazzled me."

Alec grimly absorbed that little tidbit. "Apparently the feeling was mutual."

"No, I wasn't his type at all. We were just good buddies."

"C'mon, Laura. The guy had the hots for you, admit it."

She shook her head. "I told you, we were just good—"

"Buddies. Right. Buddies play poker and swap fishing stories. They do not, in my experience, sleep together."

She turned swiftly toward the windshield, her eyes glazed, her throat working spasmodically. Her distress was very real and painful to watch, and far greater than his comment warranted.

"You want to talk about it, Laura?"

She cast him a horrified glance, then gave him her profile again—but not before he'd seen the glimmer of unshed tears. His dislike of the dazzling Michael turned primitive and ugly.

"Did he hurt you?" Alec asked tightly.

Her head snapped around. "Oh no, nothing like that. It was just..." *Don't make me say this,* her eyes implored.

God knew he didn't want to hear about her experience with another man. But it was obviously tearing her up and, if his instincts were right, filling her with self-doubt.

"Tell me what happened," he prompted gently.

She studied him for an eternity, then drew a shaky breath. "We had a standing gig at the Cactus Club on Thursdays. A lot of big names got their start there, you know. Anyway, one week a record scout showed up at the club and asked Michael to send a demo tape. He was ecstatic. We all went back to his apartment and celebrated. When everyone left, I stayed."

Alec didn't want to hear about the extended celebration.

Biting her lip, she glanced back at Jason. "He started kissing me. Things got serious pretty fast, but he couldn't..."

He *really* didn't want to hear this.

She closed her eyes, tightened her mouth and made a sound of disgust. When she finally met his gaze once more, her own was filled with resignation.

"I was nervous. And clumsy. It was my first time, and I made a horrible awkward mess of the whole thing."

The bastard had done a real number on her. "Who says *you* made a mess of it? How much had he had to drink? What other drugs were helping him celebrate that night?"

She vigorously shook her head. "He said I didn't turn him on, that he'd just felt sorry for me. That I'd looked like I could use some fun."

Vowing to track down Michael one day, Alec relaxed his fists with an effort. "The guy was saving face, Laura. Besides, the first time is awkward for everyone. The next time was better, right?"

A beat of silence, then she lifted her chin. "He didn't want me a next time."

Alec focused on her mouth—the wide sweet mouth he'd kissed, half-mad with lust once before. "Michael was a blind fool," he said, giving in to the temptation he'd fought for months.

Lowering his head, he established the lightest of contacts, savoring the feel of her lips beneath his. He waited for her protest and found himself drinking her soft sigh, instead.

His fingers cradled her chin, then slid up her cheek into thick hair. Kneading the coarse silk, he resettled his lips. Nibbled and brushed. Nibbled and brushed.

In small trembling increments, she opened her mouth. He slipped his tongue inside with a sense of homecoming. She tasted faintly of salt. Popcorn, he thought, smiling against her lips before he started a slow retreat. Her tongue followed, stroking in sensual circles until his mind emptied of all but the heat swelling his sex.

He strained forward, slanting his mouth for deeper contact. A soft feminine sound escaped her throat. He answered with a low rumble. His fingers followed the curve of her head to the soft skin of her nape. *Touch me,* he silently begged. *Touch me.*

The feel of her hands on his shoulders produced a painful ache in his loins. Each heartbeat exploded in his chest as her palms slid slowly down. *That's it, honey. Trust me.* He plundered her mouth now, stealing its pleasures with greedy abandon. Her splayed fingers burned through his shirt. Several seconds passed before he realized she pushed, rather than caressed.

Laura broke the kiss with a gasp, looking as dazed as he felt.

"We've got to stop," she said, her voice tight and breathy.

He sought her mouth again. She shoved his chest harder.

"It's Jason. He's waking up."

Alec swung toward the back seat. Jason stirred and lifted unfocused eyes. "Are we home yet, Dad?"

Nothing else could have cooled Alec's passion so swiftly.

"Yes, son, we're home." His voice sounded odd to his own ears. He cleared his throat and waited for his breathing to slow. "Tell Laura good-night, and I'll get you to bed."

Jason scrambled upright, more alert each second. His tousled blond hair shimmered like a halo. He raised huge imploring eyes—a Hummel figurine in the flesh.

"Would you put me to bed, Laura? *Please?*"

JASON PULLED HER up the stairs, his small hand warm and insistent. Smiling, Laura looked back over her shoulder.

Alec watched her from the foot of the stairs, his gaze brooding and intent. She stumbled. By the time she reached the top, Laura felt as if she'd run a marathon.

Pausing to brace her trembling knees, she felt a tug on her hand.

"You okay, Laura?" Jason's dark brows formed a worried line.

Somehow she managed a smile. "I just needed to catch my breath. I'm fine now." But she *wasn't* fine.

She'd confessed her most humiliating experience and been absolved of blame. She hadn't had time to prepare, to consider how she would feel once Alec knocked down the fence. His compassion had produced a yearning for commitment completely at odds with her career plans.

Following Jason to his room, she watched him pull pajamas out of a pine chest of drawers and turn with an expectant expression. She got on her knees and tugged off his sneakers, jeans and shirt. Standing before her in tiny jockey briefs, his slim body covered in goose bumps, he looked small and vulnerable.

Something in her expression must have strummed an answering chord in Jason. As one, they moved forward and clung to each other a long moment. Laura rubbed her cheek against his silky hair.

God, she loved this child.

The emotion was simple and pure compared with what she felt for Alec. And what did he feel for her? Had she imagined the flashes of tenderness, the longing of his spirit, rather than flesh?

By next March, it won't matter. I'll be out of both their lives for good.

Laura closed her eyes against the thought and inhaled the scent of baby shampoo, mustard and small boy. A lot could happen between now and then.

"You're squeezing me," Jason protested.

Laura released her hold and ruffled his hair. "Sorry 'bout that. Let's get you into these pj's."

She guided hands, feet and head through appropriate holes, tickled his ribs briefly, then scrambled up.

"I'll pick out a story while you brush your teeth."

"Aw, Laura. Do I hafta? I brushed 'em this morning."

"'Fraid so, kiddo. Now scoot." She patted his bottom out the door and watched him drag toward the bathroom. "And your breath better smell minty fresh when you come back, too," she warned, hiding a smile at the guilty look he threw over his shoulder.

Five minutes later, Laura snuggled back against the pillows and read Jason the story of Sister Bear's first day at school. Enchanted with the idea of entering first grade in the fall, he interrupted her a good twenty times to ask questions. At last she closed the book and looked into his drowsy eyes.

"Good night, little guy. I had fun tonight. Thanks so much for asking me." She kissed him on the tip of his nose, swung her legs to the floor and started to stand.

Jason's hand crept out and and clutched her wrist. "Don't go. Read me another story."

Were all children born knowing how to milk that adorable pleading expression? She sighed. "Your dad's going to get mad at me for keeping you up so late. Remember, you guys are supposed to play ball tomorrow, so you need your rest."

"*Please?*" he begged.

Laura chuckled. "How 'bout I sing a good-night song, instead?"

When Jason nodded, she brushed back his hair and pulled the covers up under his chin, mimicking some deep subconscious memory of her mother performing these same actions. Although she couldn't remember her mother singing, Maria had sung Laura to sleep many a night.

How did the housekeeper's favorite song go? Oh yes, now it was coming back.

The soft gentle notes of a Mexican lullaby poured from Laura's throat. As usual, the music transported her to another world. She sang of a peasant mother retiring for the night, enjoying one perfect moment after a hard day's work. The woman rocked her *bebé hermoso* to sleep and prayed for a better life for her son.

Laura watched Jason's eyes drift shut and found herself hoping he, too, would have a happy life. Knowing she would not be a part of it infused her voice with haunting tenderness.

"Ten cuidado y sea feliz, mi bebé hermoso," she sang to the little boy she loved as her own. When the final notes faded into the quiet whisper of Jason's regular breathing, Laura sensed another presence in the room.

"That was beautiful," murmured a deep voice.

She rose and turned. Alec stood leaning against the doorjamb, and his tender expression snatched her breath away. Even as she watched, his features hardened.

"You're very good with him," he said. "But I'm afraid he's beginning to depend on you."

She raised an index finger to her pursed lips and moved to join him at the door. "Afraid?"

He straightened and followed her into the hall. They walked abreast to the stairs.

"That's right. He's already lost one woman he loved. A second time could be devastating."

Laura paused with her hand on the left balustrade. "I have no intention of abandoning Jason. What makes you think such a thing?"

He slanted her an appraising look. "In eight months you'll be starting your own agency, beginning a new chapter in your life. Even if you wanted to, you won't have time to spend with him."

She raised her chin and started down the stairs, forgetting she'd thought much the same thing earlier.

"I don't abandon the people I love, Alec, even if it's convenient for you to think so."

He took the steps two at a time and caught her shoulder. "Just what is that supposed to mean?"

"It means you expect other people to be as afraid of committing to a relationship as you are. That way you're off the hook if something goes wrong. And something will go wrong, Alec, because we humans make mistakes. We lose our tempers, and break promises, and love too much or too little sometimes. We're not as controlled as you. But at least we're not frozen."

As she turned to continue down the steps, a sinewy hand shot past her and gripped the banister. Her momentum pressed her breasts into his steely arm.

He crowded her backward against the railing and clamped his left hand on the banister, padlocking her into an intimate embrace.

"Do I look frozen to you?" Blue eyes burned beneath an awning of thick black lashes.

Laura's heart beat like a trapped rabbit's. His big body surrounded hers, yet touched only the tips of her breasts. Heat seared the points of contact.

"You're f-frozen inside."

He stepped forward until their bodies merged, compact muscle against yielding flesh. The railing dug into her spine. His erection pressed into her stomach.

"Do I *feel* frozen to you?"

He felt hot. And hard. And gloriously male. Flames licked across her belly and pulsed at the juncture of her thighs.

She moaned, longing to let the blaze consume them both. But at what cost? Reaching up, she slid her palm down the hot sandpaper of his jaw.

"What do you want from me, Alec?"

He flinched as if she'd slapped his face. Wariness tightened his mouth. He stepped back, unlocking her body from his heated embrace.

"Read our contract again, partner. That's what I want."

Shivering at the absence of Alec's physical and emotional warmth, Laura straightened from the banister and rubbed her arms. She finished walking down the stairs on wobbly legs and stopped at the front door. Unlatching the bolt, she pulled the door open and turned. Alec had remained on the stairs.

"I'll serve my eight months and leave quietly," she promised. "But if you try and stop me from seeing Jason in the meantime, contract or not, the deal's off. And from now on, *partner,* keep your damn hands to yourself!"

Slipping though the door, she shut it on Alec's outraged expression.

FOR THE HUNDREDTH TIME since the scene on the stairs, Alec cursed his stupidity. This whole mess was his fault. If he'd just kept his distance from Laura, he wouldn't be hiding out in his office right now.

He'd managed to avoid everyone until Sharon had retrieved him for the regular Monday staff meeting. The sight of Laura, perched like a bright butterfly on the moth gray sofa, had confirmed his worst fears.

She'd burst from her cocoon with a vengeance.

Her royal blue jacket hugged every feminine curve with the traction of a Porsche. Her shoulder-length hair glinted with coppery highlights. And that frothy excuse for a skirt rose a good three inches above her knees. Six, with her legs crossed.

Scowling, he recalled how those legs had drawn every male eye in the room. Even Jim, the controller, had spent more time ogling Laura than his precious computer runs.

Whirling in his chair, Alec stared out the window and watched a gardener replace spent snapdragons with heat-tolerant marigolds. Ridiculous, this illogical jealousy. He and Laura had no future. No history. He'd never done more than kiss her. But he'd come close. Dangerously close.

The feel of her against the banister had reduced him to an animal—just like his old man.

Alec swallowed the sudden bile of self-loathing. Bracing his feet, he clutched the arms of his chair against what he knew was coming. What he couldn't stop. Memor swamped him, dark and ugly and choking.

He sat at a card table in the tiny apartment kitchen. A tall pot-bellied man staggered toward a thin woman standing by the stove. Jonathan McDonald grabbed the delicate wrist stirring corned beef and cabbage, and pulled.

"I got me an itch I need scratchin', woman."

"Not now, Jonathan, please. Alec's hungry," Sarah McDonald protested as he dragged her, spatula in hand, toward the bedroom.

Jonathan twisted her wrist cruelly, smiling at her cry of pain. "Alec's hungry," he mimicked in a high falsetto. His narrowed bloodshot eyes pinned Alec against the rickety chair. "How old are you now, boy?"

"E-eleven." Fear and impotent rage roiled in his stomach. He hated being young. Hated being weak. Hated his old man with a passion too big for his small body.

His father's unshaven bloated face leered. "Old enough to get hungry for a girl, eh, boy? Maybe it's time you seen how a man takes care of hunger. Come on in an' let Pop show you how it's done."

"No!" His mama stared at Jonathan in horror as he opened their bedroom door. She threw a pleading look over her shoulder.

"Run outside and play, Alec."

Jonathan's grimy fingers fumbled with the buttons of her faded housedress. Alec scraped back his chair and clenched his fists. He wanted to pound Pop till he couldn't move, couldn't hurt Mama ever again. Instead, Alec lurched to his feet and ran.

Blinded by tears, he stumbled, heard the clink of empty beer bottles and fumbled for the front doorknob. The smell of corned beef and cabbage hung heavy in the humid air. Gagging, he flung open the door, careered outside and wretched into a scraggly bush.

Long minutes later, he straightened and glanced back toward the cheerless apartment.

He wouldn't always be small.

Or weak.

CHAPTER TWELVE

SAM WIPED his shoes on the mat, resnugged his Port of Houston cap, lifted the knocker... and lost his nerve.

He hadn't called first to make certain Alec was home. He didn't have a legitimate excuse for arriving unannounced. He wasn't even sure why he was here.

He'd been driving aimlessly for half an hour and had somehow wound up in Tanglewood. 'Course, he'd had to hunt mighty hard for the house that matched the address Alec had given him for emergencies. Lowering the knocker, he grimaced.

Sam Parker, you are one pitiful son of a bitch. The last thing this family needs is an old geezer barging in on their dinner.

Turning to leave, he jumped guiltily as the front door rattled open.

"You're not Dad," a little boy declared through the narrow gap between frame and door. His eyes and voice accused with equal indignation.

Sam shifted his feet. "Now that's a fact. You must be Jason. I take it your dad's not home?"

The youngster scowled, tripling his resemblance to Alec.

"He's workin' late. I heard a car, but it was only you."

Need any more proof, geezer?

"Uh, well, you tell him that Sam Parker stopped by, but it wasn't important. I'll call him in the mor—"

"Jason McDonald! How many times have I told you not to open that door without asking me first?" The gap widened to reveal a petite woman wearing immaculate white slacks and a red knit top. Lively brown eyes contrasted nicely with chin-length silver hair.

Sam opened his mouth, but nothing came out.

Jason giggled. The woman cocked her head, reminding Sam of a sleek little squirrel.

He cleared his throat and tried again. "I'm Sam Parker, a...friend, of Alec's. I was just in the neighborhood and thought I'd drop by." *Real smooth, Parker.*

She smiled, a gracious lovely thing to watch.

"Why, Mr. Parker, do come in. I'm Evelyn Polk, Jason's baby-sitter. Mr. McDonald has mentioned you many times. I'm sure he'd want you to wait. He'll be home shortly." Stepping back, she opened the door and tugged Jason out of the way. The hands holding the boy's shoulders were dainty. And ringless.

Doffing his cap, Sam clenched it with both hands and placed one foot on the marble entry floor. "If you're sure it won't put you out..."

"Nonsense," she assured him. "Jason and I were just about to have a piece of cake. Won't you join us?"

Sam slid his other foot forward to meet the first and stood inside the foyer. "Now that *would* be putting you out."

Shutting the door, Evelyn slanted him a mischievous look. "It's devil's food with double-fudge icing."

He glanced down at Jason.

The boy made a slurping noise and rubbed his belly. "It's reeeal good."

Grinning, Sam bobbed his head. "In that case, thanks. I'd love some."

Evelyn leaned down. "Show our guest into the living room, dear. I'll be there soon."

Sam's gaze followed her to the kitchen. That was one fine-looking woman. One of the few close to his age who looked as good going as she did coming.

"Whatcha starin' at Mrs. Polk for?" Jason asked.

Sam's face heated.

"You must really like chocolate cake, huh?"

"It's one of my favorites." Chocolate gave him hives.

Jason slurped again. "Mine, too. Come on. The living room's over here."

They entered a large room with a monochromatic color scheme ranging from pale cream to dark sand. Sam's experienced eye estimated the cost of elaborate custom draperies, Italian marble coffee table, matching camel-back sofas and porcelain geegaws scattered about with a decorator's strategic touch. No expense spared.

Alec had given up some major bucks by leaving Harris, Bates and Whitman Advertising. Sam's respect rose another notch.

Heading for the sofa, he tossed his cap down, sat forward and grasped his knees. His arrival must've interrupted the kid's play. Those interlocking plastic things dotted the cream carpet like primary-colored confetti.

Jason plopped down with his back to Sam, lifted a jagged block of plastic and attached another square to the mass.

"Nice house you've got here. Lot's of room for a boy to stretch his legs," Sam observed.

The small hands stilled.

"Bet you could play hide-and-seek all day and never be found."

The slender shoulders curled forward in a protective posture.

Sam frowned. What was the matter? Oh, hell.

Nice going, jackass. The boy was locked in a tiny liquor cabinet, and you're talkin' hide-and-seek.

He searched for a way to redeem himself. "You know, son, I grew up in a house not much bigger than this one room. Had to share a bedroom with four brothers. Sometimes at night, lyin' in the dark, the walls would close in on me till I thought I'd suffocate."

Head down, Jason cocked his ear. "What's suff... suffa...?"

"I couldn't breathe. Felt like I was gonna choke or throw up. You ever felt like that?"

The slim body curled tighter.

"Well, anyway, when that happened, I used to play a little game in my head." Sam tensed.

Jason lifted his gaze. "What kind of game?" Wariness warred with hope in his turbulent blue eyes.

Sam released his breath. *Please, Lord, don't let me screw this up.*

"Well, now, I'd close my eyes and picture this great big wide-open field of bluebonnets I saw once at my granddaddy's farm. You ever seen bluebonnets, son?"

Enthralled, Jason shook his head.

"Guess not, you livin' overseas, an' all. Prettiest little flower you ever did see, though. Texas is loaded with 'em in the spring. Our highway department seeds the—"

"What'd you do then?"

"Uh...when?"

"After you thought about the field?"

"Oh. Well, I pictured myself sitting smack-dab *in* the field, breathin' clean fresh air and liftin' my face to the sun. And pretty soon, darned if I couldn't breathe easy again and fall asleep."

Jason turned the plastic block around and around in his hands.

Sam flipped on his cap and pulled down the brim. "Anyone can do it, you know, not just me. Let's say you got to feelin' bad at night or something. Why, you could picture a field of bluebonnets and put yourself in the middle."

The boy shot Sam a skeptical look. "I never seen bluebonnets. 'Sides, you had brothers. It's easier when you're not alone."

Poor kid. "You can do anything you want in your head. I'll show you. Close your eyes."

Thick dark lashes squeezed shut and trembled.

"Okay, pick a special place. Someplace that makes you feel happy and good. Then picture it in your head. Got it?"

Jason's lips curved up a little. He nodded.

"Now, pick a special person. Someone who makes you feel happy and good. Then put that person with you in your special place. Got it?"

Breaking into a half smile, Jason nodded.

"So guess what? You're not alone now. And you don't ever have to be scared or alone again, 'cause you can always go to your special place. Heck, I still go to mine sometimes."

Jason opened his eyes slowly. Shining wonder evolved into a smile so joyful Sam's heart expanded like a helium balloon.

Jason redirected his smile over Sam's shoulder. "Mrs. Polk, you shoulda been here! Sam showed me how to go to a special place in my *head,*" he explained in an awed voice.

Cringing, Sam swung around. Evelyn stood in the doorway balancing a tray of cake slices.

"I heard," she admitted, looking straight at Sam.

He caught his breath at the soft glowing admiration in her eyes. No woman had looked at him like that since ... well, since Jenny.

He felt marvelous, invincible, capable of taking on anything the world wanted to sling in his path. He rose and hurried to Evelyn's side.

"Here, let me help you with that," he offered, taking the tray from her unprotesting hands.

"Why thank you, Mr. Parker. That's very thoughtful."

"Sam. Please, call me Sam."

"All right ... Sam." Blushing prettily, she patted her smooth silver hair. "And please, call me Evelyn."

MORNING SUNLIGHT streamed through Brenda Lee's dining-alcove window and lit the glass tabletop. Laura picked up two bottles of nail polish and sighed. Alec had virtually ignored her since the night of the baseball game last weekend, and there was only herself to blame. Would he be as aloof tonight at Sam's party?

She sighed again, this time with more gusto.

Brenda Lee looked up from applying red polish. "Are you going to make a decision on that polish before Christmas?"

"Well, excuuuse me. You know I'm fashion disabled. So what do you think? Should I go with Cinnamon Spice or Apricot Kiss?"

"Cinnamon Spice. I've got some lipstick that'll match it perfectly. Remind me to give you the tube before you leave." Brenda Lee scowled at her own perfect nails. "I can't believe Alec's not taking you to the party."

Laura shuddered to think what her friend would say about her hands-off warning to Alec.

"He's got more willpower than brains, that's for sure. Thank goodness Harold doesn't have the same problem."

Laura pounced on the change of subject. "Okay, that's it. Spit out those canary feathers and talk. Just what exactly *did* happen the night you and Harold stayed late working on the Sanders proposal?"

Brenda Lee's eyes widened. "Why nothin', sugar. I was looking for a ream of copy paper when he came into the storage closet to ask me a question. Could I help it if the door accidently shut behind him?"

Chuckling, Laura shook her head. This fragile Southern belle had all the subtlety of a bulldozer. But then, who was Laura to criticize methods that worked? She'd blown it big time with Alec on the stairs that night. Frightened of being rejected, she hadn't seized her chance to expand their relationship, consequences be damned.

"Harold and I want you to ride with us to Sam's. Now don't argue. It doesn't make sense for us to take two cars when we live next door to each other."

"Why do I think Harold might disagree?"

"We've already talked it over. We can't really party hearty on Sunday, so it's settled. You'll ride with us, okay?"

Laura didn't really want to walk into the party by herself.

"Are you sure Harold won't mind?"

"Mind? Honey, with the dress you're wearing tonight, I'll be lucky if he doesn't dump me and take you, instead."

With one last stroke, she capped her polish and inspected her spread fingers. Apparently satisfied, she shot Laura a mischievous glance.

"Besides, there's always the chance Alec will offer to take you home."

The tiny nail-polish brush in Laura's fingers wavered.

"Here now," Brenda Lee murmured, taking Laura's wrist. "Let me do that before you mess up. I'm through with mine."

Laura relinquished the job thankfully and took a steadying breath. Sam had invited Regency Hotels' top management to the party, as well as many of his personal friends. She wanted to make him proud. She wanted to look beautiful.

Who was she kidding? She wanted to make Alec jealous.

There, she'd admitted it. She would flirt with every man at the party except him. Childish, yes. But she'd been raised by men and knew how their minds worked. The toy someone else wanted was always worth fighting for. It made possession that much sweeter. And she intended to make Alec both want, and possess, her tonight.

Fingers of warmth traced lightly over her belly.

Brenda Lee made short work of Laura's last four nails, then sat back and leveled a stern look. "For heaven's sake don't do dishes or anything for a couple of hours. Now, did you get the stuff I told you about?"

"Yes, and they cost a fortune, too. I don't know what's so special about them."

Brenda Lee smiled wisely. "You'll see when you put them on. What about a handbag? Did you find one at Dillard's?"

"Yes. Shoes, too."

"Let me see them."

Laura led the way to her own apartment. She wasn't offended by Brenda Lee's manner. Having different strengths and sharing them made their friendship stronger.

By the time Brenda Lee left, Laura had received a refresher course in makeup, hairstyle, perfume, jewelry—even lingerie. This process of dressing to kill would be the death of her!

When her digital clock finally flipped to five o'clock, Laura washed her hair, shaved her legs and dusted herself from head to toe in her favorite talcum powder.

Oh Mama, is this how you felt dressing up for Dad?

She closed her eyes and inhaled the lavender scent, remembering the day she'd found a frosted purple glass container in her father's bathroom cabinet. She'd been about seven at the time—old enough to know such a thing didn't belong to her rugged father. Curious, she'd lifted the lid and sniffed. The sensation of being held in soft loving arms had overwhelmed her, and she'd swallowed back tears.

She'd used her mother's brand of talcum every day since becoming a teenager.

Laura opened her eyes and glanced at the clock. Where had the time gone? She quickly applied makeup, then coaxed her hair into the windblown tumbled style she'd been taught. On impulse, she lifted a mass of locks next to her left ear and secured it high on her head with a gold comb. Not bad. Now the violet-and-amber rhinestone earrings showed to advantage. With a final uncertain glance in the mirror, she left the relative safety of her bathroom. The moment of reckoning had arrived.

Laura slipped off her robe and and stepped into a triangle of cream silk and lace. Next came the ivory garter belt, followed by sheer nylons shimmering with golden highlights. Brenda Lee had been right. The filmy underwear *did* make her feel more desirable. With trembling fingers, she opened her small closet, reached for her dress and slipped it off the hanger.

Stepping into the satin lining, she eased up the delicate fabric inch by breathless inch. Brenda Lee had insisted the dress didn't require a bra. Laura wished for one just the same. Feeling strangely vulnerable, she inserted her arms through the sleeves and leaned over to settle her breasts in the proper position. Straightening, she viewed herself in the full-length closet-door mirror.

The décolleté dress consisted entirely of gold stretch lace. Its scalloped sweetheart neckline plunged deep enough to show cleavage, but just short of looking sleazy. She hoped. Long tight sleeves of sheer gold lace reminded her of an old-fashioned wedding gown. In contrast, the body-hugging fabric stopped with modern boldness a good six inches above her knees.

She'd never worn anything remotely like it in her life.

The doorbell rang, interrupting her agonized last-minute doubts. "Just a minute," she yelled, slipping on gold leather heels before walking to the door. "Who is it?"

"It's Harold. Your coach is waiting."

Smiling, she flung open the door.

Harold gaped, then let out a low wolf whistle.

"Down, boy," came a wry voice from behind his broad shoulders. Brenda Lee pushed Harold aside to look Laura over.

Laura looked back. The sleeveless black chiffon sheath, elegant on its own, was stunning against Brenda Lee's white skin, platinum hair and curvy body. Her French twist was inspired. Just the touch of Grace Kelly class Harold would appreciate.

"I hate you," Laura said.

"I hate you more."

Both women burst out laughing. Brenda Lee glanced at Harold's bewildered expression and patted his arm.

"It's a girl thing, sugar. Don't try to understand."

Laura picked up her beaded clutch purse, locked the front door and followed the pair to Harold's Mercedes. They made a lovely couple, Harold's polished good looks and custom-tailored tuxedo a perfect foil for Brenda Lee's petite blond beauty. When he handed her into the car as if she were a piece of Dresden china, Laura suppressed a stab of envy. Just because her own love life was pitiful didn't mean she wasn't truly happy for her friend.

Sam lived in the heart of Memorial, a prestigious subdivision of towering pines and gorgeous homes. Brenda Lee exclaimed at the glimpses of softly lit paradise they passed, then gawked as they turned onto Brown Saddle Drive.

"Sam said it was valet parking," Laura volunteered from the back seat, growing queasier by the minute.

Harold followed a BMW up a bricked circular drive and waited his turn. The Mercedes advanced in line and rolled to a stop. Laura's door opened and a white-gloved valet reached in to help her out. She managed to stand without fainting.

Why had she worn this dress?

Harold held out an arm to each woman and escorted them to the door. As he rang the bell, Brenda Lee caught Laura's eye.

"You look fabulous," she mouthed, giving her a thumbs-up.

Laura felt a strengthening rush of determination. No more pulling back. She would stop behaving like a schoolgirl and respond like a woman to this attraction between her and Alec.

But first, she would make him suffer.

HE HATED CHAMPAGNE. He hated wearing a monkey suit and making small talk with people he didn't know, would never see again. Come to think of it, he hated everything these days.

And it was all Laura's fault.

Alec's gaze swept the room, searching for a glimpse of chestnut hair. Where the hell was she, anyway?

He'd taken a dozen women to bed since his divorce, but had never gotten within ten feet emotionally. Damn this need to see Laura, speak to her, *be* with her. If only he'd imagined the heart-stopping look she'd given him for praising her beauty. If only he hadn't heard her intimate confession. Maybe then he wouldn't long to be a shoulder she could lean on, a lover she could trust to repair her damaged self-image.

Sam beckoned from across the living room. Alec headed for the black marble fireplace, where the older man stood surrounded by a cluster of Regency Hotels employees.

"We'll be ready for the onslaught of calls in Reservations, Mr. Parker," a sandy-haired young man promised. "Don't worry about our department."

An attractive brunette placed her hand on Sam's arm. "Wonderful party. Just what the troops needed for morale. But I think we should personally check out the buffet and give you a report later."

Her companions laughingly agreed, and the group drifted off as Alec moved up to replace them.

He was startled to see Evelyn Polk, resplendent in a blue dress with silver beads, standing at Sam's side. His hand rested at the small of her back, and her warm brown eyes glowed with happiness.

The couple had met a week ago at Alec's house. When had their relationship progressed to this point? "Evelyn, how nice to see you here. You look lovely as usual."

"Get your own date, Alec. This one's mine." Sam slid his hand up Evelyn's back to drape possessively over her shoulder.

She blushed and made a shooing motion. "Oh, you two must want some of my devil's food cake to flatter me so. Jason could have told you it won't work." Her eyes lit with fondness. "Who's watching the little scamp tonight, Alec?"

"He's sleeping over at his friend Joey Thompson's house. Couldn't get rid of me fast enough to see that new puppy, Biscuit. The only thing Jason would have liked better is staying at your house."

"Smart boy," Sam said, his sexual nuance clear.

The two exchanged a radiant look. Apparently Sam had found someone worthy of replacing Jenny in his affections. Alec experienced a sharp pang of longing. He could be standing here with Laura, if only he'd asked her.

"Where's Laura?" Sam asked. "I thought she'd be with you."

Alec felt his face heat. "I . . . I haven't seen her." He cleared his throat and scrambled for a new topic. "You've really outdone yourself. Everything looks great."

And it did, he realized. The house was a sprawling ranch style, filled with open space and floor-to-ceiling windows. The draperies were open to reveal a beautifully landscaped backyard dominated by a free-form pool.

"It's been fun throwing a party," Sam admitted. "But then, the caterers did most of the work. 'Cept for the spinach dip. Made that myself."

Alec cocked an eyebrow.

"Swear to God. It's next to the lobster. Taste it and tell me what you think. But be prepared to lie."

Alec was heading for the dining room when a flurry at the front door caught his attention. Harold and Brenda Lee stood in the foyer, creating quite a stir by arriving as a couple. Good God, when on earth had *that* happened? The petite blonde looked radiantly happy, but no more so than Harold, Alec noted. Longing seized him again. He started to look away, only to be riveted by a pair of tawny eyes staring from behind Brenda Lee.

It was just like the day Laura had barged into his office at Harris, Bates and Whitman. Only then his heart hadn't pumped like a runaway locomotive.

Brenda Lee moved, and Laura stood alone under the crystal chandelier—as tempting and forbidden as original sin. Shimmering facets of light dusted a dress that grazed her legs at midthigh. The damn thing looked spray-painted. He glared his displeasure.

Her luminous gaze dimmed. She looked away.

Steve hurried over to greet her. Laura flashed a brilliant smile that had the handsome young art director stumbling all over himself. Alec dug a Tums from his pocket, threw it in his mouth and ground it to a chalky pulp.

"If I were you, boy, I'd hurry up and defend my claim before it gets jumped, so to speak," a voice rumbled in his ear. Alec dragged his gaze from the foyer. Sam watched him with a mixture of amusement and sympathy.

"What Laura does outside the office is her business. I have no 'claim' to defend."

Sam's sky blue gaze flicked to Evelyn and back. "Life doesn't offer many treasures, son. If you're not prepared to claim the ones that come along, you might not get a second chance." He reached up and patted Alec's shoulder in a fatherly manner. "How about a drink? And I don't mean that cow piss they're pouring, either."

"Chivas on the rocks?"

"No problem."

Sam flagged down a passing waiter and gave the order. In minutes, Alec sipped the finest Scotch whiskey made. The liquid fire hit his stomach and helped warm his strange empty chill.

"I don't need a nursemaid, Sam. Go on and see to your guests. I'll be fine."

The older man's silver brows met for an instant, then separated. He shook his head and moved off, muttering something suspiciously like "stubborn fool."

Alec resigned himself to the inevitable and began working the party, stopping to thank staff members for their hard work and giving out business cards to potential clients. The CEO of Huntington Oil actually agreed to meet for lunch the next week to discuss an annual report. Laura would go nuts at the opportunity to tackle a high-dollar project like that....

Oh, hell. There he went again.

Taking a quick gulp of Scotch, Alec slipped out the patio door into the tropical night. He stood motionless and let the tinkle of wind chimes and muffled party sounds soothe his turmoil. Several couples sat at tables. A few more stood around the pool talking quietly. No one approached him. Having perfected a back-off aura that was useful at times like this, he wasn't surprised.

Leaning against a column supporting the patio overhang, he examined an idea that had plagued him for weeks. Why was he insisting on buying Laura out? She'd proved to be a vital addition to the agency team. Sam adored her, and Alec suspected she would be a great asset in capturing other clients, if he would only let her.

If she needed the buy-out money to help her family, then hell, he could lend it to her himself. His personal funds were liquid, and she'd pay him back. Laura had more integrity than anyone he knew. Of course, that would entangle him in her life even more than he already was.

The familiar pressure built in his chest. He pulled away from the post and tossed back the remainder of his drink.

"Are you avoiding me, Alec?" asked a husky feminine voice.

He turned. From afar, she'd been dazzling. Up close, she robbed him of breath. He schooled his features to remain expressionless.

"Hello, Laura. Why would you think I'm avoiding you?"

"I thought maybe..." She glanced at the pool, took a tiny sip from her champagne flute and looked back into his eyes. "I never should have threatened to end our partnership, Alec. Especially after our talk about Michael. What you said meant a lot to me."

Alec's gut twisted at the vulnerable look in her eyes. He forced himself to shrug. "I would have done the same for any good-looking woman."

A delicate blush spread up her ivory throat. He fought an urgent desire to trail kisses along its rosy path.

"Yes, well...I just wanted to thank you. But I can see you're not in the mood for company."

She turned to leave.

"Some party, huh?" he blurted. "Sam really went all out. Hope we can live up to his expectations." It was the closest he could get to voicing his fear of failing.

She paused. "Your marketing plan is brilliant. It can't miss bringing results."

Inordinately pleased, he jostled the ice in his glass. "Your creative work is outstanding. You'll win a bundle of awards to hang at your new agency."

A warm breeze tinkled the chimes, whirled around Laura and carried the scent of lavender to Alec. He concentrated on his glass and willed himself to keep his hands off her. The patio door opened, spilling the sound of chatter and clinking cutlery into the tense moment.

"There she is, Brenda Lee! I told you she was all right." Harold smiled a greeting and walked toward them.

Behind him, Brenda Lee took in the scene and shot Laura a dismayed look. She grabbed Harold's arm and halted his progress. "Okay, you were right. Now let's go inside and get something to eat. This champagne is getting to me on an empty stomach."

Harold looked down at her in confusion. "But I just got you a pla— Ouch! What'd you pinch me for?"

Brenda Lee spun him toward the door and herded him inside, her voice trailing back to Laura and Alec. "Harold Becker, you may be a whiz with gross-rating points, but you're dumb as a fence post about some things."

Alec studied Laura's flushed profile as she lifted her glass and drained the contents. *Interesting.*

"Well, I think I'll track Sam down now. I haven't had a chance to tell him how wonderful everything is." She aimed a look somewhere near his bow tie. "See you around."

"Yeah, sure." He nodded to her disappearing back, then broke into a slow smile.

Very interesting.

LAURA SLIPPED into the bathroom, locked the door and pressed icy palms against her heated cheeks. It was one thing to want to seduce Alec. Quite another to have him know that was what she wanted.

Leaning against the marble countertop, she examined her face in the mirror. So much for appearing cool and sophisticated. The sight of Alec in a tuxedo, lounging with James Bond suavity on the patio, had reduced her to mush.

Washing her hands, she toweled them dry and remembered his smoldering appraisal when she'd first arrived, before anger had dominated his expression. She might be inexperienced, but she wasn't a fool. Alec was not nearly as indifferent to her as he would like.

Laura unlocked the door and reentered the party with chin held high. Grabbing a flute of champagne from a passing waiter, she tipped the glass and savored the tart fizz against her tongue. Call it false courage, but she'd take whatever kind she could get.

Wandering through the elegant house, she peeked into the dining room where guests were sampling the buffet. Steve glanced up from his place in line and gestured for her to join him. Smiling her thanks, she crossed to the buffet.

"Jeez, Laura, you look...incredible."

"Thanks...I think."

He flushed to his blond roots. "I mean, you look beautiful. That dress, your hair—"

"Check out the ice sculpture, would you? The new Regency logo you designed even looks great frozen," she said, diverting his attention to a safer subject. Flirting was great in theory, but Steve was too nice a guy to mislead.

Five minutes later the opening riff of Eric Clapton's "Layla" floated into the dining room, and she drifted with the curious crowd toward the sound.

The family room had been cleared of furniture for a platform stage, now supporting four male musicians playing drums, bass, keyboard and lead guitar. Boy, did this bring back memories. The guitarist even looked a little like Michael, she realized, waiting for the familiar rush of emotion.

Nothing. Not one little blip in her heartbeat. She broke into an uncontrollable grin and tapped her foot.

By the time the band segued into "Rock Around the Clock," every person in the room was swaying or dancing in some form. She had a fleeting fantasy of Alec claiming her for a dance before Steve grabbed her wrist, pulled her among the dancers and spun her under his arm. Laughing, she threw herself into an enthusiastic jitterbug. To her left, Sam whirled Evelyn and gave Laura a wink, then executed some pretty fancy footwork himself. For several carefree minutes, she forgot her personal and professional problems and simply enjoyed being young and gloriously alive. When the last note ended, she collapsed against Steve's chest. His arms quickly slipped around her and tightened.

Startled, she pushed away and assumed a teasing smile. "Okay, Fonzie, let's take a break. You wore me out." Ignoring his obvious disappointment, she turned.

Alec leaned against the wall, watching. Although both hands were stuffed in his pockets, he looked far from relaxed. He looked coiled for action. Ready for blood. Jealous.

Suddenly his eyes met hers, and everyone else ceased to exist. She walked toward him as if in a trance.

"All right folks, we're gonna slow things down now," the lead singer murmured into his microphone. "So grab yourself a partner and hold on tight."

She would have laughed if her throat hadn't gone dry. Almost within Alec's reach now, she wet her lips. The haunting notes of "Unchained Melody" swirled around them as his gaze dropped to her mouth.

She would never have a clearer invitation.

CHAPTER THIRTEEN

ALEC COULDN'T LOOK AWAY, although he cursed himself for not having the strength. She's my business partner, he reminded himself. Nothing more.

And yet, no woman had ever looked at him like this. Like he was her heaven and earth and the air she breathed. Like she would stay by his side, no matter what. Like . . . like . . . oh, God, like she loved him.

The air left his lungs. He inhaled on a rush of exhilaration so powerful it made him dizzy.

Her heart in her eyes, Laura walked toward him, stopped and stretched out her hand.

One step, and she'd be in his arms. Sweet heaven, how he wanted her in his arms. One step. And then what? his conscience chided.

What she offered was incredibly precious. More than he either deserved or could give in return.

Ignoring her hand drew beads of sweat from his forehead, but he did it. He did the right thing by Laura and walked away. Catching a glimpse of Brenda Lee's accusing eyes, he turned and met Harold's disapproving expression.

Alec broke free of the crowd and headed straight for the nearest waiter. The living room, empty save for the hired help, provided a welcome refuge. He gave his order and sank into a wing chair facing the fireplace. Safe from prying eyes, he let his shoulders slump. The pulsing guitar rhythm of a new song scrubbed across his raw nerves like a Brillo pad.

When his Scotch arrived, he huddled deeper in his chair and gazed at the empty grate. How soon could he leave without offending Sam? The last thing he wanted was to run into Laura. *Sorry coward to the end, that's me.*

Biting off a curse, he tossed back his drink and stared at the floor. The liquor burned in his belly, along with bitter regret. A stocky shadow nudged at his feet.

"Think that's gonna help?" The familiar voice held mild reproval.

In no mood for one of Sam's fatherly chats, Alec kept his head down. "Ask me again after the fourth one. Better yet, send the waiter over here."

Sam's feet edged into view. The old coot had spilled a dollop of something creamy on his right shoe. Alec's irritation dissolved, leaving him numb.

"You've got spinach dip on your shoe," he said dully.

"Best place for it. Look at me, Alec."

Sam's blue eyes shone with exasperated sympathy. "Laura's swiggin' champagne like it's lemonade. Brenda Lee took her out on the patio for some fresh air."

Alec looked down at his white-knuckled grip on the glass of Scotch. He loosened his fingers and tightened his jaw. "Brenda Lee will take care of her."

"It's *you* she needs, you stubborn jackass!"

Alec's head shot up in surprise.

Sam rubbed stubby fingers over his silver burr, obviously struggling with his temper. "You rejected that girl in front of her friends. 'Bout near broke my heart to watch her face when you walked away."

"Damn it, Sam . . ." Alec's mouth twisted at the irony. For once in his life, he'd done the noble thing, and now he was getting reamed out for it.

Sam's expression gentled. "A man's got a right to do what he think's best, no matter what other people think. But hell, Alec, Laura's not 'other people.' *Talk* to her. Explain yourself. She deserves that much at least."

For the first time, Alec allowed himself to think of Laura's feelings as he'd turned his back on her. His misery increased. Setting his empty glass on the floor, he gave Sam a grim nod.

"Okay, you win. I'll talk to her. But I have no idea what to say." He'd better get this over with. It wasn't going to get any easier.

On his way to the patio door, he searched through the glass. Just as he spotted Laura, someone grabbed his arm. He turned, concealing his annoyance at the sight of Jerry Sanders. Wooing the man's business was one thing; pretending a friendship he didn't feel was another.

Jerry leaned forward and leered. "Hey, ol' buddy. That was some invitation you turned down a little while ago. If I were you, I'd take that partner of yours home before the mood wears off, know what I mean?"

Alec swallowed his distaste. The agency could really use the extra cash flow Sanders Development Corporation would provide. "Ms. Hayes has another escort tonight." He glanced pointedly at the fingers still clutching his arm. A diamond-encrusted horseshoe glittered on the man's pinky.

Jerry lifted his hand to clap Alec on the shoulder. "Don't be modest, man. She was all over you without ever dancing a step. Just think what she'd do between the sheets."

Alec tensed under the palm resting heavily on his shoulder. He gave Jerry a look that had sent tougher men scurrying for cover.

Jerry didn't notice. His bleary gaze wandered outside and landed on Laura with prurient interest. "Yes, sir, that is one sexy lady out there." He lowered his voice conspiratorially. "You know, Alec, since you don't want her, I just might be willing to speed up negotiations with your agency if Laura acted a bit . . . friendlier. I'd give a lot for a piece of tha—" The word broke off on a strangled choke.

Alec twisted and lifted the bow tie in his fist, pulling Jerry's florid face level with his own. "If you mention Laura one more time, I'll rip your filthy tongue out by the roots. You got that, Sanders?"

Eyes bulging, Jerry managed a slight nod.

"Good." Alec released his grip and started to move away.

"Now just a goddamn minute!" Jerry had regained his breath and his bravado. "Sanders Development Corporation hasn't signed anything with your agency, yet. If you expect to do business with me, you'd better apologize right now."

Alec thrust him aside like a pesky gnat. "Screw your business. We don't want it."

Opening the patio door, he slipped into the warm night and waited for his eyes to adjust. Laura stood on the other side of the pool, resisting Brenda Lee's efforts to pull her by the arm. Alec walked over. "Can I help?"

Laura lifted wounded doe eyes to his, then averted her face. "Did you hear that, Brenda Lee? He wants to help." Her voice dripped sarcasm. She jerked her arm from Brenda Lee's hand. "Everybody wants to help. Well, I don't need anyone's help, thank you very much. I've taken care of myself just fine for twenty-six years. I can manage one more lousy night."

As Laura walked toward the door, Brenda Lee raised imploring eyes to Alec. Sighing, he followed the slim figure and reached her in four strides, encircling her upper arm with one hand. Her fragility, so at odds with her strength of character, summoned a surge of protectiveness.

"I'm taking you home now, Laura. I do believe you've had enough excitement for the evening."

She wrenched her arm free and tossed her hair. "Oh, no, you don't. I'm just beginning to have fun. You go on home, party pooper. I don't turn into a pumpkin until midnight."

Knowing argument was useless, Alec grasped her arm more firmly and propelled her forward. He threw a resigned look over his shoulder at Brenda Lee, who nodded her understanding and made a shooing motion with her hand.

Once inside the living room, Alec released Laura's arm. "Where's your purse?"

For an instant, she looked confused, then her brow cleared. She raced off to the bedroom and emerged moments later, holding the beaded bag aloft. "Found it!"

Alec cupped her elbow and steered her toward the front door.

Laura dug in her heels. "What about Sam? We haven't even said thank-you, yet."

"Sam will understand. We'll call him tomorrow." Alec opened the front door and nudged her through, then dug into his pocket for his valet parking ticket. A gold-jacketed young man plucked it from Alec's hand and ran off into the night.

Laura, so vibrant earlier, looked like a lovely wilted flower under the porch lighting. And he was responsible, damn his soul.

She loves me.

The wondrous knowledge was like a newsflash in his brain. He didn't dare examine his emotions, else he'd be forced to smother them, as he had for too many long sterile years. Some part of him rebelled at doing so this time.

His gleaming white Lexus rolled up the circular driveway. Alec handed Laura into the front seat, then jogged around to the driver's side. Tipping the valet, he slid beneath the wheel and slammed the door.

The ride to her apartment passed in silence. Laura leaned her head back against the seat and closed her eyes, obviously disinclined to talk. Relief washed through him. He wouldn't have to explain his actions, after all.

Everything in him had balked at hurting her. But he'd done the right thing and spared them both a lot of pain in the future.

Alec couldn't deny the special chemistry between them. But that same chemistry made them go at each other's throats over the day-to-day business of living. Inevitably, they would go for the heart.

And his had been ripped out one too many times already.

LAURA KEPT HER EYES closed, acutely aware of the purring engine, the butter-soft leather beneath her thighs, the faint scent of sandlewood cologne feathering her senses.

Her anger had faded along with her champagne buzz. Apparently she had no pride where Alec was concerned. And her purposes were much better served by getting him alone.

She opened her eyes and rolled her head. His hard clean profile, lit by the glow of the dashboard, filled her with deep pleasure. Although he didn't so much as glance her way, the current of awareness that always connected them crackled and hummed with increased voltage.

He knew she watched him, all right.

"It's okay, you know," she said softly.

His long fingers tightened on the wheel.

"I understand what you're trying to do, even though I don't agree."

"Is that so?"

The powerful car swept into the entrance of her apartment complex and cushioned them over a series of speed bumps. Laura waited for Alec to park and cut the engine before answering.

"Yes, that's so. But that doesn't make it any less pathetic." Opening her door, she slid quickly out of the car.

Alec caught up with her under the light in front of her door as she dug through her purse. He leaned a palm high on the door frame, his body curving over hers.

"Mind explaining that little bomb?" he rumbled in her ear.

Hoping he wouldn't notice her trembling fingers, she pulled out a key ring, inserted the proper key and glanced up. "It means that denying what's between us won't make it go away. That's a coward's solution." She shoved her shoulder against the wood and lurched over the threshold, taking care to leave the door open.

Heart pounding, she switched on a lamp and headed for the kitchen. Acting on instinct alone, she paused to bend over and remove a piece of lint from the carpet. Lord only knew if he followed, or what he thought of the view. He wasn't making a sound.

Resisting the urge to look over her shoulder, she moved on. "Would you like a nightcap? I don't have any Scotch, but I'm sure I can scrape up something."

In the relative privacy of her small kitchen, she held her breath. The silence stretched.

"No."

Her shoulders slumped in relief. Some deep feminine intuition warned her his rigid self-discipline was weaker now than ever before. She would never have a better chance at breaking through to the lonely man underneath.

"You don't mind if I have one, do you?" She risked a peek around the kitchen wall.

He paused in midprowl. "No."

Laura ducked back into the kitchen. He'd left the front door open. An escape hatch. She reached up and pulled down two liqueur glasses from a set she'd bought at a garage sale. It took some rummaging to find the dusty bottle of Kahlúa left over from a trip to Nuevo Laredo, Mexico.

She'd driven there from Austin two years ago with a group of master's degree graduates bent on celebrating in the border city. It was the last time she'd let herself forget her career goals and live for the moment, for herself.

Until tonight.

She poured the dark syrupy liquid into the glasses and took several deep breaths. Plastering a smile on her face, she scooped up the drinks and ventured into the living room. Alec stood in the doorway staring out into the night.

"Here we are. I hope you like Kahlúa. It's one of my favorites." She set one glass on the lamp table and sat on the sofa, patting the cushion beside her. "Close the door and sit down, Alec. You're air-conditioning the porch."

His wary gaze flicked to the extra glass, then back to her. "I said I didn't want anything."

"I promise not to get you drunk and have my way with you." *Not without your cooperation, anyway.* "It's only liqueur, for heaven's sake. What are you afraid of?"

Something flashed in his eyes like a subliminal frame on a movie screen. She wondered what the message was. Judging from his blank expression, he wasn't going to rewind the scene for her benefit.

He closed the door, picked up a liqueur glass and settled on the opposite end of the couch.

"Okay, Laura. You've piqued my curiosity. What's this all about?"

Stalling, she took a sip of Kahlúa. The rich coffee-flavored liqueur steadied her nerves. "It's about us, Alec. About our relationship. There's something I have to ask you. Something I need to know." She sensed his body bracing. Her own muscles grew taut. "What I... feel, when you're near me. I want to know if it's just me or if you feel it, too."

He leaned back slowly, a sultan among silk pillows, his lashes screening a gleam of male satisfaction. "That all depends on how you feel, Laura. Can you be more specific?"

She wanted to throttle him. But perhaps there was a better way. She was a copywriter, after all.

Assuming a dreamy expression, she dropped into the resonant chesty voice of a true alto. "I feel... like I just got out of a hot tub. Languid. Heavy. Weak. But at the same time, breathless. As if something wonderful is about to happen. Am I making any sense?"

Instead of answering, he took a sip of Kahlúa, the reflexive movement of his throat gaining her rapt attention. A sluggish sweet heat stole through her veins.

"I feel," she went on, "like my senses are amplified. Right now, for instance, I can see your pulse throbbing.

There, between your collar and ear, where your hair breaks into curls. I can see where your beard grows heaviest, too. That's easy. Your skin looks almost blue in those places."

She closed her eyes and turned away, intent on describing her sensations. "I can hear you breathe now, slow and steady. Well, not so slow. And you're grinding your teeth again." A smile tugged at her lips. "You do that when you're upset—did you know?

"I can even smell you, Alec. Let's see, there's Scotch. And Sam's cigar. And of course the sandalwood cologne you wear. And...and..."

Eyes still closed, she turned back toward Alec and inhaled the unique intoxicating scent that was his alone. Words failed her.

"And you," she said, opening her eyes.

Beneath heavy lids, his eyes glittered.

"How do I make you feel, Alec? I need to know."

"*Why?*"

The anguish in his voice wrenched her. Leaving his emotional vacuum was ripping him apart.

She gentled her voice. "Because if you can honestly say you don't feel anything for me, I'll tell you good-night and send you home. But if you feel even a fraction of what I'm feeling now—" she put her drink down before the trembling liquid spilled "—then it's time we find out exactly what we're dealing with."

"Meaning?"

"Make love to me, Alec."

Her heart thudded painfully. She couldn't make it any plainer than that. Couldn't make herself any more vulnerable.

He closed his eyes and lifted a hand, pressing the heel of his palm to one temple.

"Alec?"

Breath suspended, she watched him lower his arm and open his eyes at the same time, his expression hard, cynical, weary beyond measure. A chill skittered up her spine.

"Laura—"

"Is it our business agreement?" she said, desperate to prevent his rejection, unsure she could live through it. "Because we can work things out. Other couples have worked togeth—"

"Laura, please. Don't make this any harder. That's not the only reason it won't work." With a soft curse, he rumpled his hair. "Look, you're a romantic, a cockeyed optimist. You think if you dig deep enough into my soul you'll strike gold. But anything worth saving was stripped away years ago. I'm all tapped out, nothing left but a black empty hole."

His mouth twisted. He swirled his liqueur and stared into the dark liquid. "I can't give you what you want, partner. I sure as hell can't give you what you deserve. But there's a man out there somewhere with your white picket fence and two-point-one children. Go dig around for him, if you have to. But for God's sake, leave me alone."

Even forewarned, the lance of pain shocked her. She'd been so close to reaching him. He wanted her—she *knew* it. Yet, out of some twisted notion of protecting her, he'd rejected everything she longed to give him.

She lunged to her feet. "How *dare* you presume to know what I want! How dare you make decisions for me! Don't tell me you can't love, Alec McDonald, because seeing you with Jason tells me different."

She hugged her stomach in an effort to control her shaking. "You? Tapped out? My God, you're holding in so much emotion, it's giving you an ulcer!"

"That's enough, Laura." Alec set his glass down and rose, looking grim and very large.

Common sense told her to shut up. She compromised and backed away. "What are you afraid of? Tell me. Why do you insist on living like a robot? Avoiding relationships, avoiding *life?*"

His eyes glittered in warning. "That's *enough,* Laura."

"The great lord and master has spoken, is that it? Well, I've got news for you, partner. I only take orders from real men, not wimps who wouldn't know what to do with a woman if she was delivered with an apple in her mouth!"

Something broke in his eyes.

She took one step backward before catching herself up short.

Alec advanced slowly—wild, savage, alien. "Oh, I know what to do with a woman, all right. Just ask the doctor who worked on Susan three years ago."

She stared at his snarling visage, but held her ground.

"It took eight stitches to sew up the gash I put in her head, Laura. Eight. Not exactly something a robot would do, is it? But then, I'm not really a robot. I'm more like my old man. God knows he told me so often enough." Stopping inches away, he chuckled, a bitter ugly sound.

Laura winced. Wanting to ease his torment, she raised trembling fingers to his jaw.

He thrust her hand away. "Damn it, woman, what will it take to make you hear me? A bash on the head? I'm good at that. Real good. Susan's not the only one I laid open, you know. When I was sixteen, I slammed a wrench against my old man's skull, too. Would have kept on slamming it if I hadn't already thought he was dead."

In spite of herself, she gasped. "Wh-why?"

His eyes glimmered with pain and a peculiar triumph. "Because I am what I am, not what you want me to be.

Because like father, like son. Because blood will tell, and mine is bad through and through.''

Struggling with the image he'd created, Laura shook her head. ''No, no. Why did you hit your father in the first place?''

Alec leaned forward, as if to make very sure she understood. ''Because it seemed like the thing to do, *since he'd just murdered my mother.*''

CHAPTER FOURTEEN

LAURA STARED at the feral agony in Alec's eyes, at the violent rise and fall of his chest, at the corded tendons of his neck. He seemed balanced on the edge of some personal hell. One poof of breath could send him tumbling over.

This was what she'd always sensed beneath his reserve. Pain and self-doubt of such magnitude the wonder was he'd managed to keep his sanity.

His lip curled. "I'm a real prince, all right, with royal scum running through my veins. I can't change my genes, and neither can you. Don't even try." He dragged in a ragged breath. "Let me go, Laura."

She should have listened. The ugliness she'd glimpsed through the crack in his control should have scared her silly. But he hadn't left on his own. He'd asked her to free him.

She raised her chin. "Tell me you don't want me."

His eyes darkened with fury. His lips clamped in a thin line.

He couldn't say it! He'd shown her his private hell to frighten her away, because he was scared to death of himself. Of what he might do to her.

This time she succeeded in touching his rigid jaw. He flinched beneath her fingertips.

"Your father's the beast, Alec, not you. You're nothing like him, no matter what he told you. You're good and loving and honorable. I know that as surely as I know you won't hurt me. As surely as I know Susan's injury was an accident.'' Noting his dumbfounded expression, she stroked his bristled skin. "Tell me what happened.''

He covered her fingers and pressed them still against his cheek, but didn't remove either of their hands. Dazed wonder filled his eyes, before memory clouded their depths.

"I came home early, heard Jason crying in his room and went upstairs to check. He was eighteen months old, too big for his crib, really, but we hadn't gotten around to buying him a bed.

"His foot was caught between the crib spokes. He was...hysterical. I got it free and calmed him down, then went looking for Susan.''

He squeezed Laura's fingers until she had to bite her lip to keep from crying out.

"She was in bed...our bed. With the gardener. Can you believe it? The *gardener.* There wasn't an original bone in her body. I kicked the guy out, and we argued. She came at me with her nails, and I...I flung her away." His jaw clenched.

"And?" Laura prompted.

"And she hit her head on the edge of our dresser. There was so much blood, I thought..."

He thought he'd killed her, Laura knew. "Was she conscious?"

Alec came back to the present. He slid her hand off his jaw, released her fingers and stepped back. "Oh, yeah. She was conscious. Gloating, more like it. I'd finally given her an excuse for uncontested custody of Jason. It was the only thing keeping her from divorcing me before. Not that she really wanted Jason. She just knew *I* did."

Laura lowered her head. Hateful woman. No wonder Alec distrusted relationships. He'd never been exposed to a loving one. Until now.

With one step she closed the gap between them, his white-pleated chest filling her vision. Focusing on a row of shiny black studs, she followed them up past a stiff bow tie and square jaw to a mouth that snagged and held her gaze. A mouth that rivaled the most sensual courtesan's for all that it tightened under her scrutiny.

Something between a laugh and a groan escaped him. "I'm not made of stone, Laura."

Her head snapped up. The first stirrings of feminine excitement rekindled deep in her belly. "Prove it."

His eyes flared hotly, her words kerosene on a banked fire. Still he held back. "Once I touch you…I won't stop, Laura. I won't be *able* to stop. Not this time."

She met honesty with honesty. "Alec, I'm so afraid."

A ripple of emotion crossed his face, leaving cold flatness in its wake. "I understand."

She reached out and gripped his forearm. "I'm afraid I won't please you," she explained, her fingers trembling against the fine-woven cloth.

His entire body stilled. He looked from her hand into her eyes, his own questioning.

In answer, she laid her cheek against his chest. The heart beneath her ear thudded almost as hard as the one beneath her breast. When his hand cupped the back of her head, her eyes drifted shut in pleasure. For one glorious moment, she basked in the simple joy of being held by Alec.

There was no turning back, she knew. Nor did she want to. This complex enigmatic man was worth risking her pride, worth giving her heart. He insisted he had nothing to give in return, but she'd glimpsed the gold waiting to be tapped. His habitual mask of indifference hid tenderness, deep loneliness and the pain of past betrayal. How could she deny him comfort? How could she deny herself the true passion she'd glimpsed only with him?

Ear still against his heart, she slid her hand up his arm, marveling at the biceps unsoftened by two layers of cloth. Her fingers rounded his shoulder and skimmed past his collar to sink into the raven curls at his nape. As his heartbeat accelerated, she smiled in pure feminine satisfaction.

Tilting her face, she let him see all the emotion overflowing in her heart. She'd waited a lifetime for this moment. This man.

"Don't stop, Alec. I don't want you to stop."

Carnal desire exploded in his sapphire eyes. She welcomed the fierce intensity of his descending face, moaning when he kissed her roughly, ravenously, as if he was starving and she his first sustenance in weeks. His uncontrolled passion excited her, emboldened her. She lifted her left hand and framed his jaw, pressing her right palm against the base of his head in a silent plea to deepen the kiss.

Instantly his body crowded forward, forcing her to stumble backward or be crushed by two hundred pounds of solid muscle. Her spine bumped the wall, and he pressed against her, conjuring sensations and images from another time, another wall. She hadn't known what to expect then.

Anticipation swirled through her.

Alec lifted his head. "I've waited so long. You feel so good," he said thickly, peeling off his coat.

The action pushed his erection against her belly. Her eyelids drooped.

He flung the garment aside and yanked his bow tie loose, stripping it from his neck and reaching up to fumble with the row of ebony buttons. His gaze burned, never leaving hers as the tiny studs popped one by one onto the floor.

A curious lethargy seized her body, leaving her too weak to participate. But she could watch. And the sight revealed as he shrugged off his shirt took her breath away.

Broad shoulders, lean waist and sculpted muscles twisted and strained, as much a product of genes as regular weight training. His skin glowed golden, smooth and unblemished over sinew and muscle. A dusting of black chest hair arrowed down beneath his satin cummerbund, completing an image of consummate virility.

He dipped his head suddenly and captured her mouth, as if he couldn't bear losing contact a moment longer. She tasted a hint of Kahlúa and the delicious essence of Alec and was jolted from her trance. She needed to touch him. To get closer.

Her palms glided up a washboard stomach to his chest, rubbing in ever-widening circles. When she grazed his nipples, he flinched.

"You're driving me crazy. I've got to see you," he murmured against her lips.

Hot kisses nipped down her cheek and throat. A part of her registered the lace at her shoulders slipping down, his thumbs hooking under her bodice, her breasts springing free...

Gasping, she moved to cover herself. Her tight lace sleeves, now bunched at the elbows, bound her as effectively as a straitjacket.

"Beautiful," Alec breathed, before taking one sensitive peak into his mouth.

Liquid heat shot to her womb. When her legs threatened to buckle, his arm banded her waist, supporting her weight and arching her breasts at the same time. He suckled for long moments, then moved to the other breast in a nuzzling beard-rasping sweep.

Nothing in her life had prepared her for this. His dark curls against her milk white skin, the moist tugging at her nipple, the total helplessness of her position—all were incredibly erotic to her drugged senses.

With Michael, she'd had time to think. Now she could only feel. And her body clamored for more.

"Let me touch you," she begged, wriggling her arms in an effort to free herself.

He lifted his head, a wolf interrupted from feasting. As comprehension dawned, he straightened, grabbed fistfuls of lace and shucked the dress to her toes in one powerful movement. She stepped out and kicked it away, shivering as cool air swept her heated skin.

Alec stood rooted, his smoldering stare searing a path up her silk-clad legs. His gaze faltered at the garter belt and panties, rose to her breasts and finally met her anxious eyes. Any self-doubts lingering from her experience with Michael were swept away by the unmistakable admiration in his eyes.

Heady with feminine power, she moved forward and encircled his waist, groping for the clasp of his cummerbund. The exquisite feel of her breasts against his bunched muscles made her fingers clumsy. Worrying her lip, she glanced up to see Alec's eyes closed in an expression of mixed pleasure and pain. Elation swelled at her ability to affect this controlled man.

With a small click of release, the heavy satin dropped from her nerveless fingers to the floor. Holding her breath, she reached for the front of his pants.

Instantly her hands were smothered by his pressing palm. He held her still against his throbbing erection, obviously fighting for control.

"Wait," he bit out, his teeth grinding in the silence.

Unable to resist, she flexed her fingers.

A deep rumbling groan was her only warning. Sweeping his hands down her spine and pulling hard, he rubbed his straining length against her until she was damp and dazed with passion. Together they sank to their knees. She clung to his shoulders like a drowning woman.

For she *was* drowning—buffeted by whitecaps of sensation that left her struggling for breath. She was vaguely aware of his fingers at work on her garter belt before somehow, her panties, belt and stockings pooled at her knees. He pulled away, returning devastating moments later to lower her onto her back. The feel of satin startled, then warmed her, as she realized he'd spread his coat as a makeshift blanket. She lifted her arms in surrender.

He yanked off her undergarments and covered her body, molding her from chest to toe with his heavy muscled length.

Heaven. Pure heaven.

Rising on one elbow, he smoothed a palm down the swell of her hip and over her belly, stopping just short of her pulsing need. His eyes grew heavy-lidded and dark with desire.

"I've dreamed about touching you, dreamed about what you'd feel like." He lowered his mouth a fraction from hers and slid his hand downward. "What do you feel like, Laura?" he whispered against her lips, probing her curls gently.

His tongue and finger plunged at the same time, sending her back arching off the floor. He plied both hand and mouth until she broke the kiss with a restless twist of her head.

"Oh, God!" she gasped.

His finger continued its assault.

"Oh, God!" she repeated, her nails digging into his back.

He stroked and teased, relentless in his sweet torture. "I knew you'd feel like this. Hot. Wet." His eyes squeezed shut as his breathing quickened. "And so damn tight I'm ready to explode."

Laura reached frantically for his waistband, pausing in surprise when her fingers met bare skin. At some point he'd removed his pants. Relieved, she grabbed the wrist between their bodies and pulled his hand away, wriggling down at the same time until his velvety tip met the center of her being.

They both moaned.

"Son of a bitch, I wanted to wait," Alec apologized, balancing on both elbows and nudging her legs wider. "I really wanted to wait, Laura."

"For God's sake, don't wait," she choked out.

And then he was filling her, stretching her, whispering words of encouragement as her body adjusted to the intrusion inch by inch. There was no pain this time. Only awed pleasure and a desire to accommodate his full length. She eyed their joined bodies with a twinge of doubt.

"That's it, sweetheart, take me in. Oh, yes, honey, take me all in."

The erotic endearments melted the last of her body's resistance. She tilted her hips and felt him ease to the hilt . . . watched his head fall back . . . felt him throb deep inside her.

Laura's own eyes closed as he began moving slowly and rhythmically, increasing his tempo with each thrust. "Oh, Alec," she breathed in wonder at the rising tension beyond anything in her experience. Dear God, it was too fast. It was too good. It was too, too much!

She wrapped her legs around his hips in an effort to stop the unbearable intensity. But the feeling swelled like a balloon, growing larger and larger with each powerful thrust until...

"Oh, *Alec!*" She clutched his neck as the feeling burst over her in multiple ripples, leaving her tingling and dazed and feeling as if she were floating.

With a hoarse cry, Alec thrust home one last time and shuddered, his big body collapsing against her chest. Long moments later, she opened drowsy eyes and traced patterns on his back with her fingertips.

So this was what it was like with the right man. She felt more relaxed, more content, more *free* than she'd felt in four years. She wanted to absorb his pain and heal his soul. To lavish him with all the love he'd never been given. To be everything for him, as he was for her. Her eyes welled, along with her heart.

Alec stirred and rose on his elbows. Still buried deep, he studied her with a frown. "Did I hurt you?"

She shook her head, prying loose a teardrop. What did one say to a man after he'd given her the most sensual experience of her life? After he'd restored her feminine identity and self-confidence? "I thought I couldn't...I've never felt...Michael said..."

She stopped, struggling to overcome her embarrassment and express her feelings. Words were so inadequate.

Alec's thumb intercepted another tear and wiped it away. "Like I said before, Michael's a blind fool," he pronounced flatly, a tender gleam in his eye.

Happiness shimmered through her like fairy dust, spilling over into her huge smile. There was only one thing to say, after all.

"I love you, Alec."

SOMETHING WAS POKING HIM. Alec shifted, awakening fully as a mattress spring scraped his hip. What the . . . ?

Oh, hell.

He turned, noting the shapely lump swaddled in the sheets beside him. Laura slept on her stomach, one knee drawn up, head pillowed on slim arms. A tangle of copper brown hair fanned out from her face—a face he studied with a hammering heartbeat.

Half-moon feathery lashes couldn't disguise the dark circles beneath her eyes. Her wide generous mouth looked swollen, the porcelain skin surrounding it irritated and red. He reached up and dragged a hand over his bristly jaw.

Oh, hell.

She slept soundly, as if exhausted. And no wonder. He'd kept her up most of the night.

After making love the first time, he'd been terrified at her tears, afraid he'd hurt her. Laura's radiant smile and confession of love had caught him totally off guard. His body, still sheathed in hers at the time, had responded as if to a potent aphrodisiac, hardening and moving toward a second climax even more powerful than the first.

But it hadn't been enough. Not nearly enough.

After months of stored-up sexual tension, he'd proceeded to satisfy every fantasy he'd ever entertained regarding his partner, then created some new ones. Laura's eager response had broken the last threads of his control, and he'd been wild, unstoppable. His stomach knotted at the memory.

Sometime during the night they'd transferred to the debatable comfort of Laura's sofa bed. As he'd spooned her against his body, his last thought before falling asleep had been how perfectly she fit.

Too perfectly, he realized now. It made the separation to come that much more painful. He glanced toward the window, resenting the horizontal strips of dawn glowing between the miniblinds. It was almost time to leave.

You didn't hurt her, an inner voice insisted. *You don't have to leave.*

Laura stirred in her sleep, exposing one creamy shoulder to his troubled gaze. Everything in him froze at the sight of four oval bruises marring the flawless skin.

Alec swallowed sickly. He'd gripped her hard enough to bruise her tender flesh and hadn't even realized it. When she'd cried out, had it been in pain, instead of ecstasy?

He didn't know. God help him, he didn't know.

The room suddenly closed in on him, squeezing the air from his lungs. He had to get moving. Had to *think,* damn it, somewhere far from Laura's seductive warmth.

Easing from the creaking mattress, he snatched a trail of discarded clothing from the floor and dressed in the kitchen. Spying notepad and pencil on the counter, he dashed off an excuse about needing to be home when Jason arrived, signing it simply, "Alec." It was the best he could manage through the choking pressure in his chest.

Laura was still sleeping when he rounded the kitchen corner. He crept past the bed and slipped the note onto his vacated pillow. He hated like hell to hurt her with such an impersonal gesture. But it was better this way, he assured himself, slipping out the front door and closing it softly behind him.

The parking lot was deserted. Alec lifted an eyebrow at the Mercedes gleaming next to his Lexus. Harold was a lucky man. Brenda Lee was one terrific lady. Unlocking his door, he slid inside and struggled with pure irrational jealousy. He, too, wanted to be curled next to a warm loving partner. Next to *his* partner.

Snarling a curse, he slammed the door and started the engine. She was his business partner only. Wouldn't even be that for much longer, in spite of her claim to love him. He clenched the steering wheel and stared at Laura's apartment window.

He'd told her he had nothing to give, warned her not to make him into something he wasn't, damn it. But her absolute trust, her generous sweet surrender, had spoken for itself.

Alec dropped his forehead against the wheel. He'd never known that kind of giving. Had never known a woman like Laura. Kind and funny, brave and strong, a worthy partner to any man.

After learning about his father, Susan had believed him capable of the worst. But not Laura. Laura had listened to his whispered confessions of a childhood spent in fear and misery—and had cried for him. *Cried for him.* She'd insisted he was nothing like his old man. And for a brief moment, he'd almost believed her.

In the reflection of her eyes, he'd felt good and clean and whole for one magical night. He'd lost control and glimpsed heaven. He'd tempted fate and won. But he knew what *could* have happened.

And the knowledge was his personal hell.

Straightening, he backed out of the parking lot and headed for the exit gate. He'd spent the past seventeen years erecting barriers around his seething emotions. Laura had slipped under his defenses in a matter of months. Her love was dangerous, to herself as much as him. He hadn't asked for it and didn't need it.

What he needed was a shower, a cup of coffee and a hug from Jason—not necessarily in that order.

LAURA FLIPPED the sun visor down and checked her makeup in the tiny mirror. The parking garage was dim, but not dark enough to hide the combined damages of two hours' sleep and Houston's vicious humidity.

Damn this heat, damn Sam for having a party on Sunday night and damn Alec for slinking out without even a kiss goodbye!

She blotted her face with a tissue and let her anger rise. If she was angry, she wouldn't cry. And she'd been holding back tears of frustration all morning.

If ever anyone needed to be loved, it was her "unemotional" partner. So much was clear now. She ached for the little boy forced to watch his mother routinely beaten. Ached for the teenager who'd tried to protect her too late. Ached for the man terrified of becoming like his father.

Alec's deliberate insensitivity was his way of driving her off, Laura knew. Every time she got too close to the inner man, he curled up like a porcupine protecting his tender belly. The action was reflexive. But that didn't make the quills sting any less.

She raised the visor, remembering his wild abandon of the night before. Far from being frightened, she'd gloried in his loss of control, for it had freed the passionate soul beneath the cool facade. She longed to be the woman who set the real Alec free forever. Longed for it even more than she wanted a successful career.

The revelation stunned her. When had she changed?

In a rush of insight, several things became clear. A thriving career could enhance her life, true, but hardly fulfill it. A safe home, children, a loving relationship with a good man—these were the things women had craved since the beginning of time. It seemed she was no exception.

In retrospect, she realized her driving ambition had weakened as her self-identity strengthened. Had the motivation to prove herself in business always gone deeper than helping her father financially? Had she really been trying to validate her worth as a woman?

Maybe. One thing was certain. She owed Alec an enormous debt. Apparently she'd have to corner the man in order to thank him. With a last pat to her hair, she slid out of the car, locked the door and headed for the most important confrontation of her life.

All the way to the seventeenth floor, Laura rehearsed opening lines. By the time she entered the agency lobby, she'd memorized her favorite. One look at Brenda Lee's face erased it instantly.

"What's wrong?" Laura asked, her stomach clenching in preparation for bad news.

"Oh, hon . . ." Brenda Lee flashed her a sympathetic look and gestured to an outspread newspaper.

Had someone died? Was she reading the obituaries?

Laura walked forward, her focus on the newspaper. It appeared to be an advertisement, a double-page spread no less. She turned the paper around to face her—and froze.

Impossible. How had this happened?

Slashed across the top of both pages was the huge headline: Finally, A Hotel That Understands Women Travelers. Laura's incredulous gaze dropped down to the Golden Door Hotels logo at the bottom of the page, then rose to scan the copy. Bold subheads highlighted amenities designed for women traveling far from the comfort and safety of home. The appeal was emotional without being patronizing, the layout clean and elegant.

She ought to know. *She'd given final approval on the exact same ad for Regency Hotels the week before!*

"Has Alec seen this?" she asked sharply.

Brenda Lee nodded. "Dragged Harold into his office the minute we walked in. He's got Steve in there, too. I was supposed to send you in the minute you arrived, but I wanted to prepare you first."

"I owe you one," Laura said, studying the ad.

Of course it wasn't exactly the same. The model was blond, instead of brunette. And the subheads were worded a little differently, like before she'd fine-tuned the details. Like her first draft of the ad—

That sneaky bastard!

"Good Lord, Laura, you're white as a ghost. What is it?"

Laura lifted her head and stared, her mind recreating a scene from the past. "I know how this happened. I know who's responsible." She focused on Brenda Lee's worried eyes. "Tom Marsh, my supervisor at Harris, Bates and Whitman, ripped off my ideas."

Delicate blond brows arched. "No offense, sugar, but are you positive? That's a pretty strong accusation."

Remembering how Tom had tossed her layouts in the trash like so many wads of chewed gum, Laura's mouth thinned. "I'm sure."

He'd obviously fished her rough sketches out of the wastebasket after she'd left. It was the only possible explanation. She recounted her rocky history with Tom to Brenda Lee. "He must have panicked after losing the Regency Hotels account, knowing he'd run dry, creatively speaking. I can't believe he went this far, though."

"Can't we sue him or something?"

Brenda Lee's outrage was comforting, but useless. "I don't have any proof. No one else saw me submit the layouts. Tom certainly hadn't asked for them. And after he threw them away, I was too embarrassed to tell anyone." *Except Alec.*

Her awful burden lightened. Alec would take care of this nightmare. He would simply perform his usual strategic magic and force Golden Door Hotels to retract its new campaign. He'd probably mapped out a plan already. She folded the newspaper and stuffed it under her arm.

Brenda Lee reached out and caught Laura's fingers. "You've thought of something, haven't you? Is there anything I can do to help?"

Squeezing Brenda Lee's hand once, she slipped from its grasp. "You're a good friend. Just keep believing in me. I have a feeling I'll need all the support I can get in the next few days."

Brenda Lee's thumbs-up signal got her down the hall and past the curious stares from each doorway. As she neared Alec's office, the rumble of male voices grew louder. From the sound of things, they were not happy campers. It might be wise to stop and get her bearings on the situation.

Poised just out of sight in the hallway, she cocked her head and listened.

"I swear I never talked about the campaign outside the office," Steve said heatedly.

"What about that little red-haired photographer you got so chummy with? Didn't her studio do a lot of work for Golden Door Hotels?" Harold's voice dripped with suspicion.

"So what if it did, Becker? I did *not* leak campaign secrets to the enemy camp! What possible motivation would I have?"

"Oh, spare me the boy-next-door act. Money's the most powerful motivator in the world, isn't it, Alec?"

"Depends on how much you need it," came the quiet answer.

An alarm went off inside Laura's head.

"You mean someone *sold* our ideas?" Steve asked, clearly shocked.

Harold snorted. "You really are a babe in the woods, aren't you? Guess I was a little out of line, pointing a finger at you. But hell—" a newspaper rustled and snapped "—this is not a mere coincidence. Someone in this agency had an ax to grind, a grandmother's operation to pay for, a farm to save. God knows what the underlying reason was to sell us all up the river. The result's the same." He sighed. "We're up the creek, gentlemen."

Laura frowned at the hallway floor. Why was Alec letting Harold jump to conclusions? Why did he assume there was a Benedict Arnold in their midst?

"You've been awfully quiet, Alec," Steve said. "Do you know something you're not telling us?"

The silence stretched a tad too long.

Oh, no.

Steve hissed in a breath. "My God, you know who's responsible for this ad, don't you?"

"The issue here is not who's responsible, but what we're going to do about it," Alec said.

Please let me be wrong.

"I wish Laura would get here," Harold said. "Where the heck is she, anyway?"

There was her cue. Drawing a deep breath, she walked forward and stepped through the doorway. "I'm right here."

Three pairs of eyes widened in surprise. If she hadn't been focused solely on one, she might have missed the hostile suspicion swept quickly beneath lowered lashes.

But she did see it. And deep within her something fragile, and infinitely precious, shriveled and died.

CHAPTER FIFTEEN

ALEC FLIPPED through the emergency plan on his desk. A week ago, he would have bet his prized Silverado that Hayes and McDonald Advertising was finished, along with Regency Hotels' breakthrough campaign. But damned if the new marketing strategy didn't surpass the original.

Rubbing his bleary eyes, he sank back against soft leather and allowed himself to relax. God, he was tired. A good kind of tired, though, filled with satisfaction from a job well done. The entire staff had been putting in twelve-hour days without complaint.

As of this morning, all previously booked media had been canceled or rescheduled. The broadcast tapes and composed ads had been recalled for modifications. The Regency Hotel general managers had been calmed and given temporary instructions. Spirits were hopeful, instead of defeated. All thanks to Laura.

She'd organized the staff into teams and assigned a problem to each, giving complete autonomy to find solutions. There was no time, she'd pointed out, to use conventional corporate planning methods. They needed to act *now*.

Acknowledging the need for results, Alec had gritted his teeth and hoped for the best. The joke was on him. Instead of total chaos, he'd seen professionals working cohesively toward a common goal. Just like Laura had predicted.

Mentally flinching, he remembered the morning after their lovemaking. The morning he'd opened a newspaper at his breakfast table, seen the Golden Door Hotels ad and struggled for a reasonable explanation.

Damn his accurate memory! It had faithfully replayed the conversation he'd overheard between Laura and her brother.

Couldn't you hold off until August? she'd asked, referring to the sale of a valuable stallion. Scott's voice had sounded weary and resigned. *August is too late, I'm afraid. The bank has given us two extensions already. The loan committee won't approve a third...*

Alec rose from his chair, walked to the window and jammed both hands in his pockets. The blazing June sun penetrated the tinted glass, creating a wall of heat no air conditioner could combat.

What the hell was he supposed to have thought, considering what he'd heard? His buy-out settlement would obviously come too late to help Laura's family. She needed money now. Then, too, she probably resented leaving him at the end of their partnership with a prize like the Regency Hotels account. Selling campaign secrets would sure as hell lower the account's value. And it was exactly the sort of thing a vengeful woman might do.

But not Laura.

Swearing, he turned from the window and jingled his change. When Laura had walked into his office later that same morning, she'd noted his expression and stared at him like a kicked dog. He'd known immediately she was innocent. But he'd let her assume otherwise.

It would be much easier to keep his distance if she despised him, if she finally admitted he was bad news—an explosive waiting to detonate.

"Alec, you in there?" Steve's voice jerked him back to the present.

He turned toward the intercom speaker. "Yeah, what's up?"

"Can you come to the art room a minute? I just finished the print-series revisions."

"On my way."

He headed down the hallway to the undisputed hub of the agency. Ever since Laura had bought the round granite-topped table from a disbanded law firm two weeks ago, the conference room had become the site of all major agency decisions. She insisted that this table, unlike the more traditional rectangular shape, fostered productive communication and team spirit. For his own part, he enjoyed the excuse to rub elbows with the woman he'd come to respect as much as desire.

Harold, Brenda Lee, Sharon, Laura and Jim stood huddled around Steve's work, blocking the art director from view. Since Laura's back was to the door, Alec indulged in a long hungry look.

Not smart.

She wore red pumps, a slim tomato red skirt and a billowy white poet's blouse. The combination of modern sleekness and romantic ruffles intrigued him, like the woman herself. As she leaned forward and propped her elbows on the table, the red fabric cupped and molded her bottom like a lover's hands.

Definitely not smart.

He dragged his gaze upward. "Is this a private party or can anyone come?"

Laura's spine stiffened.

Ignoring the queer little twist in his chest, he walked forward and slipped into the gap Sharon had opened up. Conscious of Laura inching as far away from his left side as possible, he waved for Steve to continue his discussion of a layout.

Brenda Lee glared at Alec across the table. She'd caught him in the hall two days ago and torn into him, relating Laura's theory about how the Regency campaign had been stolen. He hadn't admitted he'd already deduced who the culprit was. Brenda Lee would have told Laura immediately.

Steve looked up from the magazine layouts and turned them toward Alec. "We won't have to take a single new photograph, can you believe it? And since we already have the color separations, these puppies can go out in a matter of days, not weeks."

The elegant somewhat generic advertising strategy of before had been abandoned in favor of a more direct no-nonsense frankness. It was risky, but a hell of a lot more interesting, in Alec's opinion. He reached forward and pulled one of the magazine layouts closer.

A large photograph featured a woman applying mascara at a well-lit vanity table in her Regency Hotel room. A cup of coffee steamed beside scattered makeup on the table. In the distance, stylish clothes could be seen laid out on the bed. Matching pumps and an attaché case sat on the floor at the foot of the bed.

A penciled headline above the photograph read Remember The Dark Ages When Hotels Catered Only To Men? Centered below was the headline We've Finally Seen The Light. Copy focused on the custom-built vanity area that was a standard feature in every room, just one more way Regency Hotels was the preferred choice of women travelers.

Alec raised his head. "I don't remember talking about this one. Is it new?"

Steve nodded. "Laura came up with it yesterday."

Against his left thigh, Alec felt the faint stirring of Laura's hip. His groin reacted as if she'd stroked him with her long delicate fingers. He ground his teeth.

Across the table, Jim pushed up thick glasses, blinked owlishly and cleared his throat. "Um...maybe this is out of line, but what's the big deal about a lighted vanity, anyway?"

"Isn't that just like a man?" Brenda Lee drawled. "Try checking your compact mirror after leaving a hotel and seeing Bozo stare back. Then you'd understand how important a well-lighted mirror is to a woman."

Alec laughed along with the rest of the impromptu gathering. He couldn't deny the increased camaraderie since he'd loosened the reins of command. Once again, Laura had been right. Too much control stifled creativity. Allocating responsibility had not only eased his stress, it had also been a damn sight more productive than trying to make every decision himself.

Harold gestured to the boards. "This series will be perfect for *Vanity Fair* and *Working Woman,* don't you think, Alec?"

"I agree." He glanced down at the cloud of chestnut hair to his left, and remembered it mink-soft against his skin. "Nice job, Laura."

Profile rigid, she nodded once.

And people said *he* was aloof and unapproachable. Hell, she could give him lessons. He pushed back from the intimate circle, perversely angry at the coolness he'd encouraged.

"Looks good to me, Steve. We'll need Sam's approval to go into final production, of course, but I don't foresee any problem. He loved the preliminary concepts."

"When is he due for your meeting?" Steve asked.

"About four o'clock. Can these be tightened up by then?"

"No sweat. I'll have them on your desk by three."

Alec nodded and cast a meaningful look around the ring of faces. "We'll leave you alone so you can get to work."

Like waves from a dropped pebble, the circle widened and disappeared. Satisfied, Alec continued on to the reception area and picked up a stack of mail from the desk. Ripping into the production invoice for a TV spot, he caught a whiff of lavender at the same time someone tapped his shoulder. He gathered his defenses and turned.

Laura stepped back, her expression wary. "I wanted to talk, but I can see this is a bad moment."

This was the first time in a week she'd spoken to him voluntarily. "No, I can look at this later." He threw the invoice down in disgust. "We've salvaged most of the campaign, thanks to you. But there are some things, like that weekend-escape TV spot, that just won't fly. Some of the vendors might cut us some slack on payment, but most will be nipping at our heels in thirty days." He glanced at Laura's thoughtful expression and shut up.

"That's one of the things I wanted to talk with you about, Alec." She nodded toward the invoice. "You've been supplementing the operating account with your personal money, haven't you?"

His mind scrambled for an answer she would accept.

She narrowed her eyes. "I've reviewed the receivables and payables with Jim, so don't bother denying it."

He hedged. "So what if I am?"

"It's not part of our agreement, that's what."

"Neither is dealing with account espionage, but that doesn't seem to bother you." Wincing at the flash of pain in her golden eyes, he made his voice cynical. "The company will pay me back every penny over time. I always collect my debts."

"And I pay back mine," she snapped. "I expect you to subtract your personal investment from the buy-out sum, whatever it happens to be at the end of August. Agreed?" Her chin lifted.

"Agreed." How had he doubted this woman's integrity for even an instant?

His gaze followed the soft white ruffles of her V-neck blouse to where they met at a point. The fabric trembled with the force of her heartbeat. "Laura, I—"

"Don't."

The choked whisper brought his head up. Her stare was smoky with memory—and accusation.

He glanced away, knowing she was right. "What else did you want to talk about?" In control now, he met her eyes squarely.

She furrowed her brow.

"We talked about *one* of the things on your mind," he reminded her. "What was the other?"

Distaste, embarrassment and rebellion flickered like heat lightning across her face. "I wanted to... I promised Jason I'd ask..." She inhaled deeply, obviously struggling for composure.

Fear clenched his stomach. "For God's sake, *what?*"

"Can you go on a picnic with me and Jason on Sunday?"

HE'D NEVER LAIN on a grassy slope and watched the stars come out before. He'd never listened to a chorus of crickets, bullfrogs and cicadas in full symphony, either. But then, today had been filled with firsts.

Alec dropped his gaze to Jason and Laura, who duplicated his sprawled position on the blanket. Hands clasped behind heads and ankles crossed, they stared at the darkening sky as if a movie was about to start. Jason reached down, slapped a mosquito, and tucked his hand back under his head without taking his eyes off the panoramic screen.

Contentment, warming as mulled wine, seeped into Alec's bones. He turned his face upward, his mind on inner thoughts.

For one perfect afternoon, he'd experienced what a family *could* be. He'd eaten pimento-cheese sandwiches salted with blowing dust and enjoyed them more than the finest rack of lamb. He'd swung on a swing set for the first time in twenty-five years and realized it still made him laugh. He'd caught a perch in the lake with a cane pole and felt as proud as if he'd landed a trophy marlin.

There'd been no fighting, no gut-clenching anger threatening to explode into violence. Only laughter and play and joy. Lots of joy.

Jason and Laura adored each other. Watching them together tapped a deep tenderness, a well of protectiveness that was both his rebirth and ruination. Because the more he cared, the greater he feared.

Alec's muscles slowly tensed, his peace fading with the diminishing daylight. Today had been wonderful, a fairy tale to cherish. But the day was over. Reality was raising a small boy who required every ounce of self-control he possessed. He simply didn't have enough to spare for a woman who shattered his restraint as easily as cracking an egg. The thought of what might spill out terrified him.

Jason was stuck with him.

But Laura wasn't.

"See that bright star, Jason?" Laura pointed to a dot glowing in the twilight. "That's really the planet Jupiter. You can't see them, but there are four little moons surrounding it."

"For real?" Jason squinted at the single pinpoint, obviously doubtful. "How do you know?"

"My father showed me. He used to set up his telescope on nights like this and let me look at all the planets and constellations. If I stood on my tiptoes, I could just reach the viewer."

"You were prob'ly smaller'n me, huh? I bet *I* could reach it."

Laura shot Alec an amused glance before answering seriously, "I'll bet you could, too. Although I was about your age when he first started teaching me. We would sit on the back porch for hours at a time." Her voice grew absent. "I think it gave him some peace after losing Mother."

"Where'd you lose her?"

Obviously startled, Laura rolled to one side, propped her head in hand and regarded him gently. "She went to heaven to be with God."

"Like my mom," Jason said matter-of-factly. "Were you sad?"

Laura's eyes met Alec's once again, questioning. He nodded, ashamed of himself. He'd been too busy coping with his own disrupted life to think about a small confused boy. He'd never once talked with Jason about his mother's death.

"I was very sad at first," Laura admitted. "Then my dad told me she was happy and healthy in heaven with Grandma and Grandpa Davidson, and I felt a lot better." She reached out and rubbed Jason's stomach in slow circles with her fingertips. "What about you, sweetheart? Were you sad when your mom went to heaven?"

He lifted his elbows an inch. "I guess. Mostly I was scared. Nanny Howard cried an' said she couldn't take care of me anymore 'cause I had to go live with my dad. I didn't like bein' alone."

Laura's hand stilled. Jason instantly slipped an arm from beneath his head and held it out for her attention. She continued her soothing ministrations from wrist to elbow. "You don't feel alone now, do you?"

Like a lizard being stroked, Jason's eyes drifted shut. "Nope. I got Dad now. An' you. You're better 'n Miss Howard." He yawned, ending with a sleepy smile. "Can you teach me the consuh...consuhla..."

"The constellations?" she asked huskily.

"Yeah, those. Can you teach 'em to me sometime?"

Starlight illuminated her stricken eyes.

Alec fought the urge to tell Jason of course she would teach him; she would teach him that and a thousand other things throughout his life. Swallowing painfully, Alec clamped his lips together and looked up.

"We'll see," came Laura's throaty whisper. "Just look at those stars now, would you?"

During the last ten minutes, it was as if someone had unfurled a vast bolt of ink black velvet, then scattered a fifty-gallon bin of diamond chips from end to end. A dazzling sight.

Too bad his vision kept blurring.

LAURA SIGNED her name with a flourish, slipped the thick stack of papers into an envelope and dropped the plain brown square into her desk drawer. Exhaustion battled with relief.

She'd been pushing her stamina to the limits, arriving
at the office before seven and staying past midnight. Other
than meeting an old friend for lunch to call in a marker,
she hadn't eaten a decent meal in the three days since the
picnic. When her stomach had grumbled too loudly to ignore, she'd simply grabbed a snack out of the vending
machine and continued working.

Tonight she would pick up something on the way home.
Something nice and healthy—like a greasy burger and
fries. She checked her watch. The only thing open at one
o'clock would be a fast-food establishment.

Lifting her arms high, she uncurled her fingers in a
mighty stretch, then collapsed back against the chair.
Alec's phone line glowed, although she couldn't imagine
who he might be talking to at this hour. No doubt he was
waiting to escort her to her car as he'd done the past two
nights. Considering how he avoided her during the day,
she found his chivalry more baffling than flattering.

Suddenly the thought of another tense walk, each of
them avoiding the other's eyes, became unbearable.
Reaching for her purse, she checked his extension line,
slipped off her pumps and padded down the tiled hall to
the lobby. He'd be mad as hell when he discovered she'd
left, but if she didn't put some space between them, there
was no telling how she might humiliate herself.

Easing out the front door, she closed it quietly and slid
into her shoes. The carpet muffled her footsteps to the elevator. She pressed the Down button and watched the
hallway for Alec until the motor whined to a stop. Rushing inside, she let out a grateful breath as the doors closed.

They opened with a soft swish onto the cavernous
lobby. Laura stepped out and headed for the parking garage. Ficus, philodendron and dieffenbachia stood sil-

houetted in the dim light. Absolute quiet enfolded her. Even the maintenance crew had come and gone.

Digging among the debris in her purse, Laura produced her key chain and the palm-size container of mace she'd bought upon arriving in Houston. Thus prepared, she pressed the exit button and slipped out a side door into the clear summer night. Three steps down, a bricked walkway roofed with Plexiglas led to the garage. As she strode forward, a balmy breeze stirred the tendrils surrounding her face. She'd pinned her hair into a loose knot that morning in deference to the heat, but no telling what it looked like now.

Tonight, only a third of the stars visible at Brazos Bend State Park had managed to penetrate the city's cloak of polluted air and electric lights. What a difference forty miles made! Jason and Alec's awe over the jeweled sky had renewed her appreciation for something she'd taken for granted while growing up in the country.

If only she could share her knowledge of astronomy with the two of them. Wishful thinking, she knew. After their wonderful day together, Alec had become as distant as the planet Pluto.

She stepped off brick onto concrete and sighed. Only two more days until the weekend. She could last that long, surely. Tomorrow, she would— *Oomph!*

A beefy hand clamped over her nose and mouth, choking off her air supply and rising scream. Adrenaline blasted through her veins as she was dragged against a massive chest. Driving an elbow into barrel ribs, she rammed her two-inch heel down like a pike. The hand covering her nose slackened. She dragged in a ragged breath. A man's howled obscenity filtered through the roar of blood in her ears.

This can't be happening.

His hand clamped back down against her mouth. Sinking her teeth into flesh, she twisted sharply and raised her can of mace. In the split second before she sprayed, recognition dawned.

"Help!" she screamed, depressing the button.

Jack Brewster, the slime who'd nearly raped Brenda Lee three months ago, clutched his streaming left eye with a bloody hand and knocked her mace, purse and car keys aside with the other. Currents of white-hot agony shot up her arm. Heart slamming, she turned and lurched forward. She had to get back inside the office building. To Alec.

Her feet were cement blocks. Too slow. Too clumsy on the slick concrete.

"Come back here, you *bitch!*"

His tackle caught her ankles. She toppled forward and hit concrete with a teeth-jarring *whoosh*. Mouth working, she gasped silently for air. She couldn't breathe. Her lungs burned. Tears of pain and self-recrimination blurred her vision.

Why didn't I wait for Alec?

Then her lungs inflated. Never had oil and gas fumes smelled so sweet. A dim part of her brain registered that the concrete beneath her stomach was moving. No, *she* was moving. Jack pulled her toward him hand over hand like an anchor.

"I was startin' to think you never went nowheres without that tall fella doggin' your tail. 'Course, now I seen it up close, cain't say as I blame'm none," Jack said, snickering.

Alec wouldn't save her. There was only herself to blame. Only herself to rely on.

"Know what I thought about waitin' for my trial? I thought about what I was gonna do to you and that slut, Brenda Lee, when I got outta jail."

The hands had slipped beneath her dress now. They grasped her thighs and pulled with the strength of a bull. She choked back a scream. He would enjoy knocking her senseless, and her only chance of escape was to remain alert.

"I woulda waited long as it took. But my lawyer, he got me off on a technicality. Ain't America great?" He laughed, an obnoxious donkey bray of sound, then hauled her across his lap. "I got me a van over there. You and me are gonna take a little ride in a minute and have a real good time now that you're cooperatin'." A callused hand slid up over her buttocks, alternately stroking and squeezing.

She closed her eyes and shuddered. If only she had a weapon. Her fingernails would have to do. If she left this garage with him, she was a dead woman.

"At first I was mad 'cause Brenda Lee always had that guy with the glasses hangin' around. Then I seen you up close, with all that wild hair around your face. Man, you were somethin'."

Hair. Laura's eyelids popped open. The ceiling whirled as she was flipped over and inspected hungrily.

"Hell, you're classier 'n that trash, Brenda Lee, and just as hot." He licked thick lips and thrust out his hips. "I'm gonna show you what a *real* man feels like."

With one eye swollen shut and a yellow leer on his broad flat face, he looked grotesque—as ugly as she remembered. She prayed he was also as stupid.

She reached up to pat her head in a coy gesture. "I must look terrible."

His gaze latched onto her uplifted breast. The minute his hand followed, she frantically probed her tumbled hair knot. There! Yanking out a long pin, she looked away and stabbed the two-pronged weapon in the vicinity of his undamaged eye.

Bile rose in her throat as metal pierced something resilient. A high thin scream raised the hairs on her neck. She scrambled off his lap before the sound died.

"I'm gonna *kill* you, you goddamn bitch!" Virtually blinded, he swiped the air like a wounded grizzly.

Laura scuttled backward on hands and knees, panting in shallow breaths.

"You hear me, whore? I'm gonna make you wish you'd never been born a woman." He lunged forward as she leapt up.

"Nooo!" she wailed, straining against the vise grip on her foot. Oh, God, he was too strong! She couldn't resist much longer. What a senseless way to die. Alec would blame himself, and Jason... Jason would be devastated at losing another woman he loved.

In one final surge of defiance, she threw her full weight forward, stumbling to catch her balance when her foot jerked free. She glanced back in shock.

Jack sat holding her leather pump like some macabre Prince Charming from hell. She fought down an hysterical bubble of laughter, kicked off her other shoe and ran.

Pounding down the brick walkway, she tuned her senses behind her. Jack's maddened roar of frustration curdled her blood. The entry door seemed miles away. Her muscles screamed in a hundred different places. Pebbles jabbed the soles of her feet. Her breath wheezed raggedly.

She leapt up the steps and hit the metal bar at full speed, recoiling in a daze of pain. *Locked.* A security panel to the right displayed rows of buttons, similar to a telephone. The code. What was the entry code? Numbers tumbled in her mind, none of them falling into place. She glanced wildly over her shoulder.

Jack was staggering toward her in a nightmarish parody of Frankenstein's monster's walk.

Laura spun back and stabbed five buttons. A red light winked mockingly. Jack was yelling, but she couldn't make out his words over the jackhammer in her chest. What was it Alec had said about the code? Something about food. Remember Jason's favorite food.

Pizza!

Punching the code with trembling fingers, Laura sobbed with relief when a green light flashed. She shoved her hip against the bar and burst inward, whirling to slam the door shut. The automatic door closer resisted her efforts to hurry. *Come on, come on.* She peered through the narrowing gap in horror as Jack groped his way up the steps and launched himself toward the door. The blessed click of a lock sounded only an instant before a jarring crash shook the frame.

She was safe.

Sinking to the floor on rubbery legs, she stared vacantly into space. The bar outside the door rattled several times, then stopped.

Alec. She had to get to Alec. Her body felt boneless. Cold. She would never be able to stand, much less get to the seventeenth floor.

Setting her jaw, Laura pushed against the floor and slowly rose.

CHAPTER SIXTEEN

ALEC HUNG UP the phone, templed his fingers and smiled. Good thing Jason was on a camping trip with the Thompsons. Working late definitely had its advantages.

On a hunch, Alec had caught Daniel Merrick in his office at 7:30 a.m. London, England, time during the lull before the storm of a busy day. If their meeting next week went as well as the conversation they'd just had, Hayes and McDonald Advertising would take a giant leap in billings.

He owed Sam a big one. Over the years, the hotelier had made a point to cultivate relationships with the more prominent businessmen frequenting Regency Hotels. And Daniel certainly qualified.

When Sam had casually mentioned he'd referred Hayes and McDonald Advertising to the vice-president of Littlefield, Ltd., Alec had been thrilled, but cautious. The London-based company was an international retail giant, way out of league for a midsize agency. But it seemed the company was seeking four American regional agencies to coordinate efforts with its London agency of record. Hayes and McDonald Advertising was now in contention for handling the Southwest region. Alec would call a staff meeting tomorrow and—

A door clattered open. He shot to his feet. "Laura?"

Silence.

Checking his watch, he frowned. The cleaning crew had finished hours ago. He entered the hallway, trotted past Jim's and Harold's offices and stopped at the next doorway. Damn.

"Laura?" he called louder.

A small choked sound from the reception area tunneled straight to his heart, stopping it cold. Panic jump started the muscle into overdrive. He ran up the hall and paused, bracing one hand against the curved archway as the blood drained from his face.

"Laura?" he whispered.

She stood swaying on shoeless feet, in the middle of the lobby. Black oily stains smeared the front of her dress from collar to hem. The remains of a loosely wound bun sagged drunkenly over one ear, the majority of hair having slipped free to tangle about her shoulders. Her huge golden eyes, stark with shock, stared above cheeks blanched of any color save streaks of drying blood.

Blood. Alec fought a wave of dizziness and stared, numb with horror and guilt. Blood again. The women in his life seemed destined to wear it.

Laura's knees sagged.

Shaking off his paralysis, he rushed forward and crushed her against his chest. "What in God's name happened?"

A small whimper escaped her throat.

He stroked her back. "Shh. It's all right. You're safe."

Tremors rippled through her body. Her ribs rose and fell with her quick panting breaths.

His mouth tightened. "What happened?"

She burrowed her face into his shoulder and shook her head.

"Laura, I've got to know what happened so I can help you." He pulled back and rubbed his thumbs against her forearms. "Take a deep breath. There, that's it. Now, one word at a time."

"I wa...wa...was..." Her chin quivered between stammers. "A...t-t-tacked!" She doubled over, fist to her mouth, obviously fighting off nausea.

He massaged her shoulders and helped her straighten, a terrible coldness lending calm to his voice.

"You were attacked by a man?" At her mute nod, the ice inside him broke, shattered by a burst of hot violent fury unlike any he'd felt before. "Did he hurt you?"

Her shrug and half sob could have meant anything.

He unclenched his jaw. "Did you see who it was?"

She nodded. "J-Jack B-B-Brewster." Her eyes reflected inner revulsion. "He was h-hiding in the g-garage."

Alec spun around and slammed his fist on the reception desk. "Damn it! I thought that slime bucket was behind bars." The idea of the big ugly brute touching Laura—or worse—hazed his vision. He picked up the phone receiver and started to dial.

Laura stumbled forward and clutched his arm. "No police! N-not yet."

The haze lifted and hovered, waiting to drift back and enfold him completely. "I have to call, Laura. He'll get away."

"He can't s-see. I s-stabbed him. In the eye. W-with my hairpin."

Alec stared in amazement. She'd defeated a man twice her size with only her wits and courage. Even so, she shook so hard he heard her teeth rattle.

Without a word, he swung her into his arms, carried her to the couch and settled her on the soft leather. When he tried to straighten, she clung to his neck.

"D-don't call the police. Don't leave me. Promise," she begged.

"I promise," he said, removing her hands with a reassuring squeeze. "Lie still. I'll be right back."

Alec raced down the hallway to the small kitchen. As he gathered the items he needed, his mind prioritized actions. The police would have to be called, but first he would make Laura as comfortable as possible and determine the extent of her injuries. If she'd been raped, he'd bypass the cops altogether and go after the son of a bitch himself.

He squeezed a dishcloth in his hands, wishing it was Jack's neck. One way or another, Alec would make sure the bastard never hurt another woman again.

LAURA OPENED her eyes at Alec's approach and struggled to sit up. He set a loaded plastic tray on the coffee table and sat beside her, studying her with brittle intensity.

"Some of your color is back. Feeling better?"

"A little." She tried to smile and winced at the sharp stab of pain in her head.

He reached over and uncapped the bottle of Chivas Regal sitting on the tray. Splashing an inch of Scotch into a small juice glass, he held the liquor under her nose. "Drink this. I personally guarantee it will put roses in your cheeks—or hair on your chest."

This time she managed a tiny smile. As she took the glass, her fingers brushed his. The odd little catch in her heart had nothing to do with lingering fear and everything to do with Alec's worried regard. She knocked back the liquid fire in one swallow, then shuddered.

"Tastes like turpentine."

He set her glass on the tray, picked up the wet dishcloth and began cleaning her face. "John Bates insisted I learn to tolerate the stuff. Said it was a man's drink, and together with playing golf, indispensable to doing business. After a while, I learned to like it." He snorted. "Drinking Scotch, that is."

She let her eyes drift shut and hugged her stomach. The liquor hadn't vanquished her terrible chill.

"You're going to have a hell of a bruise here tomorrow," Alec said after a moment, dabbing gently at the lump on her forehead.

Numb, she barely noticed the pain.

"Want to tell me now how you got it?"

"P-probably when he tackled me." Her teeth chattered intermittently. She felt so cold. So violated. Felt huge paws grasping her ankles, pulling her backward into terror....

Alec dropped the cloth and grabbed her hands. "Hang in there, Laura. We've got to call the police, but I need to know whether to ask for medical assistance. Do you understand?"

She flushed, but held his gaze. "Yes. I'm a little bruised, but he didn't rape me. Jack could use a good doctor, though." Memory of the nightmarish struggle came surging back, swamping her in horror. "Oh, Alec, it was so *awful*."

In one smooth motion, he pulled her forward and hitched her onto his lap. She curled one arm around his neck and snuggled her cheek against his heart. Toying with the buttons of his shirt, she sighed. If only she could stay here forever, his hard muscles cradling her, his heat surrounding her, his end-of-day scent more man than cologne. If only she could stay, she would ask nothing more from life.

His arms tightened. "What happened, honey?"

The endearment unraveled her. Haltingly, she recounted her experience from the time she'd left the building to the impact of Jack's body against the locked door. By the time she finished, the contrast between remembered terror and the safety of Alec's arms shattered her calm.

"It's time to call in the hounds," Alec pronounced, his voice hard and clipped. He sat forward and prepared to slide her off of his lap.

Laura wound her other arm around his neck and clung. What did her pride matter, when life could be snuffed out in an instant? Each moment was a gift. She was in the arms of the man she loved. And she needed to feel alive. Needed desperately to replace the feel of Jack's touch with Alec's.

"All I could think about all the time I thought I might die was getting to you," she whispered in his ear. Taking the lobe of his ear in her mouth, she nibbled the soft skin.

"What are you doing?"

She trailed kisses down his neck, pulling his starched collar away with one finger to give her better access. His pulse throbbed hotly against her mouth. She flicked his skin with her tongue and thrilled at the corresponding surge beneath her thighs.

"Jeez, Laura. What's gotten into you?" His voice sounded strangled. He clutched a fistful of her hair and tipped her head back.

Neck arched, she watched him under lowered lashes. "Nothing . . . yet. I'm hoping you'll change that."

As awareness dawned, his fingers loosened. It was all the invitation Laura needed. She was beyond shyness, beyond anything but the swollen heat, the musky smell, the leashed power of Alec. Her hands reached for the top button of his shirt. He intercepted them by grasping her wrists.

"Laura, *think*. It's the danger, the whiskey. I don't want to take advan—"

She stopped his protests with her mouth. Take advantage of her? She almost laughed. But the taste of him, the texture of his lips and teeth and tongue was so glorious she moaned, instead. It was a long drugging moment before she realized he wasn't participating.

Laura drew away to study him. They were both breathing hard. His mouth might be passive, but his eyes could have smelted ore. Reassured, she reached up and clasped his cheeks.

"Don't think. *Feel*," she ordered, pulling him down to her lips.

Her hands worked two buttons loose on his shirt and burrowed through the crisp hair on his chest. She squirmed against the ridge in his lap and nipped and laved and teased his lips until she thought she would die if he didn't kiss her back. He twisted his head and broke the connection.

"Laura, stop," he pleaded, his voice and expression tortured. His chest rose and fell like ocean swells. "This isn't what you want. I can't give you what you want."

"Then give me what I need."

Running her palms down his ribs, she hit his belt, pulled his shirt free and fumbled with his buckle. At the first tug of his zipper, Alec groaned.

The next instant she was lifted, turned and dropped on her back against the couch. He followed her down and pressed her into the cushions from chest to toe.

Dazed, Laura reached up and stroked his jaw. "No strings. No regrets. I promise."

His eyes darkened. "You'll regret it," he predicted in bleak tones. Then his mouth slanted hungrily over hers, making up in spades for his earlier lack of participation.

If she lived to be a hundred, she would never forget how this man made her feel. He didn't want the words, so she told him with her body.

I love your hair, said her fingers, caressing the curls at his nape. *I love your strength,* said her palm, gliding over contoured muscles in shoulders and arms. *I love your kisses,* said her lips, softening beneath his devouring mouth.

He lifted his head a fraction.

"I love you, Alec," said her heart, bursting with emotion. Only when he pressed two fingers against her lips did she realize she'd spoken aloud.

"Don't talk. *Feel,*" he ordered, lowering his mouth once again.

It was as if he'd been playing and had decided only now to get serious. His tongue twined, meshed and explored with succulent greed. One hand found her breast and kneaded gently, the other plucked the remaining pins from her hair and plunged deep.

She forgot Jack Brewster, forgot her aches, forgot her very name. The only things existing were Alec and the sensations vibrating her body like a plucked harp. The throbbing below her belly begged for appeasement. Her pelvis tipped up and pressed.

Alec caught his breath, then sat up, pulling her with him. He unbuttoned his shirt with sharp jerky movements and shrugged it off. Stripping off his belt, he sent it sailing across the room like an airborne snake. He yanked off his shoes, then peeled down pants, underwear and socks in one movement to stand unabashedly naked in front of her.

She couldn't help him remove her clothes. She was too entranced with the sight of powerful legs, broad chest and muscular arms. And of course, that other part of him. The part that jutted and pulsed and elicited an empty ache between her thighs in response.

Careful of her bruises, he pressed her gently back down against the cushions, a sacrificial lamb at the altar. The shock of her bare skin against soft leather widened her eyes. The shock of his hot mouth on her nipple closed them.

With hands and lips and tongue he worshiped her, leaving no part of her body untouched. She trembled beneath his tender homage. Her body twisted, her moans grew more tormented. She fisted her hands in his hair and tugged, beseeching him to join her. "Alec, please."

Suddenly he lunged up, warm and solid and heavy. She parted her legs and gasped at his single powerful thrust. Quivering, she watched his taut beautiful face as he struggled to give her time to adjust. But her body had been well prepared and demanded satisfaction. *Now.*

She ground against him until he threw his head back and growled. When finally he looked down, his gaze mesmerized, dominated, glittered with primal possession.

"Hold on," he warned.

The ride was wild and rough and incomparably thrilling. It carried her up and up and up until the sweet agony had her clawing at his back. Just when she thought the climb would destroy her, Alec reached between their bodies and found the hub of her femininity. One flick, two, and she careened over the edge in a whirling exhilarating fall that made her cry out in wonder.

Alec followed, groaning his pleasure into her throat as he convulsed within her body.

Laura lay silent, waiting for her heartbeat to slow and reality to return. She wanted . . . she wanted a lifetime of such moments. She wanted more than he could give her. Alec had been right about that.

But he'd been dead wrong about the other.

Never in a thousand lifetimes would she regret what had just happened between them.

ALEC FLIPPED ON the track lighting and watched the Hayes and McDonald Advertising logo light up. If anything, the sight gave him more pleasure now than during those first heady weeks of opening the business. Funny how a logo without the name "Hayes" would seem strange now, when not so long ago it would have thrilled him.

Jason nudged through the doorway. Alec caught his shoulder as he slipped past. "Where do you think you're going?"

"To the art room. I'm gonna draw."

"You know the rules. Everything is to be put back *exactly* like you found it. And no touching anything you don't have permission to play with."

"Yes, sir."

Hiding a smile at the boy's angelic expression, Alec released Jason's shoulder and watched him race off down the hallway. Having free run of the place would keep him occupied on this rainy Sunday while Alec caught up on billing.

Moving to the reception desk, he sorted through a thick stack of mail and messages. One would think he'd taken a week off, instead of only Friday afternoon. Not that he regretted his action. Nothing had been more important than preventing Jack Brewster from getting off completely free this time. Alec had spent hours with his lawyer making damn sure the bastard didn't. Laura had no idea, of course. She'd just been thankful Jack was behind bars.

Justice was closing in on another scumbag, too, Alec suspected. He'd had an interesting conversation with an old colleague at Harris, Bates and Whitman Advertising. It seemed once the initial Golden Door Hotels campaign broke, Tom Marsh hadn't produced a single idea the client liked. The industry had a way of culling the has-beens with cruel efficiency. Stealing Laura's concepts had only postponed Tom's downfall.

Alec returned the pink message slips to their proper slot and tucked the mail under his arm. Unable to resist the pull a moment longer, he glanced at the couch. Of the dozen thoughts twisting in his mind, one steadied and held constant.

He was in love with his partner. And he wanted her to stay.

Heading for his office, Alec paused in the art-room doorway. Jason looked up from the drafting table. One hand clutched a fistful of colored markers, the other rested on a small layout pad.

"Hi, Dad." His smile was as welcoming as if hours had passed, instead of just minutes.

Thank you, God, for giving me Jason. "Hi, son. What are you drawing?"

"A card for Laura, so she'll feel better." Jason had seen the bruise on Laura's face and been told she'd fallen down. "You think she'd like a real card better, Dad? I can't draw as good as the store."

Alec cleared the huskiness from his throat. "No. She'll like it more if you make it yourself," he promised, warmed by the truth of his words.

"Good, 'cause this is gonna be my best heart ever."

The boy bent over the table once more, chewing his lip in concentration, absorbed in his task of love. With a bittersweet smile, Alec walked on to his office.

A large brown envelope propped against the back of his executive chair snagged his attention. Unease prickled his spine. He approached the chair slowly, dropped his mail on the desk and picked up the envelope.

His name sloped in longhand across the front. He would know Laura's elegant handwriting anywhere. With increasing dread, he sat down, opened the flap and pulled out a sheaf of papers.

Centered on the first page was the title "Advertising Campaign, Regency Hotels Final Revisions." The next ten pages were filled with notes on refinements to earlier print and broadcast advertisements, as well as promotional tie-in opportunities for the new campaign developed two weeks ago.

She'd spent a considerable amount of time finalizing these details. But why?

Suddenly nauseous, he flipped to the last sheet, a document of some sort, and scanned the page. Unbelieving, he reread the middle paragraph:

"In order to effectuate an orderly dissolution, my client is prepared to relinquish any and all claims or interest in the Partnership assets and future income, provided you will agree to hold her harmless from all outstanding liabilities...

The legalese blurred together as one fact became clear. Laura wanted to dissolve the partnership! She was prepared, in fact, to hand it over without compensation. The letter slipped from his fingers.

Not work with Laura? Not see her laugh, hear her sass, share her love of life?

According to her lawyer, Alec had ten days to respond to the letter of intent. But surely she wouldn't end things so impersonally?

Grabbing the large brown envelope, he turned it upside down and shook. Sure enough, a small note fluttered out. As he picked up the scrap of paper, a subtle fragrance wafted from its milled fibers. He breathed in the familiar scent of lavender and squeezed his eyes closed. He didn't want to read this. Didn't want to confirm his worst fear. Only the lure of her handwriting overcame his cowardice.

Dear Alec,
I hope you'll find these notes helpful in finalizing details of the Regency campaign. For obvious reasons, I think it's best we dissolve the partnership before our private-contract term has expired. Sam has

agreed to continue using your services with no revisions to the original agency/client agreement. (He doesn't like it, but he'll do it.)

At the last minute, I was simply not brave enough to tell Jason goodbye personally. Please tell him I love him and will be in touch soon.

At this point, the stationery grew puckered and the ink smeared, as if something wet had spattered on the paper. Alec looked away, swallowed several times, then brought the note closer.

You're a good father, Alec. Always believe that. Jason's a very lucky boy. I know I can trust you to explain my leaving so he'll understand.

Best wishes for the success of McDonald Advertising. You deserve it.

Love, Laura
P.S. I don't regret a thing.

Alec stared blindly at the note resting on one thigh. He was so damn tired. Tired of the constant struggle not to feel. When he'd made an agreement with a hotheaded spitfire to form a temporary partnership, he'd never expected to ache so at the actual separation. But then, he hadn't known—really known—Laura at the time.

Outside, the summer storm raged. The darkened windowpane wept a steady stream of raindrops.

LAURA HALVED three ham sandwiches with a butcher knife, added a pickle to each plate and carried them to the chipped formica table. After two weeks at her father's home, the routine was depressingly familiar. So much had happened to her in the past three months. Yet nothing had changed in this old kitchen since the day she'd left for college.

There hung the same blue gingham curtains, faded and in need of a thorough washing. There sat the same ancient gas-burning stove that had given her fits on winter mornings. Even the same clunky refrigerator, one of the first models General Electric had ever manufactured, still hummed valiantly in the corner. Everything was just as it had always been. Dull, dull, dull.

She lifted the hair off her nape and noted its heaviness. She needed a shape-up cut. But finding a stylist in Luling or Gonzales who possessed Marilyn's skill would be next to impossible. Why bother? Who cared?

Letting her hair drop, Laura grimaced as the strands clung to her sticky neck. Of all the modern conveniences, she missed air-conditioning the most. Although the house boasted two window units, one in her father's bedroom and another in the small living room, she knew the electric bills they generated were steep. The last thing she wanted was to cost her father more money now that she was home.

Footsteps on the back porch alerted her to the men's arrival. The screen door twanged open, and suddenly the kitchen shrank to miniscule proportions. She clenched her hands against a wave of claustrophobia.

"Hi, honey. Don't you look pretty." Grant Hayes swept off his sweat-stained hat, tossed it onto the refrigerator and bussed her on the cheek.

Laura forced a weak smile for her father, pleased to see more color in his face. Even with the weight he'd lost, he was a strikingly attractive man.

Whereas Laura and Scott had inherited their mother's golden eyes, their father possessed irises as green as spring leaves. His lean face might have weathered and his mahogany hair silvered, but in Laura's opinion, the changes only enhanced his rugged appeal. As tall as Scott, her father had also been as strong as a bull until his recent heart attack.

"Sit down and quit buttering me up. I already fixed your lunch. And you—" Laura nodded to her grimy brother "—wash your hands and get the milk."

When the men were seated, she turned to Scott. "How's the east pasture? Still holding on?" A movement flashed in her peripheral vision. "Dad," she warned sternly, "you know you're supposed to cut back on sodium."

Caught in midair, Grant threw her an exasperated look and thwacked the saltshaker down.

To Scott's credit, only his eyes smiled. "If we don't get a good rain in the next week, we'll have to burn cactus for the cattle. But after that gives out..." His voice trailed off, leaving no doubt about the dire consequences. The current drought made the ranch's bleak outlook even more dismal.

Laura noticed her father's pinched face and diverted the conversation to safer subjects. As both men wolfed down their sandwiches, she chatted between desultory bites about the vegetable garden reviving under her care, the new curtains she wanted to hang, the roast she'd thawed for dinner. Ignoring Scott's odd expression, she concentrated on her father. He seemed pleased, but tired. If he kept pushing himself this way, he'd wind up back in the hospital.

Crossing her arms, she steeled her voice. "Okay, Dad. You know what the doctor said. I want you to go stretch out on the bed for a few minutes and relax."

A mutinous scowl darkened Grant's face. "Damnation, Laura, I've managed to muddle through the last seven years without your help. Quit treating me like a child."

The heart she'd thought incapable of feeling proved her wrong.

Grant exhaled through his teeth and turned away. When he met her eyes again, his own were contrite. "Aw, hell, sweetheart, I'm sorry. This bum ticker's making me mean as a rattler. You know I'm tickled as can be you're home...don't you?"

I thought so.

"It's just that I want you to know I can take care of myself, if you ever decide to leave." He glanced at Scott, and something passed between the two men. Fingering the saltshaker, he twirled the glass bottom on the table and frowned.

If Laura hadn't known better, she'd have sworn her father was embarrassed.

"After the heart attack, a lot of things fell into perspective for me. I...I was wrong to hope you'd follow in your mama's footsteps, Laura. This ranch was our dream, not yours. She would have encouraged you to follow your own heart. It took courage for you to strike out on your own, and I'm proud of what you've accomplished. Fact is, I always have been." The saltshaker wobbled and stilled. His imploring green gaze held her motionless. "Can you forgive me, honey?"

The invincible Grant Hayes looked...vulnerable.

Overwhelmed by her shifting perceptions, unable to speak past her amazement and tender triumph, she nodded.

Relief flooded Grant's face. Scraping back his chair, he rose and grinned. "Think I'll take that nap now. I have a feeling I'll sleep like a baby." At the kitchen door, he turned. "Confession is mighty good for the soul, Laura. Any time you want to try it, I'll be glad to listen."

Laura stared at the empty doorway until she heard his bedroom door shut. Shaking her head, she got up and reached for the empty plates.

"Just a minute, runt," Scott said, grabbing her wrist.

Laura's stomach lurched. "I've got a million things to do. Can't this wait?"

He snorted. "'Fraid not, chicken. I've kept quiet since the day I drove home the blubbering wreck who used to be my tough little sister. You've had two weeks to pull yourself together. Now sit your fanny down and talk." He pulled downward until she had to either sink to the chair or fracture her wrist.

She sat. "Some woman is going to bring you to your knees one day, Scott Hayes, and when she does, I'll send her a dozen long-stemmed roses." Laura rubbed her wrist and glared at the handsome lout sprawled beside her.

"Yeah, yeah, yeah. Don't hold your breath. And don't change the subject." His penetrating gaze pinned her to the chair. "Just what's with all this Donna Reed crap, anyway? You always hated domestic stuff before."

Laura lifted her chin. "Maybe I've changed."

"Yes, you have," he agreed, his deep voice gentle. "You've become a woman, Laura. A woman who deserves her own life and her own home. Dad doesn't want you to sacrifice that for us, no matter what you might think.''

She reached out and scooted a pickle round and round her plate. When it collided with the uneaten half of her sandwich, she looked up. "When things got bad for H & H Cattle Company, I made a promise to myself that if I couldn't send money home, I would at least help out by sharing the workload. I love this ranch just as much as you do, Scott." The sentiment sounded halfhearted, even to her own ears. With a defiant surge of energy, she pushed back her chair, carried the dishes to the sink and wrapped her sandwich in foil. Twisting the water tap, she attacked the chipped blue plates with a soapy rag.

He strode over and leaned one hip against the counter. "There's something you love more. Some*one* you love more. What happened between you and Alec, Laura?"

Her hands grew still. What happened?

She'd wanted to exorcise his demons, to free him of the past and be a part of his future. Instead, he'd used suspicion and distrust as shields. She knew that now. Knew that as long as Alec thought himself unworthy of her love, he wouldn't accept it. So she'd refused to torture them both by sticking out the remainder of their contract term.

Laura raised her face and met Scott's compassionate gaze. "You know me. It's all or nothing. I gambled and lost."

Suddenly she felt as fragile as a Chinese lantern in a storm. One more word, one more sympathetic look, and she'd shred into tiny pieces and scatter in the wind. Turning off the tap, she wiped her hands on a towel and cleared her throat. "I'll be out in the garden if you need me." Knowing he'd seen her weeding just after breakfast, she avoided Scott's eyes.

After a long pause, he relented. "Sure, runt. I'll tell Dad when he gets up. Take all the time you want."

Slipping out the door, Laura stood on the back stoop, squinted at the noonday sun and swallowed a miserable chuckle. Time. Take all you want, he'd said.

As if she coveted the stuff. As if each minute didn't crawl past, each hour didn't yawn ahead. As if each day she didn't wonder how she'd get through the next.

As if each night she didn't hope she wouldn't.

CHAPTER SEVENTEEN

"COULD I SEE your driver's license, sir?"

Alec passed his wallet through the truck's open window and controlled his urge to squirm. Damn, he hated mirrored sunglasses. They gave him the creeps. He stared at his own grim-faced reflection in the other man's shiny silver lenses and waited.

"Very good, Mr. McDonald. Would you step out of the truck now, please?" The man moved aside, his gray short-sleeved uniform neat and crisp, despite the withering heat. A .357 magnum rested on one hip.

With persuasion like that, Alec sure as hell wasn't going to argue. He opened the door, slid out and watched his Chevy systematically searched for weapons.

Apparently finished, the young man turned, his stern features and shielded eyes reinforcing the impression of an emotionless android. "That should do it, sir. The gate house is straight ahead." Holding the cab door open, he motioned for Alec to climb in, then slammed the door shut. "Have a nice visit."

"Yeah." Alec rolled up the window, started the engine and drove slowly up the narrow road. Have a nice visit. What a joke! As if this were some sort of resort hotel, instead of a state penitentiary.

He could turn back now, before it was too late. Everyone thought he was still in San Antonio pitching a new account. Brenda Lee had practically shoved him out the door yesterday morning in her haste to be rid of him. Not that he blamed her. He'd been insufferable since Laura left.

No one, least of all Alec, had fully appreciated her contribution to the agency until she was gone. Buzzing from office to office, she'd boosted morale and pollinated ideas that blossomed into some of the finest creative work he'd ever seen. Without Laura, work was flat, but bearable.

It was his personal life he couldn't tolerate.

Clenching the steering wheel, he kept his foot on the gas pedal by sheer force of will. He'd been a martyr and a coward long enough. Perhaps after today, he could be the man Laura deserved.

Pulling up at the gate house, he again rolled down the window and provided information to the guard on duty. Five minutes later he'd been cleared to enter the compound. Stomach churning like an outboard motor, he parked the truck and slid out. As a child, confronting his father had often made him nauseous. Age hadn't improved the sensation one whit.

His legs moved him toward the entrance gate as if they belonged to someone else. Inside the towering picket guardhouse, a shadowed figure waved. Seconds later, an angry electronic buzz jolted Alec's heart.

A chain-link gate slowly opened. The sally port enclosure, fifteen feet high and topped with a double spool of razor wire, sat waiting to trap him within. Taking a deep breath, he walked through and stopped. What would his father say after all these years? Would he apologize for making his family's life a living hell? Would he retract the words that haunted Alec to this day?

And what in God's name would he say to his father?

The second buzzer broke his speculation. He moved through the gate and headed for the only bricked structure in the complex. All other buildings were of the metal warehouse variety. One of these functional cheerless dormitories housed Jonathan McDonald. By contrast, Alec's plush Georgian home seemed palatial—exactly the sort of house his father would both covet and sneer at.

Which is exactly why you bought it, pal.

Alec shook off the disturbing thought and entered the one-story office building. Stale chilled air hit his perspiring skin. Shivering, he studied the typical institutional waiting area. A soft-drink machine, two green vinyl chairs and a plastic laminated end table huddled on dingy white linoleum squares. An ivy, gasping for water, drooped over a chipped yellow pot on the table.

A stocky middle-aged woman dressed in a guard's uniform entered from a hallway on his left. Her hard hazel eyes, devoid of all makeup, studied him without interest. She looked entirely capable of subduing any convict who crossed her path.

"You Alec McDonald?"

He dug into his pocket for his roll of Tums. "Yes."

"You'll need a visitation slip." She glanced at the paper in her hand, did a double take, then read it more closely. "Well, if that don't beat all. Johnny-boy has a visitor. I didn't think the old man had any family—still *living,* that is."

Alec winced. Where were those antacids? Pulling out a handful of change, he sifted through for stray tablets.

Oblivious, she gestured to a doorway on the far end of the waiting area. "Take this slip into the chain room. Eddie'll fix you right up."

Alec dropped the coins back in his pocket and reached for the computer printout, startled when she clutched his wrist with the grip of a stevedore.

"That there Johnny is mean as they come. Can't quit fighting long enough to make parole. He gives you any lip, you call Eddie now, hear?"

"Thanks. I'll do that." Much to Alec's relief, she seemed satisfied and released his wrist. He felt her eyes on his back all the way across the waiting area.

Some twenty visitation slots dissected the large rectangular "chain room." Unlike TV-show versions, there were neither telephones nor privacy partitions at each slot. A Plexiglas and wire-screen barrier separated inmates from visitors. Eight conversations were in progress at the moment. Scanning the visitors, Alec guessed there were four wives and/or lady friends, three mothers and a possible lawyer.

Handing his slip to Eddie, Alec grimaced at the trembling paper. He was shaking like a woman, damn it. No, like the sixteen-year-old kid he'd been the last time he saw his old man.

"Have a seat at number eleven, Mr. McDonald. It will take a few minutes to get your father." The brawny guard motioned to a spot between a bleached blonde smacking her gum and a well-dressed man with a briefcase.

Nodding, Alec pulled out the folding metal chair at slot eleven and sat down. God, this was worse than he'd imagined. Good thing he could sit, because his legs wouldn't have held out much longer. His muscles ached from repressing his shivers. His gaze wandered.

After ten minutes, he'd memorized the sign warning visitors to supervise small children, the six soft-drink brands offered in the vending machine and the many flaws of Sue Ann's stingy mother-in-law who wouldn't fork over rent money but could afford weekly manicures. He'd just tuned in to the lawyer's conversation on his right when a door opened on the prisoner's side.

Jonathan McDonald walked through and stared straight at Alec. For one burning moment, their gazes locked as each studied the changes seventeen years had wrought in the other. Surprise and grudging respect flashed in his father's eyes before hostility nudged them aside. Raising one eyebrow at his son, he deliberately turned his back.

Alec released his pent-up breath. The physical changes in his father stunned him. Despite the baggy white prison garb and silver hair, he seemed leaner and younger at age fifty-one than the bloated thirty-four-year-old alcoholic etched in Alec's memory. Years of forced sobriety and prison fare had improved Jonathan's appearance. His belligerent attitude, however, was all too familiar.

Alec's stomach picked up the cues and roiled automatically, instinctively.

After logging in his name and inmate number with the guard, Jonathan turned and sauntered forward, his black lace-up work boots scuffing the linoleum. Pulling out a chair, he sat down and crossed his arms.

"Well, well, well. If it ain't my loving *son,*" he sneered, pronouncing the last word like an obscenity. "Makes me feel all warm and cozy, you visitin' your old pop like this. Leastways, it would have . . . seventeen years ago."

How could Alec have forgotten the contemptuous tone that had always made him want to snap and snarl? "As I recall, you said you never wanted to see my ugly snitch's face again."

"Yeah, well, your testifying against me kind of stuck in my craw for a few years. But bein' a generous man, I forgave you. Anyhow, you ain't so ugly now that you're all growed up."

Deep blue eyes, the legacy of all McDonald men, squinted at Alec in lazy appraisal. "You're bigger'n I thought you'd be. Spittin' image of me, too. Don't say I never gave you nothin', boy." He laughed softly, revealing even white teeth that somehow appeared sinister. "Bet that face gets you laid free."

Alec fought back sick panic. He did indeed bear an uncanny resemblance to the man in front of him. Booze and forty pounds must have distorted the similarities before. "I may look like you, but that's all we have in common."

"That's what your mama used to say. She thought you hung the moon, sure enough. Always braggin' about how smart you were, how perfect." He lowered his voice conspiratorially. "But we know different, don't we, *son?*"

Alec stared, mesmerized by the unholy gleam in his father's eyes. Jonathan McDonald could smell fear a mile away. Alec prayed his staccato heartbeats weren't audible through the Plexiglas. "You don't know anything about me."

"I know all about you, hotshot. You were written up in the *Houston Business Journal* last year. Some joker put the article on my bunk. Let's see if I got this straight." He cocked his head and stroked his chin. "You coasted through college on a scholarship, got a cush job, dipped the boss's daughter and knocked her up. Married her, reorganized her daddy's company, fired a lot of deadbeats and dumped a loyal client for a bigger one."

Alec's hands slowly clenched and unclenched.

"Along the way, you divorced the little woman and then abandoned your brat, too." He raised a mocking brow. "Your mama's probably turnin' in her grave right now. She always did think you were better 'n me. Better 'n me, ha! You're *exactly* like me. I got the mark to prove it." Jonathan leaned forward, parted his cropped hair and revealed a pink jagged scar. "Remember this? You damn near split my head like a pumpkin with that wrench. Would've done it, too, if you'd had any meat on your bones."

Alec's nausea increased at the images flickering like flames in his mind. Pounding fists, maddened blue eyes, battered flesh, heartrending terror and blood...so much blood. The helpless rage of a teenage boy swelled in his breast. His fingers itched for a wrench.

"I should've killed you that day," Alec said low in his throat.

Jonathan's face lit with triumph. "Blood lust, that's what we got, son, you 'n me. Once you've felt it, ain't nothin' any better. Not booze. Not sex. Nothin'. Look at you, for chrissake. You're ready to bust through this glass and tear me apart."

Shaking with the effort, Alec kept his fists in his lap. *You're nothing like your father! You're good and loving and honorable.* Laura's passionate assurance rang through his fevered mind.

"Why'd your fancy wife divorce you, boy? Get a little too rough with her, maybe?" Jonathan cackled knowingly.

I know you won't hurt me. Just as surely as I know Susan's injury was an accident. The throaty feminine voice soothed Alec's fury, pulling him back into rational territory.

"Only reason you're not in this shithole with me is money. That and luck."

Alec shook his head, as if awakening from a bad dream.

Jonathan sniffed. "Yep, if I'd had me a fancy degree and a fancy job, things woulda turned out different. I'd be on top of the heap now, too."

"No, you wouldn't," Alec heard himself say.

Jonathan's double take was almost comical. "The hell you say." He thrust out his chin.

A rather weak chin, Alec noticed for the first time. Details registered fast and furious. The petulant mouth, the flicker of insecurity in narrowed eyes, the soured expression of a petty mean-spirited soul. Seen through the eyes of an adult, this was the face of a bully—not the all-powerful man he remembered.

His voice strengthened with conviction. "You would have looked for the easy way to success and blamed everyone else for your inadequacies. Once a loser, always a loser. Nothing you do or say will change that, *Pop*."

Jonathan's reddened face heightened the silver color of his hair. Gripping the laminated ledge with both hands, he lowered his voice to a biting hiss. "You wise-ass punk! I'd like to hear you say that on this side of the wall. Just wait until I'm outta here, boy. You and yours better look to your backs, 'cause I'll be comin'."

Conversations flowed around them, undeterred by the drama being played out between father and son. Alec was glad of the noise. He leaned forward to within inches of the glass and looked his father in the eye. "I'm only going to say this once, so listen carefully, old man. If you *ever* come near me or my family, I'll split your head open without blinking. You understand me, Pop?"

"You ain't got the guts."

"In case you hadn't noticed, I've got a lot of meat on my bones now. And unlike you, I prefer going up against someone my own size rather than women and children." How had he thought he could hurt Laura or Jason, no matter what the provocation? The very idea made him sick. But protecting them from harm... "Believe me, I'd split you open and laugh doing it."

Jonathan's gaze widened, then faltered.

Sweet liberating triumph swept through Alec as he realized his father not only believed him, but was afraid. The powerful mystical monster was in reality a pathetic cowardly bully, unworthy of stealing another moment of Alec's time or thoughts.

At long last he was free!

Recovering his bravado, Jonathan leaned back and sneered. "Go on, then. Go back to your big house and rich friends. It don't change what you are, boy, and that's trash. Always have been and always will be. We're two of a kind, you 'n me, and don't tell me no different. You always were—"

Alec scraped back his chair and rose, interrupting the venomous flow. "Shut up, Pop. I have it on the best authority—I'm nothing at all like you."

It wasn't the first time Jonathan spewed obscenities at his son's back.

But it was the first time Alec smiled as he walked away.

LAURA STUMBLED toward the barn door. Damn, damn, damn! She would not cry. Not again. She'd watered the garden yesterday with enough tears to ensure a bumper crop of vegetables.

The interior of the barn welcomed her like a dear friend. She clutched the lopsided paper heart against her breast, closed her eyes and inhaled the distinctive scent of new-mown hay, warm horses and ammonia-sharp urine. Knees trembling, she let the dusky embrace soothe her as it had when she was a child.

Evelyn had found the handmade card in Jason's room and mailed it to Laura with a note. The child had not been himself since she'd left. Would she please call or write soon to let Jason know she wasn't mad at him?

Laura opened her eyes and held out the card. He'd misspelled everything, including her name. But he'd labored over the letters without help, cut and colored the paper heart with earnest six-year-old fingers. "I luv u lora" merged into a hopeless blur before her eyes.

He thought she was mad at him. A choked sob racked her body.

Fleetwood nickered her distress from a nearby stall. The mare had a sixth sense where her owner's mood was concerned. Laura had raised the Appaloosa from a foal. Leaving her had been almost as hard for Laura as leaving the two men she loved, although periodic visits home had kept the bond alive.

Slipping the card inside her jeans back pocket, Laura backhanded the tears from her face. She plucked Fleetwood's worn halter from the hook beside her stall, unlatched the door and slipped inside. "Hello, girl. Worried about me?"

Fleetwood whuffled softly, nudged Laura's neck with prickly muzzle whiskers and blasted warm moist breath against her sensitive skin.

She managed a shaky smile. "I love you too, girl."

As well mannered as ever, the mare lowered her head for the halter and followed Laura meekly into the main corridor. Scott's Arabian stud, Twister, whinnied from the barn's largest box stall. When Laura ignored him on her way back from the tack room, he slammed his back hooves against the cedar boards with an explosive double crack.

"Men," she muttered. "Always throwing their weight around."

Minutes later she swung into the saddle and broke free of the barn. Space. She needed space. Scott had been right about her hating domestic chores. She felt smothered in the small clapboard house—but she would die before admitting such petty feelings. She'd had a shot at her dream and blown it. The least she could do was help Scott and her father salvage theirs.

Bypassing the graded gravel road leading to the county highway, she took a deeply rutted track to the west. "You know where we're going, don't you, Fleetwood?" Laura smiled as one black ear swiveled back like a satellite dish. Leaning forward, she patted the sleek freckled neck. "All right, old girl. Let's see what you can still do." Laura tightened her knees and jabbed with her heels.

The mare responded gallantly, erupting into an earth-eating gallop on the smooth flat center between tire ruts. Laura gloried in the whistling wind, the drumming hooves, the awesome power of surging muscles. She raised her face to the broiling sun and, for the first time in two weeks, felt glad she wasn't dead.

After a quarter mile, she sensed the mare tiring. "Whoa, there, girl. That's enough for you today." Slowing Fleetwood to a walk, Laura settled back in the saddle. Everywhere she looked, mesquite trees, cactus and sagebrush threatened to swallow up the grazing land. Scott and her father waged a constant war against the encroachment, but Laura secretly liked the sense of isolation it gave the ranch. She felt like the only person within a hundred miles.

Fleetwood snorted, nodded against the bit and pricked her ears. No doubt she smelled the water ahead. Urging her into a trot, Laura spotted the levee surrounding a one-acre stock tank in the distance. The mare scrambled up the outer bank and then down to the water, sinking deep in the mud to sip from its surface.

After Fleetwood drank her fill, Laura headed for a towering oak tree at the mouth of the tank. Dismounting at the tree's base, she tied the reins securely to a branch.

It was still there, she saw with relief. Her sanctuary. The place she'd run to whenever she needed to dream. And she'd had big dreams then.

Laura tilted her head and examined the weathered structure nestled within the tree's center. How had it fared over the years? She eyed the rickety series of boards nailed into the massive trunk, shrugged her shoulders and started climbing. Midway up, her left boot slipped, ramming her knee into the coarse bark. Glad she'd worn jeans, Laura clamored up the last few boards.

The original structure had been built to last, with walls about six feet high all around. Interlocking branches swaying overhead served as the roof. She swept aside a layer of leaves from the floor with her toe and surveyed the eight-by-ten-foot platform for dry rot. The tree house had survived the elements with surprisingly little damage.

How many hours had she spent here imagining herself in glamorous settings and exciting new places? Too many to count. She sat on the bench her father had built against one wall, hugged her chest and closed her eyes. The rumble of Scott's pickup heading toward the west pasture blended with the droning cicadas. In this place of dreams, all her pretenses crumbled.

Her father and Scott thought she'd sacrificed her happiness for them, that she was noble and unselfish. But they would survive, dignity intact, with or without her help, she knew. In truth, she would have stuck by Alec like a burr on a saddle blanket if he'd so much as crooked his finger.

But he hadn't.

Oh, God, how would she endure life without him or Jason? How would she endure canning vegetables and hanging curtains, instead of breaking new campaigns and reading bedtime stories to an angel? How would she endure the nights, now that her body had known rapture?

She'd experienced more emotional intensity during her short time with Alec than the rest of her life combined. He'd given her so much, really. Shown her that independence, without discipline, lacked purpose and meaning. All she'd given him was a pain in the neck.

Unaware of passing time, Laura rocked back and forth on the bench, her aching hollowness too deep for tears. Eventually little things penetrated her senses. The creaking branches and rustling leaves. The dappled sunlight warming her bare arms. The biting smell of dust and decomposed leaves. Fleetwood's soft nicker. Life went on, whether one enjoyed it or not.

She would endure, and possibly learn to enjoy life again, all the wiser for her experience. But far, far lonelier.

Fleetwood jangled her bit and whinnied. Poor girl. She was probably hungry and couldn't reach the grass with her reins tied high—

"You can climb pretty good—for a girl," the deep familiar voice broke into her thoughts.

Laura froze.

"I've only climbed a tree once in my life, but I suppose I could do it again."

Alec! Her heartbeat galloped like a Thoroughbred. She listened to the squeaking protest of rusty nails strained to the limit. Seconds later, a blue-black crown of hair bobbed into sight, followed by a frowning, sinfully handsome face.

With a loud curse, Alec maneuvered his broad shoulders through the narrow opening and hoisted himself onto the platform. He flicked a leaf off his red polo shirt, dusted the seat of his faded jeans, retied the shoelace of his right sneaker and straightened.

The oxygen left her lungs.

His glossy black hair lifted and fell with the stirring breeze. Her gaze wandered over the planes and angles of his bronzed face, lingered on his sensual mouth and rose to meet his eyes. They were narrowed, bluer than the triangles of sky peeping through the leaves, and fixed with smoldering interest on her lips.

"Hello, Laura."

She stared at the apparition her yearning soul had conjured up out of nowhere.

"You're looking well," he said.

Dazed, she touched her windblown hair, her sunburned nose, her powderless cheeks and silently groaned. "How…" she squeaked, cleared her throat, and tried again. "How did you find me?"

"The Luling feed store gave me directions to the ranch. Scott dropped me off in his truck about a hundred yards from the tank. Your horse gave you away from there."

She didn't know where to look. Those eyes of his were magnetic, narcotic. Settling for the opened neck of his shirt, she watched the rhythmic pulse at the base of his throat. Edging the lower V of fabric, curly black hairs quivered with each heartbeat.

"I've gone to considerable trouble to get here. Aren't you glad to see me?" he asked.

What kind of game was this? Why was he torturing her? As his shirt loomed closer, her nails bit into her palms. She looked at her feet and concentrated on the pain.

"I'm glad to see *you*." His sneakers butted her boots. "I've missed you, Laura."

Her heart lodged in her throat. She trembled, not daring to raise her eyes, not daring to hope. "You'll get over it," she assured him.

"And Jason? Will he get over it? He cried when I told him you'd left."

She curled over as if punched, then drew in a shuddering breath. "That's pretty low, Alec, even for you."

"I'd sink lower, if I thought it would bring you back." His tone was wry, humble, completely sincere. "Come back to us, Laura."

Her mind whirled in confusion. She fought for equilibrium. "Why are you doing this? You don't even trust me."

"I didn't trust myself. I've always trusted you, Laura. I knew right away you weren't responsible for leaking campaign secrets, but it was easier to keep my hands off you when I knew you hated me." He shifted his feet, then stilled. "I went to see my father yesterday."

Her gaze flew upward at that, recoiled from his passionate intensity and dropped to her lap. She couldn't concentrate if she looked at him. And she desperately needed to concentrate.

"He was just like I remembered, Laura, only different. Physically we look alike, and that scared the hell out of me. But then he started talking, and a funny thing happened." The toe of one sneaker rubbed her tooled leather boot in slow circular movements. "I kept hearing your voice, telling me I wasn't really like him at all."

She clasped her hands and held her breath. Tingles shimmered up her shin.

"Pretty soon it was like a veil had lifted, and I was seeing him for the first time. Seeing myself, too. And you were right. I'm not like that bastard. I could never be like that bastard!" His voice rang with triumph. "Would you look at me, please?"

Disappointment crushed her chest. He was grateful. That was why he'd come, to thank her. Self-preservation kept her chin down.

"Stubborn as ever, eh? Okay then, I'll look at you. I don't think I'll ever get my fill of doing that." His voice gentled, deepened to an intimate caress. "Want to know what I see?"

She waited, entranced—and hating herself for it.

"I see a thick mane of hair, the kind a man wants to stare at in the office and run his fingers through at home. I see long beautiful legs, the kind a man wants walking beside him every day and tangled with his at night."

His low throbbing croon matched the sluggish hot beat in her veins. Her gaze rose and snagged on his straining zipper. Blood surged to her face and loins.

"I see cheeks that blush a pretty rose pink and make a man want to know if the skin he can't see is half as lovely. I can still feel your skin in my dreams, like ivory satin. So creamy, so smooth..." He made an odd sound, a cross between a choke and a laugh. "I'm dying here, Laura. *Look at me, please.*"

"Oh, Alec..."

Her face lifted, but she was already being hauled into his arms. She had a brief impression of glittering blue eyes before his mouth covered hers. Laura could no more prevent her uninhibited response than tame Twister's wild spirit. Twining her arms around Alec's neck, she gave herself up to the magic of kissing a man she'd thought never to kiss again. A man she loved more than life itself.

It was Alec who broke away first. Breathing hard, he looked into her eyes. "I tore up the letter from your lawyer. As far as I'm concerned, you're still my partner. The agency needs you, Laura."

The pain caught her by surprise, doubly worse in contrast with the pleasure of seconds before. Her mouth twisted. "The agency will do fine without me. You'll find someone to replace me. There are hundreds of talented copywriters out there—" The sentence merged with Alec's kiss.

After a long moment he lifted his mouth a scant inch. "What I meant was, *I* need you, Laura. I need you to make me laugh when I get too serious." He dropped a kiss on her parted lips and continued as if she wasn't stunned. "I need you to mother Jason and help guide him into manhood." He dipped his head for a longer deeper taste.

"I need you to warm my bed, and give Jason brothers and sisters, and love me, Laura, until I'm old and senile and hard of hearing. *I need you to marry me.*"

Joy exploded throughout her. Still, she bit back her glad cry of agreement.

"What is it? What's wrong?" Alec scowled. "Don't you want to marry me?" His arms tightened, as if to squeeze out the answer he wanted to hear.

Laura pushed against his chest, succeeding only in straining her arms. She glared into his face. "Is there something, maybe, you've forgotten to tell me?"

Honest confusion clouded his eyes.

She would have to spell it out, the dolt. "You seem to admire some of my body parts. And you say you need me. But those things seldom last a lifetime. I'll get saggy and wrinkled, Jason will grow up, someone else will run the agency eventually. You won't need me then. What's to keep you from tottering off with some cute young thing hanging on to your cane?"

He frowned. "That's stupid. I—" He broke off, looking sheepish. "Ah, Laura. I've never told you, have I? But how could you doubt it?"

She grabbed two fistfuls of shirt and shook. "Doubt *what?*"

Grinning, he grabbed her shoulders and shook back. "I love you! I love your smart mouth and smarter brain, your generous heart and loyal soul..." He cocked a brow, eyes sparkling. "Have I finished, yet?"

"No way, pal. I just went through two weeks of hell."

"Me, too," he breathed. Every trace of amusement fled, replaced by heart-stopping tenderness. "I love you, Laura Hayes, because without you, life is calm and predictable and completely, utterly boring. You brought joy and happiness into my life when I thought I'd never experience either emotion again. There's no one else in the world I'd rather be partners with, in business—or in life."

He paused, looking boyish and hopeful. "Did I get it right?"

"Almost. When you say partners, what exactly do you mean?"

"Two halves of a whole, give and take, fifty-fifty. *Equal* partners all the way."

Laura smiled radiantly. "By George, I think you've got it." Wrapping her arms around his waist, she slipped both hands inside Alec's back pockets. The man had some body parts of his own she particularly admired.

When her fingers encountered a small cylindrical object, she frowned. Pulling out a roll of antacids, she leaned back and tossed them up and over the tree-house wall.

"Hey! I need those," he protested.

"Not anymore, you don't." Laura gave him a long sultry look. "Surely we can come up with a more... creative way of relieving your tension, hmm?"

His answering grin curled her toes. "Funny, now that you mention it—" he pulled her close, his gaze filled with delicious promise "—I feel a helluva stress attack coming on."

HARLEQUIN®

PRESENTS
RELUCTANT BRIDEGROOMS

Two beautiful brides, two unforgettable romances...
two men running for their lives....

My Lady Love, by Paula Marshall, introduces
Charles, Viscount Halstead, who lost his memory
and found himself employed as a stableboy by the
untouchable Nell Tallboys, Countess Malplaquet.
But Nell didn't consider Charles untouchable—
not at all!

Darling Amazon, by Sylvia Andrew, is the story of
a spurious engagement between Julia Marchant
and Hugo, marquess of Rostherne—an engagement
that gets out of hand and just may lead Hugo to
the altar after all!

Enjoy two madcap Regency weddings this May,
wherever Harlequin books are sold.

REG5

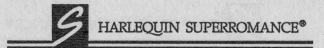

HARLEQUIN SUPERROMANCE®

A Superromance *Showcase* book.

Legacy of Fear
by
Evelyn A. Crowe

Ten years ago, when she was just thirteen years old, she'd been found clutching a bloody knife, her murdered grandmother in her arms. Ten years ago, with her memory a total blank, she'd been committed to a very private, very luxurious sanitarium.

But now she remembers...everything. Except who the real killer is. And now, although she's finally been released, she can't tell anyone about her innocence or even that her memory has returned. Because now she knows she can't trust...anyone.

Not even the man she's falling in love with.

Watch for *Legacy of Fear* in June, wherever
Harlequin books are sold.

SHOW5

HARLEQUIN SUPERROMANCE®

Coming in June 1995

Father Takes a Wife
by Ginger Chambers

"If Sharon wants to be with you, that's all that matters."

Brave words, but it had seemed so straightforward in the beginning. After all, Hallie's wonderful new husband, Kyle, has every right to custody of his daughter. Still, whatever had made Hallie think that Sharon would welcome *her* with open arms?

It's hate at first sight—at least on Sharon's part. And the child's grandparents…! Not content with fighting tooth and nail to retain custody of Sharon, they're actively trying to poison Hallie's mind against Kyle. They're hinting at terrible secrets in Kyle's past—*dangerous secrets.*

Even worse, Hallie has come to realize that her handsome husband *is* keeping secrets.…

Look for *Father Takes a Wife* in June,
wherever Harlequin books are sold.

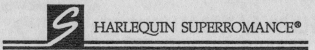

HARLEQUIN SUPERROMANCE®

presents

Major Attraction
by Roz Denny Fox

This June, meet the second of our FOUR STRONG MEN:

Major A. C. Bannister grew up on the mean streets of a Texas town. The army was his one chance to get out, and he took it. He worked his way up through the ranks and now, as head ROTC instructor at a Texas college, he's admired by all the young men—and adored by all the young women. Truly a "major attraction"....

Needless to say, he doesn't appreciate being landed with a new instructor straight out of West Point. Worse, Captain Meredith St. James has a general for a father and an attitude that doesn't mesh with the major's. Her belief in a "new" army, a "softer" army, doesn't sit well with him, either.

He soon learns that St. James isn't as soft as she looks. And that sometimes a major defers to a captain—*especially when he's in love with her!*

**Look for *Major Attraction* in June 1995,
wherever Harlequin books are sold.**

ANNOUNCING THE

FLYAWAY VACATION SWEEPSTAKES!

This month's destination:

Beautiful SAN FRANCISCO!

This month, as a special surprise, we're offering an exciting FREE VACATION!

Think how much fun it would be to visit San Francisco "on us"! You could ride cable cars, visit Chinatown, see the Golden Gate Bridge and dine in some of the finest restaurants in America!

The facing page contains two Entry Coupons (as does every book you received this shipment). Complete and return *all* the entry coupons; **the more times you enter, the better your chances of winning!**

Then keep your fingers crossed, because you'll find out by June 15, 1995 if you're the winner! If you are, here's what you'll get:

- Round-trip airfare for two to beautiful San Francisco!
- 4 days/3 nights at a first-class hotel!
- $500.00 pocket money for meals and sightseeing!

Remember: The more times you enter, the better your chances of winning!*

*NO PURCHASE OR OBLIGATION TO CONTINUE BEING A SUBSCRIBER NECESSARY TO ENTER. SEE REVERSE SIDE OR ANY ENTRY COUPON FOR ALTERNATIVE MEANS OF ENTRY.

VSF KAL

FLYAWAY VACATION SWEEPSTAKES
OFFICIAL ENTRY COUPON

This entry must be received by: MAY 30, 1995
This month's winner will be notified by: JUNE 15, 1995
Trip must be taken between: JULY 30, 1995-JULY 30, 1996

YES, I want to win the San Francisco vacation for two. I understand the prize includes round-trip airfare, first-class hotel and $500.00 spending money. Please let me know if I'm the winner!

Name_____

Address _____ Apt. _____

City   State/Prov.   Zip/Postal Code

Account # _____

Return entry with invoice in reply envelope.

© 1995 HARLEQUIN ENTERPRISES LTD.   CSF KAL

FLYAWAY VACATION SWEEPSTAKES
OFFICIAL ENTRY COUPON

This entry must be received by: MAY 30, 1995
This month's winner will be notified by: JUNE 15, 1995
Trip must be taken between: JULY 30, 1995-JULY 30, 1996

YES, I want to win the San Francisco vacation for two. I understand the prize includes round-trip airfare, first-class hotel and $500.00 spending money. Please let me know if I'm the winner!

Name_____

Address _____ Apt. _____

City   State/Prov.   Zip/Postal Code

Account # _____

Return entry with invoice in reply envelope.

© 1995 HARLEQUIN ENTERPRISES LTD.   CSF KAL

OFFICIAL RULES

FLYAWAY VACATION SWEEPSTAKES 3449

NO PURCHASE OR OBLIGATION NECESSARY

Three Harlequin Reader Service 1995 shipments will contain respectively, coupons for entry into three different prize drawings, one for a trip for two to San Francisco, another for a trip for two to Las Vegas and the third for a trip for two to Orlando, Florida. To enter any drawing using an Entry Coupon, simply complete and mail according to directions.

There is no obligation to continue using the Reader Service to enter and be eligible for any prize drawing. You may also enter any drawing by hand printing the words "Flyaway Vacation," your name and address on a 3"x5" card and the destination of the prize you wish that entry to be considered for (i.e., San Francisco trip, Las Vegas trip or Orlando trip). Send your 3"x5" entries via first-class mail (limit: one entry per envelope) to: Flyaway Vacation Sweepstakes 3449, c/o Prize Destination you wish that entry to be considered for, P.O. Box 1315, Buffalo, NY 14269-1315, USA or P.O. Box 610, Fort Erie, Ontario L2A 5X3, Canada.

To be eligible for the San Francisco trip, entries must be received by 5/30/95; for the Las Vegas trip, 7/30/95; and for the Orlando trip, 9/30/95.

Winners will be determined in random drawings conducted under the supervision of D.L. Blair, Inc., an independent judging organization whose decisions are final, from among all eligible entries received for that drawing. San Francisco trip prize includes round-trip airfare for two, 4-day/3-night weekend accommodations at a first-class hotel, and $500 in cash (trip must be taken between 7/30/95—7/30/96, approximate prize value—$3,500); Las Vegas trip includes round-trip airfare for two, 4-day/3-night weekend accommodations at a first-class hotel, and $500 in cash (trip must be taken between 9/30/95—9/30/96, approximate prize value—$3,500); Orlando trip includes round-trip airfare for two, 4-day/3-night weekend accommodations at a first-class hotel, and $500 in cash (trip must be taken between 11/30/95—11/30/96, approximate prize value—$3,500). All travelers must sign and return a Release of Liability prior to travel. Hotel accommodations and flights are subject to accommodation and schedule availability. Sweepstakes open to residents of the U.S. (except Puerto Rico) and Canada, 18 years of age or older. Employees and immediate family members of Harlequin Enterprises, Ltd., D.L. Blair, Inc., their affiliates, subsidiaries and all other agencies, entities and persons connected with the use, marketing or conduct of this sweepstakes are not eligible. Odds of winning a prize are dependent upon the number of eligible entries received for that drawing. Prize drawing and winner notification for each drawing will occur no later than 15 days after deadline for entry eligibility for that drawing. Limit: one prize to an individual, family or organization. All applicable laws and regulations apply. Sweepstakes offer void wherever prohibited by law. Any litigation within the province of Quebec respecting the conduct and awarding of the prizes in this sweepstakes must be submitted to the Regies des loteries et Courses du Quebec. In order to win a prize, residents of Canada will be required to correctly answer a time-limited arithmetical skill-testing question. Value of prizes are in U.S. currency.

Winners will be obligated to sign and return an Affidavit of Eligibility within 30 days of notification. In the event of noncompliance within this time period, prize may not be awarded. If any prize or prize notification is returned as undeliverable, that prize will not be awarded. By acceptance of a prize, winner consents to use of his/her name, photograph or other likeness for purposes of advertising, trade and promotion on behalf of Harlequin Enterprises, Ltd., without further compensation, unless prohibited by law.

For the names of prizewinners (available after 12/31/95), send a self-addressed, stamped envelope to: Flyaway Vacation Sweepstakes 3449 Winners, P.O. Box 4200, Blair, NE 68009.

RVC KAL